D1571056

Sarah Goode spoke: "All of us have so much *power*, Stephen. You, especially. And we have been using that power, and nurturing it for a long time." Stephen had never heard her speak with such rabid enthusiasm and it confused him. "And this chance, Stephen, this opportunity, this challenge, this *responsibility* is not something we can lightly turn aside."

"What opportunity, Sarah?" He wanted desperately to understand.

"To bring the children back to us. To unlock the door, to knock down the wall"—she looked him squarely in the eye now; he felt a chill settle into his body—"between their world, and ours!"

"My God!" It was all he could manage.

"Soon, Stephen. It will happen very soon."

The Playground

T. M. WRIGHT

TOR

A TOM DOHERTY ASSOCIATES BOOK

THE PLAYGROUND

"The End of the World" from *New and Collected Poems 1917-1976* by Archibald MacLeish. Copyright©1976 by Archibald MacLeish. Reprinted by permission of Houghton Mifflin Company.

A Tor Book

Published by Tom Doherty Associates, 8-10 W. 36th St., New York City, N.Y. 10018

First printing, November 1982

ISBN: 0-523-48046-6

Printed in the United States of America

Distributed by Pinnacle Books, 1430 Broadway, New York, N.Y. 10018

*With love and gratitude
for Miles and Carolyn Wright*

AUTHOR'S NOTE

The people you will meet in this book existed solely in my imagination before I brought them forth on paper. And now they will exist in your imagination.

To the best of my knowledge, they exist nowhere else in this world, and so, any similarity between people and places within these pages and people and places in the real world should be seen to constitute only a wonderful, if chilling, coincidence.

T.M. WRIGHT
April 23, 1982
Rochester, New York

With dimming eyes I watch, and then;
the glimmering phantom fades, and lo,
The ashy form of what I've been
Comes stalking in the firelight glow.

— from *The Wraith*
    by Charles E. Wheelock (1864-1938)

And there, there overhead, there, there, hung over
Those thousands of white faces, those dazed eyes,
There in the starless dark, the poise, the hover,
There with vast wings across the canceled skies,
There in the sudden blackness, the black pall
Of nothing, nothing, nothing—nothing at all.

— from *The End of the World*
    by Archibald Macleish (1892-1982)

1

The Discovery—November 21

Rick Armstrong—telephone lineman for the Greater Adirondack Communications Company—pushed the Snowcat's door open, swung his legs around, hesitated. He thought about playing golf in all that bright white snow just inches below his boots. He pushed off with his hands from the driver's seat and landed in snow up to his crotch. He cursed, loud, and heard it come back to him from a small stand of white pines a hundred yards to the west.

It was cold here. Not the kind of brisk, chill cold that you fought off with goose-down-filled coats and Timberland boots, but the kind of cold that stunned, that made your lungs ache. Nothing moves in this kind of cold—not animals, nor man. Unless it's absolutely necessary.

The call had come six hours earlier:

"Rick? This is Jasper."

"You woke me up, Jasper. What do you want?"

"We need you, Rick."

"It's Sunday. I don't work Sunday—it's part of my contract."

"Rick, this is in the nature of an emergency."

"'In the nature of an emergency'? What does *that* mean?"

"Okay, it *is* an emergency."

"I'm happy for you, Jasper, but I still don't work Sundays. If you don't like it, fight with the union."

"I know what the union says, and I know what your contract says, Rick, and it says that under 'Emergency Situations'—"

"Read the contract closer, Jasper, my boy. Because nowhere does it say that you—Jasper Yackel—have the power to declare this situation or that situation an 'emergency situation.' It doesn't *say* that."

"Double time, Rick. We'll give you double time."

"I'd get that anyway, Jasper."

"Okay, triple time. What are you making, now—"

"Give it up, Jasper."

"A bonus, Rick. Triple time, plus a bonus. One-fifty. What do you say?"

"Make it three hundred and I'll think about it."

"Bastard!"

"Beg pardon?"

"I called you a 'bastard,' Rick."

And that was exactly what he was, Rick thought now—six hours later. And a stupid bastard, to boot. Because money could buy most things, but not new fingers and toes.

"Ever been to Goode's Crossing, Rick?"

"No."

"Would you *like* to go to Goode's Crossing?"

"Not particularly."

"Because that's where the trouble is. At least we think it's where the trouble is. Miles tried to go in there with his jeep but got bogged down almost before he got started—"

"And how do you propose that *I* go in there, Jasper?"

"A Snowcat—number eight's available."

"Number eight?! Isn't that the one that quit on me last December?"

"It's been overhauled, Rick. It's almost like new. We even overhauled the radio."

Rick glanced behind him at the Snowcat's cab. He grinned; a lot of good a CB radio did in these hills. But that was no problem, as long as he had access to telephone lines.

"So what am I looking for in Goode's Crossing, Jasper?"

"I don't know, Rick. Could be a downed pole, a shorting transformer. It could be anything."

"You're a big help, Jasper."

"It's all I can tell you, Rick. Goode's Crossing has been snowed in for a couple days, now. Maybe a week. Not that they haven't been snowed in before—they get snowed in a couple of times a year, so that isn't the problem; it's not the big problem, anyway. The problem is, they apparently have no phone service. And that's where you come in."

"Why don't you drop a chopper in there, Jasper?

You've done it before, haven't you?"

"Rick, do you have any idea the shit and the hell you've got to go through with Albany trying to get a chopper up here?! Those things are expensive, and the pilots tell me they're a bitch to fly around these mountains. Albany lost one up here a couple years ago and there was pure hell to pay."

"Okay, Jasper, I get the message. I'll take the damned Snowcat in."

Rick turned his body around sluggishly in the heavy snow until he was facing the Snowcat. He thought that people shouldn't try to live where they needed big, ugly machines like this. He moved forward, lifted the engine cover, and peered in. He admitted at last that he didn't have much of an idea what he might be looking for. The last time the machine had quit on him it had turned out to be because of a cracked distributor cap (and so this time, someone—some damned idiot, Rick thought—had put a brand new distributor cap in the tool chest. Just to be sure).

He considered a moment, closed the engine cover, and climbed back into the cab. "Jesus, please," he whispered, and turned the ignition on.

The engine started at once.

"You know where Goode's Crossing is, Rick?"

"Uh-huh. Jan and I drove through it about a year ago."

"I thought you hadn't been there."

"We didn't stop, Jasper, we just drove through. Why would we want to stop?"

"I don't know—lots of people do."

"For God's sake, why?"

"For seances, fortune telling, that kind of thing. Don't tell me you don't know what Goode's Crossing is all about?"

"That's what I'm telling you, Jasper."

Jasper chuckled. "Well, you'll find out, Rick. Might even be fun for you, you never know."

Rick pushed the accelerator pedal gently. The Snowcat bucked and harrumphed and moved very slowly forward.

Just as Goode's Crossing came into view—still a mile off, a very pretty, picture-postcard kind of town at that distance, settled so comfortably into the bright white snow—the Snowcat died again. And for good, Rick knew—its final wheeze and sputter were almost reminiscent of other deaths ("C'mon, Barney, old boy, don't die. Please?!"). Rick cursed the machine quickly, hotly. He hit the steering wheel hard, hoping—futilely, he knew—that the wheel would break ("Aw, God, Mom, he's dead. Barney's dead!"). He stared blankly at Goode's Crossing for a full two minutes. Sure, he told himself, someone had seen him, someone was probably watching him right at that very moment: ("Dad, the telephone lineman's here! Now we can call Aunt Mary.") Because, damn, it was colder than a witch's tit out here, and there was still a lot of deep snow to trundle through with fifty pounds of gear around his waist. "Jasper, my boy," he said tightly, "I hope you really and truly value your short hairs because I am going to pluck them out one by one!"

He turned in the seat, pulled his gear belt onto

his lap, hesitated a moment, then climbed out of the cab.

His double-take when he saw the thing in the snow was almost theatrical. He laughed a quick, shrill, and nervous laugh, as if, he thought, the thing had frightened him. He strapped his gear belt on, bent over. The thing was half-buried in snow just inches from the Snowcat's tread. "It's Donald Duck," he said, still unaccountably nervous, as if the thing might suddenly talk back to him. The head and neck and part of the body—with the replica of a saddle on it—were visible. (It reminded him of the Seventh Street Playground, from twenty five years before, and the large metal replicas of Goofy and Mickey Mouse and Donald Duck, all bolted firmly on top of heavy iron springs; some poor damned kid had gotten his foot crushed in one of those springs, he remembered.) He looked about; but this place—so out in the open, so far from town—was a strange place to put a playground. He shrugged, and waded into the thigh-deep snow, his gaze fixed on Goode's Crossing.

Ten minutes later, snowblindness began creeping up on him. It destroyed his peripheral vision first, then the small town ahead lost its geometry, as if it had become a dark, shimmering blob of pudding in the snow. It lifted, descended, widened, flattened, became a thick and undulating black line. Then, for a moment, it was Goode's Crossing again and Rick could see that it was not really the pretty, picture-postcard kind of town he had seen from his vantage point at the playground.

He put his gloved hands over his eyes. "Jesus God," he murmured. He groped at his gear belt, found the empty space where his goggles should have been. He swore again, opened his eyes to slits ("Dad, the telephone lineman's here. Now we can call Aunt Mary."). Goode's Crossing sat stiff and silent a half mile off. Its big Victorian homes seemed to lean very slightly at odd angles; it was almost one-dimensional—like a pop-up town in a badly planned children's book.

Rick cupped his hands around his mouth. "Hello," he shouted. "Hello." He waited a moment, got no answer, expected none at this distance. He moved forward, more easily now—the snow was not as deep here as at the playground.

"Jasper, this is Rick!"

"Rick?! Where have you been, we thought you'd—"

"Shut up, Jasper, this is important. I'm in Goode's Crossing."

"Goode's Crossing? Then you found the problem?"

"Shut up, Jasper. I want to ask you something; I want to ask you if this is your idea of a joke?"

"If what's a joke, Rick?"

"Because if it is a joke, if it *is* a stupid, goddamned joke, you are going to live to regret it, Jasper. . . ."

"Rick, I—"

"Because, first of all, I am *not* one of your biggest fans, Jasper—I guess you knew that. At least you should know it. And secondly, I do not like practical jokes, I think they're dumb!"

"Rick, please, I don't know what in hell you're talking about!"

"There's no one here, Jasper, and from what I can see there hasn't *been* anyone here for a long, long time—"

"But—"

"A *long* time, Jasper. Years. Literally years! But I don't have to tell you that, do I? You know that. That's why you *sent* me here!"

"Rick, listen to me, just shut up and listen to me. You are in the *wrong town!* Somehow, you wound up in the wrong fucking town!"

"Jasper, your ass is in the blender for that! You sent me to Goode's Crossing, and that's where I am!"

"But you don't understand, Rick—you *can't* be in Goode's Crossing, you—"

"Jasper, this has gone beyond simple animosity; I'm going to sue your ass till it falls off! Do you know that I've got frostbite?"

"Rick, please listen to me. Please! You're obviously in some kind of trouble—"

"No, Jasper, you're the one who's in trouble—"

"You're either not playing with a full deck, Rick, or you're telling the truth. Either way, you're in deep trouble. I'm calling Albany for a chopper. Just stay where you are."

"Where am I going to go, Jasper?—tell me that. Where—" But Jasper Yackel had hung up. Rick gritted his teeth, slammed the receiver down. He stood very stiffly, very silently a long while. Then

—suddenly and totally exhausted—he plopped into a big, high-back Naugahyde chair near the phone. He closed his eyes. "Dad, the telephone lineman's here. Now we can call Aunt Mary." But there was no Aunt Mary, was there? Just a lot of open doors, and cold rooms, and dust. Tons of dust. And tons of rot. He supposed that if his ears were just a little better he'd be able to *hear* the decay going on all around him.

("Aw, Mom, he's dead—Barney's dead.")

("I know, Rick. I know.")

("Why'd he have to die, Mom?")

"Dad, the telephone lineman's here. Now we can call Aunt Mary up."

("It happens to all of us, Rick. Today it happened to Barney. Maybe twenty years from now it will happen to me. Maybe twenty or thirty years after that it will happen to you.")

"We can call Aunt Mary up and when we've got her we can ask her how things are. Do you think she'll tell us, Dad?"

("It's a fact of life, Rick, just like growing up, or having your first date, or buying your first house.")

("What can I bury him in, Mom? Can I bury him in his bed? He liked that bed a whole lot, Mom.")

"Do you think she's happy, Dad?"

"Well, I think she's at rest."

"You mean like she's just sleeping?"

"Yes, in a way."

("Barney's really just sleeping, isn't he?")

("In a way.")

"In what way?"

"Well, I don't know—I don't think anybody really knows for sure."

("Everything dies, Rick. Barney died because all dogs die, in time. And all cats. And trees. And you and I. And your father. We'll all die, sometime.")

("How about houses, Mom? Do *they* die? And hats and coats? And sandy beaches?")

("Well, of course not, Ricky.")

("But why not, Mom?")

("For Christ's sake, Ricky, for Christ's sake—")

"I don't know, I don't know, I don't know!"

It was a pleading, senseless, agonized scream. And when he woke because of it, Rick knew that—impossibly—it had come from his mouth, had torn through his brain. He murmured, "Oh God, Oh Jesus!" And with immense effort he pushed himself to his feet. He stumbled toward the door, noticed, obliquely, that it had come open again, fell through it, onto the porch, crawled across the porch and rolled very slowly down the steps.

He lay quietly in the snow. He felt that he might be smiling.

Part One
A FEW OF THE PLAYERS

2

SARAH

July 1921: In a Cottage on Oneida Lake,
New York State

Sarah could hear their voices clearly because
the warm night air was still, and because, at her
request, they had left the door open a crack.

She could hear Aunt Lucy's voice—very high-
pitched, but not hard to listen to; Sarah had
thought once that if certain large and graceful
birds could talk they would sound much like Aunt
Lucy. And Uncle Merlo's voice, broken every few
seconds by those awful, stiff hacking sounds that
were a cross between a cough and a hoot ("Merlo's
not long for this world, either," she had recently
overheard Aunt Jessica say). She could hear Aunt
Jessica, too. Her clipped, harsh whispers—as if,
despite some imagined handicap, she were strain-

ing to be heard from a far corner—always quieted everyone and made her the center of attention.

She said now, "I think we have to make some arrangements. It's not too early."

Uncle Merlo hacked.

Aunt Lucy made soft, unintelligible piping sounds, as if she were underwater and trying to talk through a long wooden whistle that broke through the surface.

"*Never* too early," Aunt Jessica reiterated. "And there *is* the child to think about. Of course the child." Her last remark was sharp, and offhanded; from her tone, she could as easily have been talking about something as bothersome and mundane as closing the windows when it rained, or feeding the dozen cats that roamed in and about the cottage.

Sarah didn't actively dislike Aunt Jessica (she actively disliked no one). She viewed her in much the way she would have viewed the presence of a third ear on the back of her head—Aunt Jessica was a permanent fixture in her life and it would do no good at all to let that fact upset her.

Sarah was a very reasonable child.

(She did actively dislike the small attic room they put her in when she visited the cottage. The room was always too warm, even in winter, when the two woodburning stoves below were kept constantly working and the adults sat around in a permanent sweat, bottles and cans of beer in hand, stuffing themselves on the never-ending flow of sandwiches that Nana provided. There were spiders in the room, too—"Nothing poisonous," she had been assured, and although she had no great fear of them, she felt very uncomfortable about sleeping with them, so she itched a lot in the room. And while the adults slept in the noticeably cooler and far less infested main-floor bedrooms, Sarah never for a moment thought of the arrangement as unfair. Between adults and children, of course, the concept just did not exist. You did what you were told and if you asked questions, you got your mouth slapped. That was fair.)

Aunt Lucy spoke now. "We haven't even gotten the call from the hospital, yet, Jessica. Don't you think we're being a little premature?" It was not really a question so much as the statement of a question, as if Lucy were inviting Jessica to pick it apart and tell her where her error lay.

"I think we're being realists," Jessica said.

Uncle Merlo hacked again, louder, and longer. Afterwards, he apologized shortly, out of habit.

"Yes," said Aunt Lucy, though without conviction.

Sarah's left arm began to itch, inside the elbow. She scratched it and felt something small and soft, like a ball of dust, roll up under her finger. It moistened quickly, and she brushed it from the bedsheet.

In the attic room, the smell of the lake—mixed with the smells of old wooden beams, and vaguely damp bedding—was heavy and sickly sweet. It was the odor of use and age, but, on this particular night, Sarah did not think of it as unpleasant. She sensed in the smell an almost spiritual kind of permanence which, despite the spiders and the sticky warmth, made her feel very secure, and very comfortable.

She could see the lake. In the summers, she swam in it regularly because it was a predictable kind of lake. There were no dropoffs. The rocky bottom sloped casually, almost unnoticeably, to a maximum depth of fifty feet or so. And it was a clear lake, brimming with catfish and bullheads and bass—a fisherman's paradise, and the fishermen were out on it season after season, either in their little wooden boats, or moving about stiffly on the ice, pulling the fish up, accepting from the lake what it had to give them.

"And one reality," Sarah heard Aunt Jessica say, "is whether we will want her embalmed or not." She paused briefly; Sarah, because she had known Aunt Jessica all her life, imagined that Jessica smiled very slightly. "It's an extremely expensive procedure, and, you know, it is a procedure that is *not required by law*. Did you know that?"

Sarah heard Uncle Merlo mumble something that could have been a negative, and Aunt Lucy say, "Is that true?" as if it were something terribly interesting and maybe they could talk about it at length.

"It is true," Aunt Jessica said.

Tonight, for Sarah, from the small attic window, the lake was massive, black, and featureless. The rough little pier one of her uncles had built decades before was a slight, pale imperfection on it. The light from just one pulsating kerosene lamp was visible on Frenchman's Island, a mile and a half from shore. The family that lived there had probably gone to bed early, Sarah thought. "Good people," her mother had once said, though Sarah had never met them.

Sarah missed her mother. She hoped fervently that her mother would not be "away" for long: "We love her, too," Aunt Jessica had said a week before. "We do hope she'll be all right, Sarah." Sarah remembered thinking, *No, you don't!* "And it was not your fault, Sarah," Jessica went on. "You must believe that." But Sarah did not believe it. Deep inside herself, she knew better.

A breeze started, small and soft and erratic, like the lamp on Frenchman's Island. It moved quietly about in the attic room; it found the narrow stairway, and went down.

"It's a crime what she did to that child," Jessica said. "It's little wonder the child reacted that way."

Uncle Merlo hacked, then he said, "She had her reasons, Jessica."

"Reasons?" Jessica said tightly. "We *all* have *reasons,* Merlo!"

Sarah closed her eyes lightly so she could better enjoy the breeze, and the smells of the lake, and the room. She thought it was wonderful what she was feeling now, and she realized that she was caught up in a very precious moment, that she had better hold on tight to it. And let it go when it was time. Let it go quickly. So she'd always have it.

She opened her eyes.

She watched the dark figure climb gracefully out of the lake and up onto the pier. She watched the figure stand on the pier quietly. She listened to the small, dull plopping sounds of water dripping on old wood.

(Mother loved to swim. She was an expert—a lifeguard, once.)

"Merlo," Jessica said, "she's *your* sister; you explain her."

"Explain her?" Merlo said, confused. "Jessica, I can't *explain* her."

The phone rang. Merlo hacked grotesquely. Lucy made her soft, piping sounds.

The figure on the pier took one slow and measured step, then another; and in the hot attic room, Sarah watched; she was smiling slightly, as if at something pleasant.

(Before leaving, Mother had told her, "Watch for me, Sarah.")

"Hello," Jessica said; she had answered the phone. "Yes," she said a moment later, and paused to listen. "I agree completely. Thank you," she said; Sarah heard the receiver being put down.

The cottage was almost on top of the lake, so it was a very short walk from the pier to the cottage wall. Sarah pressed her face into the window screen. She watched the figure move gracefully up the wall.

From behind her she heard, "Child?" It was Aunt Jessica.

The figure pulled itself up, over the little edge of roof below the window. The figure did not grunt or groan with the effort. The figure stayed quiet.

Sarah heard again, "Child?" Then, "I'm talking to you."

The figure sat quietly below the window. Its

eyes found Sarah's, then its head turned and its eyes found the lake.

"Child?" Aunt Jessica said a third time.

Sarah whispered into the window screen, through a smile, "Aunt Jessica, Mother is alive. Mother is alive, Aunt Jessica."

"Oh, child," Aunt Jessica said, her voice choked with false pity. "Oh, child, my poor child!"

Sarah lived to be seventy two years old.

3
WEYRE

April 1934: New York City

"What kind of a name is that?" asked Weyre Goodall's new friend. And Weyre (pronounced "Weere") answered smoothly, because of practice, "My father says it's a Germanic-Slav name." He lifted his chin slightly, proudly. "A prince's name."

"Yeah? Prince who?"

"Prince Weyre, of course," Weyre answered, as if stating the obvious.

"Well," said his new friend, "*I* never heard of him."

"Why should you? He was prince over the Germanic Slavs. And he died ten thousand years ago."

"Bullcrap! There wasn't nothin' *living* ten

thousand years ago. I *know* that. You're fulla shit!"

Weyre smiled a long-suffering smile. He had been told he was full of shit more than once and so had devised what he considered the most effective response. "I will pardon you your lack of education and vocabulary," he said.

His new friend laughed suddenly, loudly—a grating and humorless noise that moved about in the empty building like a ball of lead.

The boy's name was Martin. Like Weyre, he was twelve years old; the resemblance ended there. Martin was tall and well-muscled and even sported the faint beginnings of a mustache. No one called him "Martin." Everyone called him "Red," because his hair was red, and because such nicknames—nicknames in general—are always reserved for boys like him. (No one would have given Weyre Goodall a nickname. Nicknames, of course, are familiarities, and people do not become familiar with things they don't understand.)

Red stopped laughing as abruptly as he'd started. He became deadly serious. "Let's go jack off, Weyre," he said.

Weyre's muscles tightened. He said nothing.

"On the roof, Weyre. If you go out on the edge, on this one corner—you gotta be real careful—you can see into the YW, into the locker room, Weyre. Through the skylight."

"I don't want to," Weyre said, his voice a nervous whisper.

Red grinned. "Sure you want to. Wait'll you see the *boobs*, Weyre, bouncin' all around!" He stuck his chest out and moved it quickly from side to side. "Like this, Weyre." His grin softened. He looked suspiciously at Weyre. He went on, "You ain't never *seen* boobs, have you?"

Weyre said defensively, and still at a whisper, "Yes, I have."

Red shook his head slowly. "Just your mom's, I bet. *They* don't count. And your sister's don't, either."

"I don't have a sister."

"Yeah? Then whose boobs you seen?"

Weyre looked away. He suddenly hated being here, in this empty building, with Red, and the day just beginning. He glanced about, half expecting one of the jillion or so rats that lived in the building to pop out of a wall and grab him by the throat —*that* would sure be the proper punishment, wouldn't it, for disobeying his father?

"You're a chicken shit!" Red taunted.

And Weyre said, "You go on up."

"What?"

"You go on up." He smiled as if happy he'd found the answer, at last, to some great problem. "You go and do what you have to do and I'll wait right here."

Red looked hurt. "You want me to go up there and do it *alone?*" He paused, thought a moment. "It ain't *right* to do it alone." He paused again, very briefly. "You don't drown cats alone, do you?"

Weyre said, "Uh-uh." He didn't want to admit that he didn't drown cats at all.

"Sure you don't. And you know why you don't?

'Cuz it'd mean you were sick in the head if you did. Same thing with jackin' off, Weyre. You do it with your buddy. Ain't I your buddy?"

"You go on up," Weyre said again. "I'll join you directly."

"How directly?"

"A minute, that's all."

Red grinned. He nodded briskly at Weyre's crotch. "You gotta get it ready, Weyre?"

"Yeah," Weyre answered. "I gotta get it ready."

"How long's it take ya? It takes me"—he snapped his fingers—"that long."

"Yeah," said Weyre.

Red said, "Okay. I'll go on up." Then he turned abruptly and headed for the open concrete stairway that led to the fourth floor and eventually to the roof. He held his hand up as he walked; his back was to Weyre; he snapped his fingers again. "That long," he repeated, chuckling, and disappeared up the stairway.

Weyre stood very still. He felt sticky, and uncomfortable—though the morning was cool—and he felt dirty. He wanted suddenly to be at home, away from here, anyway. And away from Red and his nastiness. But he couldn't move. Something was holding him.

The building he was in had been a hotel once— The Elmgrove. From the start, because of its location, it catered almost exclusively to transients, and hookers, and eventually—after its reputation had gone from bad to very bad to downright ugly —the city fathers decided that it had become a hotbed of disease and crime and would have to be condemned. So, in 1928, they condemned it. The Elmgrove's owners slunk off quietly to the Sun Belt, where things were beginning to open up, and the city fathers had the building stripped of all its reuseable items—couches, chairs, beds (mattresses, of course, were burned), lamps, dressers, etc.—and sold at public auction. After that, the building sat unoccupied (except by rats and hobos), and unwanted, open to the elements, decaying quickly. It was only one of scores of similar eyesores in New York, and no one paid much attention to it.

Except the children.

Like Weyre Goodall, who heard now (several minutes after his new friend had gone to the roof), very faintly, a long, hissing whisper, as if a radiator were spouting in the next room. He looked to his left, toward the source of the sound, through one of The Elmgrove's one hundred or so smashed windows. He saw nothing unusual—the gray wall of the YWCA next door, and the lower half of a window in it.

Then the hissing noise stopped and he heard, just as faintly, a quick, hard, thumping sound, at a distance, from outside, and below.

And moments later, from the open stairway, he heard, "It really is no fun alone, Weyre." It was Red, and he was pleading with him. "Let's do it together; let's please do it together!"

Weyre looked. He saw, at the top of the stairway, where the ceiling joined it, the lower half of Red's pantlegs, and Red's incredibly worn out sneakers. Weyre called to him, "You go on up,

Red." He paused; Red said nothing. "I'll join you directly."

"You're lying, Weyre." He said the words with great, fluid confidence. "I know you're lying. I'm going to have to come down there for you, aren't I, Weyre?"

"No," Weyre said, and he noticed his voice was trembling slightly. "I'll be up directly." And he watched as Red took first one, then another slow step down, until his knees were visible, then the tops of his thighs.

Weyre heard what could, he supposed, have been a bee. But it quickly grew louder and he realized it was a siren—an ambulance, the police; he wasn't sure. Sirens of all kinds were a constant part of the city's background noise and he wondered why he'd noticed this one in particular.

And he realized at once that he was a little scared, that he did not want to do what Red wanted him to do. But that, for Red, it had grown very, very urgent.

"Please don't leave me all alone up here!" Red was whining. His great, fluid confidence was gone completely. He sounded on the verge of tears.

Weyre answered, his voice straining, "I gotta go now, Red. I really gotta go now." And he turned toward the stairway to the second floor. He stopped. The siren was much louder, now, just outside the building. "Red, there's a cop or something down there . . ." He moved quickly to the window.

He heard, from the stairway, "Weyre, I hurt! I hurt real bad! Don't leave me all alone! Don't leave me all alone here!"

"Red?" Confusedly, because Weyre could see a dozen or so people huddled together in the alley three floors below, and he could see the ambulance on the street. "Red, there's an ambulance down there."

He heard Red move further down the stairway. "I never hurt so damned bad, Weyre! Why does it hurt so damned bad?!"

Weyre looked toward the stairway. He wasn't sure what he was seeing, at first. He supposed momentarily that Red's body was at a different angle on the stairs than he'd first thought, or that maybe there'd been a subtle change in the light, because Red's left arm looked as if it were hanging backward, or inside out, from the shoulder, and his right hip seemed to jut queerly several inches above where it should have been, and for one quiet moment, Weyre convinced himself that he was looking at some poor, broken marionette that had wandered down from the roof to take Red's place. But he knew in the next moment that that was not what he was seeing at all.

So he screamed.

And he ran.

And halfway home, in his panic, he crossed in front of a slowly moving truck. The driver tried valiantly to stop in time but hit Weyre a glancing blow that sent him spinning to the sidewalk.

Later that day, the doctor would tell Weyre's parents that the break at Weyre's knee was clean and would heal well. But the break wasn't clean and it did not heal well, and for the rest of his life

Weyre Goodall not only walked with a limp but suffered, as well, from moments of extreme pain.

He lived to be sixty-one years old.

4

MARJORY

June 1954: On a Dairy Farm in Minnesota

She liked the smell of the barn. She was twelve years old, and she was unquestionably happy with her life, happy with her mother and father, and with her little brother, Ike, and her dozens of cats and dogs, and with the geese, and the cows, and the sunshine, and the warmth. And the smell of the barn. She liked the smell of the barn.

She inhaled deeply of the air in the barn. There was some grain dust in it and it tickled. She sneezed once, and again. Then she smiled. "Pappy, bless me," she said to her grandfather, dead two years then. And she imagined that he said, "Bless you, Marjory." She could hear his voice clearly; it was rough-edged, and loving, like when he used to play games with her. Marjory had come to the conclusion that those games were okay, now that he was gone. "They're only games, Marjory," her grandmother had once said.

She found that she was thinking very often about Pappy in the past six months or so. She didn't know why. Of all her relatives (and it seemed at times that there were hundreds of them, especially on Sundays, when the ones who lived in Gwynne Township came over after church for lemonade, or Coca-Cola, or tea) Pappy was the one who stuck hardest in her memory. She remembered that when he died, and after her father had come into her bedroom and told her, "Pappy's gone, Marjory. He's with your grandmother, up in heaven," she hadn't cried at all. It had even made her a little happy. Because, she told herself, he had been very sick, and in great pain—they hadn't been able to keep it from her. And so, now that he was with Grandma, he wasn't sick anymore, or in pain. And that was good. She could love him, and she could forgive him. And she could feel better about herself. Because it was right, after all, to love and forgive your grandfather.

He had liked the smell of the barn, too. "That's the smell of the earth, Marjory," he'd told her more than once (he always called her "Marjory," not "Marge"—"It's more dignified," he said).

It was a very large barn, even as dairy barns go, and it was kept in good repair. It housed seventy-five cows, several draft horses, and four dozen or so chickens and geese (the number fluctuated with the family appetite), so, consequently, it was always alive with sound. The mooings and bellowings of the cows predominated, of course, there were so many of them, but the chickens managed a close second, because their squawks were high-pitched and jarring, and the geese had no trouble making themselves heard. "You know, Marjory," Pappy had once said, "there's a saying that goes, 'You ain't got the brains that God gave geese.' Well, I'm here to tell you, Marjory, that that particular saying ain't fair, because geese, Marjory, are among the very smartest of the barnyard animals. Not as smart as a pig, it's true, but lots smarter than the average horse, or the average cow, and *tons* smarter than the average insurance salesman." It was a joke he'd obviously concocted on the spur of the moment and he laughed long and hard at it. Marjory did, too—not because she understood it (What was an insurance salesman, anyway?) but because Pappy's laughter was infectious, and when it got her laughing it made him laugh even harder, which made her laugh harder, until, very soon, they both found themselves weak-legged and wobbly because they'd been laughing too hard and too long.

She thought she heard him laughing now. When the cows stopped bellowing for a moment, and when the chickens stopped squawking at the same time, she imagined that she heard him, off in a far corner of the barn, near the horse stalls, laughing hard and nonstop at one of his jokes. But the cows bellowed all the time, it seemed, and the chickens squawked almost continuously, so she found it nearly impossible to pin down what she was hearing.

It'd be great if it really was Pappy, if she really was hearing him.

"Pappy?"

"It's just wishing," he'd say. Because he'd said it before, about other things. And she knew in her heart that he was right. He was right most of the time (almost always he was right about the weather, and almost always he was right about if someone was going to have a girl baby or a boy baby, and he was *always* right about wishing).

It's just wishing, he'd say. And of course he'd be right, Marjory told herself.

Then, for a moment, there was silence in the barn. Dead silence. As if all the cows and the chickens, and geese, and horses had somehow gotten together and agreed that, if only for the briefest moment, they would give Marjory the quiet that she wanted. And deep within it, as if from deep within a well, from deep within the mud and the debris at the bottom of that well, she heard Pappy.

And even at that great distance, and for that brief moment, she could tell that he was enjoying himself immensely.

5
LILY

July 1949: Passaic, New Jersey

Lily's father, a tall, well-muscled man sporting a crew cut, patted the big, darkwood console TV that the men from Alhart's Appliances had just delivered; he smiled proudly. "It's quite an invention, isn't it?"

Lily, not quite eight years old, thin, blonde, pixieish, nodded and smiled her slight, pretty smile. "Uh-huh," she said, "it is, Daddy." She was standing in front of the set. She reached for the ON/OFF switch. Her father grabbed her hand. "No, you don't," he said gravely. "You may watch this television receiver, Lily, but you are not to touch it. Do I make myself clear?"

She nodded again. Her smile had vanished. "Yes, Daddy." She looked very solemn and apologetic.

"This is a very fragile instrument, Lily. Do you know what that means?—Do you know what 'fragile' means?"

"No, Daddy. What does it mean?"

"It means if you touch it it'll break and Daddy will be very angry and he'll yell. You don't want Daddy to yell, do you?"

She shook her head. "No, Daddy. I don't."

"That's my princess." He patted her head in much the same way that he'd patted the TV. "And besides," he went on, "those men are still up on the roof, I think, adjusting the antenna. They'll let us know when to turn the television on, Lily."

"Yes, Daddy."

Lily's brother, Larry, appeared in the living room doorway. He'd been outside playing cops 'n robbers with several of his friends. He was a year older than Lily, but big for his age, and sassy. "We got it, huh?" He came over and studied the set critically a moment. "I thought we weren't gonna get it till tomorrow."

"No, Larry, today," his father said.

"Uh-huh," Larry said. "Well, Jackie's folks got a bigger one."

"Yeah?" his father said, and he sounded vaguely concerned. "How big is it?"

Larry announced, "It's a nine-incher, Dad."

"Larry, they don't make nine-inchers, and that's a fact."

"Yes, they do, Dad. I seen it."

"Yeah, who told you it was a nine-incher? Did Jackie's father tell you it was a nine-incher, 'cuz if he did, Larry, you oughta know that he's a bullshi—" He stopped suddenly and glanced at Lily, who was looking questioningly up at him. He went on, "You oughta know that he don't always tell the truth, Larry."

"Yeah," Larry said, "I know. But me and Jackie we measured it ourselves, Dad."

"Which way'd you measure it? Up and down?"

"We measured it diagonal, and it's nine inches, like I said. This one here's a seven-incher, ain't it?"

"Is theirs made of cherrywood like this one is, Larry?"

"Jees, I dunno, all I know is it's a nine-incher."

"Daddy," Lily interrupted, "can we watch it now?"

He ignored her. "Did Jackie's father say how much he paid for his TV receiver, Larry?"

"Naw. All he said was, 'It cost a bundle.' "

Lily said again, "Can we watch the TV now, Daddy?"

He leaned over Larry, put his big hands on Larry's shoulders. "Is that what he said, Larry— he said it cost 'a bundle'?"

"Daddy," Lily said, "are those men still on the roof?" She took hold of the bottom of his shirt and tugged on it to get his attention. "Daddy?"

He slapped at her hand. "Not *now*, Lily!"

She dropped her hand; her lower lip quivered. She reached out and turned the TV on. Her father, facing away from it now, didn't notice. He continued questioning Larry. "He didn't say how much, Larry?"

"No, Dad." He nodded to indicate the TV. "Dad, Lily turned the TV on."

"Oh, for Christ's sake!" He shoved Lily angrily to one side. "I told you *not* to touch it, didn't I?" He shook his forefinger at her.

"I'm sorry, Daddy," she said. "Daddy, is that man dead?" she went on, very concerned, and she pointed tremblingly at the TV screen. He looked. A war movie was on and a soldier lay quietly in his foxhole, his mouth open slightly and his arms and legs splayed out.

Larry said sarcastically, " 'Course he ain't dead, Lily! What're you, stupid? He's just playacting, right Dad?"

He didn't answer immediately. He was considering whether or not to punish Lily for her disobedience. He said finally, "That's right, Lily. It's all playacting; do you understand that?"

"Yes, Daddy," she answered obediently, though it was a lie.

"And besides," he added, "I don't think programs like this are right for little girls."

"Yeah," Larry chimed in. "It might make them *throw up* or something!" He laughed.

"Now, Larry," his father admonished, "that's not very nice, is it?"

Larry didn't answer. His father turned back to Lily. "I'm not going to punish you this time, Lily, but next time—" He gathered up a look of great sternness. "Next time, Lily—" He hesitated. "Do you understand?"

"Yes, Daddy," she answered, smiling gratefully at him.

"That's my princess." He patted her affectionately on the rear end. "Why don't you go help your

Mom, now."

"She's lying down, Daddy. She said she doesn't feel good."

He glanced toward the stairs and harrumphed. "Well, why don't you go outside, then, while your brother and I watch this show?"

Larry asked, with much enthusiasm, "Can Billy and Tommy and Dick come in, too, Dad?"

"Sure they can, son."

Larry left immediately.

Lily's father said again, "Go on outside, Lily. Stay close to the house, though, okay?"

She nodded sullenly. "Okay."

"Promise?"

"I promise." She did not want to go outside. It was hot and muggy, and what she really wanted to do, of course, was watch the new television receiver. She nodded at it, thought very briefly about asking why they couldn't watch some other show—one that was okay for little girls to watch—decided against it, and shuffled from the house.

The house had been built at the end of a cul de sac. Behind it, beyond the small backyard, was a shallow gully that had once been used as an illegal dumping site, a practice which had been effectively stopped upon the request of the local neighborhood association. Still, cleanup efforts in the gully had not yet begun. Although there was much talk about broken glass, and rats, and erosion, most of the people on the street had decided to let it be for the moment—it kept the kids happy, and it was certainly a better place to play than the street itself.

The kids on the street thought of the gully as a kind of treasure hunter's paradise. Larry's friend, Jackie, had found a working wristwatch there several weeks earlier, and other kids had found, among many other things, old broken radios (the tubes brought a couple cents apiece at a local fixit shop), and bald tires, and yellowing magazines, and telephone wire, and so every afternoon after school, the kids on the street descended into the gully and started picking it apart.

Lily had been in the gully with her brother only once. She had complained that it wasn't safe, and that it had gotten her dirty, and had agreed at once when he told her, with much authority, that it was "not a place for girls." She had stayed away from it ever since.

Today was no exception.

She crossed the front yard and started down the street. She was preoccupied with the image she had seen on the TV—the image of the man lying dead—and was wondering distractedly why the TV had to show things like that, why it couldn't show nicer things. She had decided that it probably did show nicer things when she remembered her promise to her father that she'd stay close to the house. She turned around quickly and ran back.

"Hey, Dad," Larry said.

"Yeah, son?"

"I think somebody's been dumpin' stuff in the gully again."

"Yeah," Bobby murmured. He was sitting next to Larry on the couch. Dick and Tommy were seated cross-legged on the floor in front of them. All eyes were on the TV. The war movie was coming to an end.

"This is bigger than Jackie's TV," Tommy said.

"No it ain't," Larry said. "Jackie's is a nine-incher."

"No it ain't," Dick said. "It's a six-incher."

"Yeah, well me and Jackie *measured* it," Larry protested.

Dick chuckled. "Yeah, well you got the number upside down then."

"It doesn't matter, boys," Larry's father said, and he glanced quickly at Larry, then back at the screen. "You said somebody's been dumping in the gully again, Larry?"

"Yeah," Tommy laughed, "they're dumpin' *farts*!"

The other boys giggled at the mention of the magic word.

Larry said, when his giggling had ended, "That's what it smells like, Dad. It smells like farts—bad ones!"

His father grimaced; he wondered if there might be some kind of gas pipe leak in the gully. "Uh-huh," he said, "well, maybe you boys shouldn't play down there for awhile, okay?"

Lily peered over the short chain-link fence that separated the backyard from the gully. She pursed her lips; why would anyone want to play down there? Sure there was some good stuff you could find—like that wristwatch of Jackie's—but Criminy!—it was where other people threw their *garbage*, and who would want to play in other people's garbage? Ha!, she answered herself, Larry would, and his dumb friends, that's who! She shook her head slowly.

She wasn't used to climbing fences and was wearing a dress besides, so when she was halfway over, and was straddling it, the top of the chain-link fence pushed several long, thin, white scratches into her thigh. She drew her other leg over, and hopped to the edge of the gully—a kind of path several feet wide.

She put one hand on the fence, the other one up, as if she were balancing herself (though there was no need; the path was wide enough) and moved very slowly to the east, eyes scanning the gully all the while. She enjoyed the little breeze that pushed up from the gully floor—on this unforgivingly hot day it was refreshing. She thought she was beginning to understand why her brother and his friends came here.

She walked for several minutes on the path. Every now and then she probed the scratches in her thigh with her fingertips to see if they'd started to bleed. They hadn't. And when she had gone beyond her family's property line, and had found that the path narrowed considerably, she stopped at once. "Fiddlesticks!" she whispered. She looked down the path. It continued for another twenty-five yards or so and then appeared to come to an end at the edge of a dense stand of weeds and woods—a place she knew was alive with bees and mosquitoes and poison ivy. "Fiddlesticks!" she said again, and she turned around.

She lost her footing very quickly when the outer edge of the path, weakened by recent heavy rains, gave way. She sat down immediately—she'd slide on her fanny, she decided; it would be fun. She slid that way for a few yards until her feet hit the upper edges of a partially buried rock and she tumbled forward, out of control. Her forehead hit another partially buried rock immediately and by the time she reached the floor of the gully she was unconscious.

It was the rain that brought her around a half hour later. And the smell. She pushed herself to a sitting position, put her hand to her forehead, and started whimpering, though the pain was minor. Her nose wrinkled up. She glanced about, through the downpour, and thought for a moment that she had had "an accident," (as her father put it) but when she reached around and checked she found that she hadn't, that the awful, sickening smell had to be coming from somewhere else, somewhere close by.

"Daddy?" she called. She was crying hard, now. "Daddy?!" she screamed. "Daddy?!" And she pushed herself to her feet, automatically swiped at her dress—various shades of black and brown mud streaked it—and took a few steps forward. She stopped. The rain had revealed the edges of what looked like a refrigerator buried in the mud, and it was from inside it, she realized, that the awful smell was coming.

She heard a loud, crackling noise, like a peal of thunder. She looked up, toward the source of the noise. She saw that, incredibly, a fifty-foot section of the gully slope had broken away and had slid forward a couple inches. And, because she was a fairly bright girl, if timid, she started backing away from it. The hill gave way abruptly. She ran. She had acted none too soon. When the fifty-foot section of hill had stopped moving, its leading edges were over her shoes and halfway up her calves.

She screamed very loud. Then, because she was convinced that the mud was going to crawl over her and smother her, and because the smell from within the refrigerator (she could see now that that was what it was; the mud slide had set it loose and it lay close by, on its back, its door thrown wide open) was making her sick. She took a step backward, tried another. Her foot stuck in the heavy mud and she fell again. She scrambled to her feet, panic-stricken.

The floor of the gully was flat, and only a few yards across. Its north slope, shallower than its south slope, was clear of debris because there was no access road to it. She started climbing the north slope, glancing, awestruck, through the rain every now and then, at the refrigerator behind her.

When she saw the thing's hand she saw it unclearly, because it was nearly the same color as the refrigerator, and because the rain was cutting off her vision. She stopped. She took another step up the slope. It was enough. She saw the head, then, and the body—doubled up into a fetal position, its arms high and bent hard at the elbow. And the first thought that came to her was, *It's not like the TV shows it, Daddy!* because the thing didn't look like it was sleeping, as the man on the TV had. It looked more, she decided, like a big, wrinkled, naked, gray doll made of papier-maché.

And it wasn't frightening at all.

It was kind of sad.

Six years later, long before going to Goode's Crossing, she awoke screaming, and in a heavy sweat, from a dream she did not want to remember. The dream haunted her for the next decade.

6
HARRY

May 1945: Fort Bragg, North Carolina

Harold March—everyone called him 'Harry,' though he asked them not to—lay in his Government Issue cot (the smoking lamp had just been turned off) and thought that he hated his drill sergeant most of all, but that that was okay, because everyone hated their drill sergeant, it was part of the process of becoming a soldier. He was pleased that he'd figured that out for himself. Not everyone had—poor Kenny McConnell, for instance, who spent a lot of his private moments weeping quietly, in obvious fear that someone would notice. He never should have left home. He was probably one of those poor slobs who'd lied about his age. He was probably twelve years old, or something.

And of course Harry hated barracks living, hated the idea that he was being constantly watched by strangers, and being judged by them. But that, too, he'd figured out, was something he'd learn to cope with because it was required of him. He had prided himself, lately, on knowing what his duty was, and how to go about fulfilling it.

He had also been chastising himself often, and harshly, for not having been born several years earlier, because if he had he could at least have seen some action. He might have been there during the landing at Normandy, or—for Christ's sake —helped out in the cleanup of the Philippines. Now all he'd probably get would be a clerking job somewhere in the States and spend four years shuffling papers around instead of, as his Uncle Nate put it, "coming to a death grip with the grim enemies of freedom and democracy." He liked his Uncle Nate, corny as he was. Hell, these were corny times!

Too bad that Uncle Nate was going to die. Suddenly, and soon.

Harry knew this was true because he had seen it happen the night before, just before sleep had overtaken him. And though he didn't know exactly when it would happen, or exactly how (he had heard a heart beating hard, and irregularly, so he assumed that Uncle Nate would have a heart attack), he knew beyond doubt that it would happen.

He had foreseen other deaths. His mother's, his Aunt Lucille's, the death of his English Setter, Trilby, twelve years earlier, and several others.

His Uncle George had told him, "Harry it's what they call a 'wild talent,' and it's a gift from God, so you be careful with it." Harry wasn't sure, now, how much of a 'gift' it was—why should he know when someone else was going to die, and what was he supposed to do with the knowledge? Was he supposed to share it with the world at large?— "Hey, Aunt Lucille is going to die next Tuesday. She's going to choke on a piece of baby-beef liver." Was he supposed to spread it around?

"You're a very sensitive boy." Uncle George again. "Not many's as sensitive as you, and I'll tell you something—you got to make your own decisions about what you 'see.' You feel it's worth sharin', well then, share it. But ask yourself this first; ask yourself, 'Who's going to benefit?' And if the answer is, 'No one but me,' well, then—" He hadn't needed to say more.

Harry put his hands behind his head and focused on the upper part of the wall on the opposite side of the barracks. A single bright light a hundred yards away, on the perimeter of the parade grounds, lit the wall dully. Around him, some men were snoring already, but most were still awake. He heard a few belches, someone else broke wind, someone—at the other end of the barracks—was humming softly; Harry didn't recognize the tune. Another man, close to the man humming, said, "Stop that, wouldja?! Jesus Christ!" and the man humming fell silent. Here and there, bed springs creaked rhythmicaly, tellingly; Harry wondered where those guys got all their energy. Probably just real nervous, he supposed.

And what he was hearing now—the belches, the farts, the squeaking bed springs, the snoring—was, he guessed, no doubt a carbon copy of other nights in these barracks, in the years just passed. Only those were other men, with different names and different faces, and maybe even different drill sergeants. But other than that it was probably all pretty much the same, probably exactly the same. The only real difference was that a lot of those men were dead, and buried (most of them, anyway. They'd find the others in crashed planes, and in caves, and foxholes. Harry knew all about such things from Uncle Nate, who'd been in the First World War and had a thousand grisly stories to tell).

And this place, inside these barracks, within these walls, had been their jumping-off point. From here they'd all marched out to meet eternity. Harry smiled to himself. These are indeed corny times, he thought. And he became aware that someone was standing very quietly beside his bed. He turned his head slightly. The face above him was clear, round, and expressionless—and was illuminated dimly by the light near the parade grounds. It was the face of a boy sixteen or seventeen, no older.

"Yeah?" Harry said, trying to sound annoyed. "You want something?"

The boy merely nodded slowly, and meaningfully, at the bed.

Harry decided that the boy was probably Kenny McConnell—it was hard to tell in the dim light.

"You wanta talk?" Harry said. "You got a problem?"

The same man who'd told the man humming to
be quiet said now, "Hey, pipe down over there!"

Harry whispered, "Is something bothering you,
Kenny? You got a problem?"

The boy nodded slowly at the bed again.

Harry sighed. "Why don't you just go and lie
down, Kenny?"

The boy nodded again, again slowly.

Harry stared quizically at him. He pushed himself up on his elbows. "What in the hell do you
want?" he said.

The boy nodded again at the bed.

"Pipe down, I said!" It was the other man.

Harry said aloud, "You aren't Kenny
McConnell. Who in the hell are you?" Because he
could see the boy's face more clearly, now, and he
didn't recognize it. "What're you?—In the wrong
barracks or something?" Harry said.

The boy put one knee up on the bed. Harry
glanced incredulously at it. "Hey, get offa here!"
The boy bent over, put his hands on either side of
Harry's pillow. He was obviously going to lie
down on the cot.

Harry saw the wound in the center of the boy's
chest, then. It was a wide, round wound, and deep,
and the blood surrounding it had coagulated into
a half-inch thick rim, like debris thrown up
around a crater.

Harry leaped from the bed. The boy looked up at
him briefly, his eyes glazed over with gratitude,
and then he laid down on his back, his hands

behind his head, and his eyes on the ceiling high above him.

Harold March was given a Section Eight Discharge from the Army two weeks later.

He lived to be fifty-four years old.

7

The October Sixth Meeting of The Goode's Crossing Spiritualist Society

Fairclau House was a cavernous, octagonal building made of oak, and white pine, and walnut. A dozen sitting rooms, each equipped with a small wooden table, a half-dozen straight-backed wooden chairs, and an oval mirror, had been arranged, six to a floor, around a large, open, circular discussion area.

From the September 24, 1983 issue of *Update:* An article titled RISE, TABLE, RISE!

It's a village where, for a usually modest fee, the supernatural can be made commonplace, the dead brought back to life, at least in spirit, and futures read as easily as tomorrow's TV listings. Or so the people who live there would have you believe.

The village is called Goode's Crossing. It was founded almost 100 years ago by a man named Lucius Fairclau, who later hanged himself; it boasts a summer population of 32, a winter population of 18—a number which varies from year to year—and its sole purpose for existing is to give psychics, mediums, mystics, and seers a place to practice their trade. Some do it full-time, others part-time, and a few claim to have gone into retirement. And if you're interested in visiting Goode's Crossing, getting there, from Rochester, may be quite a chore indeed.

By 1925, two decades after the wife of Lucius Fairclau had died, the sitting rooms in Fairclau House had fallen into disuse—they'd been stripped of most of their furnishings, anyway, by residents of the village, and by clients, and the occasional transient. The rooms had only rarely been used. In the summer they had proved to be unbearably hot, and humid, and in the spring and fall much too clammy. Winters in Goode's Crossing were vacation periods. Many of the residents went south, to a village called Thendara, in Florida. Most of those that stayed took winter jobs in nearby Merrimac, while others did various types of home work—envelope stuffing, typing; one man, Lester Stanhope, fashioned passable replicas of deer and grizzly bears and moose from native pine and gave them, to be sold on consignment, to a crafts store in Merrimac. Another resident, Lily Krull, did pleasant, stylized oil paintings of the village itself, and the surrounding woods and high foothills (which people in the area were loath to call "mountains"). She was able to sell many of these paintings to people visiting the village, and the money always proved quite valuable in getting her and her husband, Stephen, through the always long and cold winter.

From Rochester, take Route 90 sixty-three miles east to Utica, then, still going east, another 58 miles to Speculator, a little town at the very edge of the Adirondacks. From Speculator, travel southeast another ten miles on Routes 8 and 30 until you hit Route 8 again, then limp another 24 miles northeast to Weverton, a small town whose chief product appears to be isolation. In Weverton, ask Bill Thompson, a fifty-year resident whose house is the only one with an ad for a well-known chewing tobacco painted on its side, where Goode's Crossing is.

Shortly before his death in 1904, Lucius Fairclau built Fairclau House as, he proclaimed, "A place for the communion of souls, passed over and present, for the common good of us all." When someone confessed that they didn't really understand what he was driving at, he said that it didn't matter if anyone else understood, as long as he—Lucius Fairclau—did, because it was, after all, his village, and his house.

Bill Thompson will chuckle a bit, and then he'll point due south: "See that stand of poplars there?" he'll ask. And if you look closely you'll see it, about a half mile off. "Well, sir," he'll continue, "that's Johnson's Road. It's not a good one, for sure, but it's flat, and if you follow it a couple miles you'll come to Shoemaker Road. It's not a very good one either, but it's paved, and if you go east on it it'll take you to Goode's Crossing before long."

Bill readily admits that he's never been in the village—"Never had no need to," he says with a chuckle. "I'm happy to keep all *my* dead relations right where they're at."

Upon his death, Lucius Fairclau was sealed in a large and elaborate vault deep in the underbelly of Fairclau House. Because he was violently afraid of being buried alive, he'd extracted promises from his family that the vault would be equipped with an alarm, which it was—a system of eight large cowbells attached to a length of strong rope. For nearly half a year after his death, his wife and daughters took eight-hour shifts waiting at Fairclau House in case the cowbells should ring. The bells remained silent.

It was the black fly season in the Adirondacks when I left Bill Thompson and took Johnson's Road five miles south to Shoemaker Road, and though it was unbearably hot, and my '76 Celica is not equipped with air conditioning, I found it more than a good idea to keep the windows rolled up. (For those few uninitiated among you, black flies are the scourge of the Adirondacks. They swarm, they bite, they get into your hair, and mouth, and nose, and I've heard more than a few reports, from reliable sources, that they've driven livestock insane.)

The meetings of The Goode's Crossing Spiritualist Society were held in the Discussion Area of

Fairclau House on the first Sunday of every month. It was Sarah Goode who had begun the meetings in 1946, "as a forum for the discussion of all matters of concern to the residents of Goode's Crossing," and Sarah Goode who had suggested that the meetings be held in Fairclau House. She had even suggested that a large, circular, wooden table be used, and identical chairs, because, she explained, "there is no head to a circle; all sides are equal because there are none." The meetings were to be a perfect exercise in democracy. But, although the required trappings were present (someone took minutes; someone else, Sarah usually, called the meetings to order, "motions" were sometimes made (often frivolous: Stephen Krull had once offered, "that we change the style of the lettering on the sign at the front of Fairclau Close" —which read, simply, GOODE'S CROSSING—VISITORS WELCOME—"I think *Gothic* would be nice," and there was general, easy laughter in the building. Someone else once made a motion that, "All spirit forces be allowed in at half price," which also elicited laughter, though of a more nervous kind. The one-dollar fee to get into the village had long since been dropped, anyway, because of the logistics of collecting it), people were "recognized," which usually drew bad jokes about "familiars," and meetings were quite properly "dismissed"), they had rapidly become gab sessions where the village residents could get together and gossip, and swap an occasional story about clients, or—on rare occasions—about something "genuinely spooky" that might have gone on during a private sitting.

On this particular evening, special attention was being paid to a recently published cover story in the Rochester, New York *Post Dispatch*'s Sunday magazine, *Update*—RISE, TABLE, RISE! which included photographs, in moody black and white, interviews with several of the residents, and a light, this-is-really-bullshit kind of style that many in Fairclau House that evening resented. Especially Sarah.

> If you don't break any speed limits, you should be able to reach Goode's Crossing, off Shoemaker Road, from Johnson's Road, out of Weverton, down from Speculator, east from Utica, Syracuse, and Rochester, before the black fly season starts up again next May. Bill Thompson neglected to tell me, however, that the village is not actually on Shoemaker Road. It's on Fairclau Close, which is off Shoemaker Road. Fairclau Close is passable, but not magnificent. My notes also tell me that in winter Fairclau Close is pure hell. Which is why, I imagine, there were so many four-wheel-drive vehicles, of various ages, and in various states of repair, in the village.

Sarah held the magazine stiffly in front of her and shouted—though only a few people, Marjory Gwynne and Harry March and the Krulls, had seated themselves at the big table—"This magazine says we're all fakes and liars!", which got the attention of most of the people in the room, though not all of them, so she repeated, much louder, "This magazine says we're all fakes and liars!" And there was immediate silence.

Sarah was generally considered to be the village's matriarch, and nothing of substance happened in the village without her knowledge and consent (things of "substance" usually involved okaying the extension of the season a few weeks, or allowing a new resident in, or asking certain long-time residents to "alter their business practices"—Irene Atwater Janus, for instance, who had once begun soliciting new clients through various obituary columns, which Sarah frowned upon because it was so public a practice and invited criticism). She was possessed of small, dark eyes, a long, beak-like nose, a prominent chin and jawline, and shoulder-length black hair which had, incredibly, not a trace of gray in it. She usually wore it in a tight bun covered by a net, but when she let it down—as she did several times a year, though not tonight—it usually drew exclamations of amazement and praise, which she very privately enjoyed. No one in the village supposed for even a second that she dyed her hair. She was simply not that kind of a woman. She was, they imagined, much too honest for that.

Goode's Crossing is, at first glance, a rather charming little place. The streets—three altogether; Fox Street, Main Street, and Fairclau Close—are tidy, and the houses, big Victorian things, appear simple and rustic, in a strange, anachronistic way. And Leslie's Mountain (2,840 feet, according to my atlas) looms very green and pretty just behind the village.

It's only upon closer inspection that you begin to realize there's not a lot of money here. Many of the houses appear to have gone without a paint job for decades. Here and there, a junk car sits out in the open, rusting to nothingness. A stray dog can occasionally be seen routing in trash cans kept plainly in view. It quickly became obvious that whatever reason these people gave me for doing what they do, money would not be at the top of their list.

At first glance, Sarah did not look to be seventy-one years of age, but it was not hard to imagine—studying her face a while—that she was at least that old. Some would have called it the "aura of wisdom" about her, others the presence, as well, of crow's feet, and liver spots. She was, at any rate, very much aware of the effect she had on people—that, if nothing else, they *had* to listen to her—and she cultivated it beautifully.

"This magazine," she shouted once more, "says that we are all fakes and liars!" She held it high above her head, as if she were auctioning it off.

Lester Stanhope, a tall, gaunt man of fifty-six who'd been in the village a decade and a half, raised his hand and said, "It doesn't say that directly, Sarah," his tone implying strongly that he wasn't so much objecting to her comment as offering up his own for her quick rebuttal.

She stared silently at him a few moments, then a slow, wide grin appeared on her face. She held the magazine at eye level, opened it, and turned it around, so the group cold see it. She pointed at a black-and-white photograph showing an old and badly rusted car, up on blocks, sitting next to a big, weather-beaten house. "Lester," she said, "is this your car?"

He lowered his head, as if ashamed. "Yes," he answered. "It is. But it's a '53 Dodge, Sarah. It's a collector's item."

She said, to the group, now, "The caption—I'm sure you've all seen it—reads, '*The psychic powers of the residents of Goode's Crossing do not, apparently, extend to the resurrection of junked cars.*'" She focused on Lester again. "I want it removed, Lester. Before the week is out. You have a garage, don't you?"

He nodded.

"Okay, then, put it in there. It's an eyesore."

Lester took a seat at the table. "Sure," he said, his voice low. "If that's what you'd like, Sarah, I'll see what I can do." And though he sounded hesitant, everyone in the room knew that within a few days the '53 Dodge would be gone.

Sarah addressed the group again. "Please, can we all sit down now?" And after much murmuring and shuffling of chairs, the dozen or so people who still were standing took their assigned seats. Shortly, they grew quiet and turned their attention to Sarah. She nodded at John Yount, the only one in the village who knew shorthand and so had been appointed Group Secretary, who took a thick spiral notebook from his briefcase, laid it flat on the table, opened it to the middle, and nodded at Sarah.

"The Goode's Crossing Spiritualist Society will come to order," she said, without particular emphasis. "John Yount will review the minutes of our September 4th meeting." She looked at him. "John?"

He flipped back in the notebook a few pages, paused, flipped back a few more. He grinned an apology at Sarah. "I guess we had a lot to talk about, Sarah." She said nothing. He went on, his forefinger marking his place as he read, "First item of business: Marjory Gwynne reported a strong sulfurous, uh, sul*furic* odor behind her house on Fox Street. Investigation disclosed"—he flipped the page—"nothing of consequence in that area, which"—he cleared his throat softly— "skirts Fall's Pond, which, it was noted by Marcus Breeze, has been the source of strong sulfuric odors in the past. Stephen Krull suggested that Beelzebub, which he said was another name for the devil, had gone skinny-dipping in the pond." There was quick laughter around the table. John grinned. "Further investigation will be postponed for the winter." He paused again and looked up confusedly at Sarah. "I can't . . ." he began, and looked quickly back at the notebook, then back at Sarah. "I can't quite decipher my shorthand, here. I'm sorry. I think it says something about fleas."

Irene Atwater Janus, at the opposite side of the table from John, raised her hand, got a nod from Sarah, and explained, "It was about the raccoons coming into the houses, Sarah, and infesting them with fleas. That's what it was about."

"Yeah," John exclaimed, smiling. "I remember that." He studied the notebook closely a moment. "It was resolved," he read, "that an exterminator from Merrimac be hired to look into the problem. Said resolution to also be postponed until spring." He glanced around. He was a pale, round-faced man of forty-nine, pleasant and good-natured, if not exquisitely bright, who'd been in the village for fourteen years and whose specialty was bringing grieving parents and their departed children together, however briefly. It was a task he took very seriously. "Maybe that exterminator," he said, "can go after the roaches in my house. 'Course he'd need a bazooka!" Again there was laughter in the room, and John looked very pleased by it. Sarah raised her hand; the laughter died. "John," she said, "is there much more?"

He flipped the pages. "Gee, yes there is, Sarah. A couple of pages of shorthand here."

She looked distressed by this. "Okay," she said, "I think we can forego further reading of the minutes and get on to more pressing matters."

"Sure, Sarah," John said. He flipped forward in the notebook, put his pen to the page. "Whenever you're ready."

In 1883, Lucius Fairclau came to the area where Goode's Crossing now stands from Bethlehem, Pennsylvania. His purpose?—"To establish a place where prophets, and seers, and sensitives can congregate and be free from the awful ridicule of others." He apparently had been kicked out of Bethlehem (and before that out of Harrisburg, Pennsylvania, and Troy, New York), for "practicing witchcraft, which is in direct violation of the laws and covenants of our Creator." Or so said the Bethlehem Town Council. It was a charge that he vehemently denied: "I am not a *witch!* I practice psychism. I *see!*"

He came to the Adirondacks with his wife, Melnora, and two teenaged daughters and fashioned a crude, but liveable house out of native white pine. His fame, or infamy—depending on who you talked to—followed him, and within months other "practitioners of psychism" had joined him.

Within a year, "Fairclau Village" had grown to an approximate population of 30. An ad in *The Merrimac Bee* for June 21, 1885 reads: "Bring your suffering and your grief to Fairclau Village. We will show you that Death steps to one side for us." It worked. People flocked to the village in search of departed relatives, and friends, and loved ones. And apparently the people there gave them what they wanted, because the village continued to grow, slowly, but surely, until, in 1901, it was revealed that one of the village's most respected residents was not so much a practitioner of "psychism" as a practitioner of an extremely smooth con game. So, due to the zealous work of an early investigative reporter, the village fell into disrepute. It did not close down, but it did slow down considerably.

There are two churches in or near the village. One is The Goode's Crossing Presbyterian Church, and appears to have been abandoned for decades. The other, a small, Methodist Church on Shoemaker Road, just outside the village boundary, is closed down during the fall and winter and serves only a couple dozen people, anyway—a few residents of Goode's Crossing included.

Sarah held the *Update* magazine high once again: "I would like reactions to this, please," she said.

Marjory Gwynne raised her hand. Sarah nodded. "I think," Marjory said, "that it was pretty clever. And besides, maybe some of us *are* fakes and liars." Several of the people in the room gasped audibly.

Marjory was forty-three, auburn-haired—it had begun turning gray at the temples—gray-eyed, and, as Marcus Breeze and Francis Eblecker, two other residents of the village, had once agreed, "the only really sexy woman east of Merrimac." Most of the men in the village had entertained various fantasies about her, though only Harry March, eleven years her senior, had succeeded in doing anything about it. Marjory was a quick-witted, discriminating woman who had few illusions about herself, or about her place in the village. She felt that she might possess a certain "sensitivity" (a word many of the villagers liked to use to describe themselves) but beyond that she freely admitted that much of what she did was formulated out of whole cloth. She took a certain pride, however, in the fact she never let anyone leave her home without feeling that they had been somehow comforted, that their grief was just a little less than when they had come in. It was a philosophy she thought some of the others in the village did not understand.

Sarah stared hard at Marjory now. "My dear woman," she said, "you are, of course, speaking for yourself?"

"I can speak for no one else," Marjory said, grinning. Harry March, seated next to her, nudged her with his knee as if to say, *That's enough!* She nudged him back, hard enough that Marcus

Breeze, next to her, heard a distinct knocking sound. A small *Ah* of pain erupted from Harry.

"Are you saying that *you* are a fake and a liar?" Sarah asked. "Because if you are, then we have no use for you in this village."

"Does it really make any difference what I say, Sarah?" Again there were several audible gasps in the room.

"It makes a difference to *me*, Mrs. Gwynne!" Sarah was clearly angry.

Marjory said nothing for a moment. She was considering her response. At last she said, "No. I'm not saying that I'm a fake and a liar, Sarah. I apologize."

Harry March sighed.

Someone whispered, "Well, I should say so."

Someone else cleared his throat nervously.

Marjory felt suddenly as if she had committed treason against herself, and it felt awful.

Sarah looked at John. "John," she said, "for her own sake, why don't you strike Mrs. Gwynne's conversation with me from the minutes of this meeting. I can't see that it serves any real purpose."

Don't do me any favors, Sarah! Marjory thought. But she said, to John, "It's *Ms.* Gwynne, John. Not Mrs.—Ms."

John nodded once, quickly, as if embarrassed. "Yes," he said, "I know." And he tore a page from his spiral notebook, crumpled it up, then looked at a loss as to what to do with it. He shoved it in his pants pocket.

Sarah asked, "Any other reactions?" She glanced around the table.

Anna Breeze said, "It made us appear, I don't know . . . tacky, I guess." She had her own copy of the magazine in front of her. She put on a pair of glasses, and continued, "Like when it talks about 'Well-worn couches, and thrift-store interiors.'" She glanced up; she looked offended. "There is no need for that kind of talk," she said. "I myself told the reporter that many of us do not make much of a living from this."

"Yellow journalism," Weyre Goodall offered glumly. "It sells papers."

Anna shook her head sadly. "I take pride in what Marcus and I have done with our house, regardless of how little money we have. It might not look like a page from *House Beautiful*, but—"

Weyre Goodall interrupted, "When that reporter talked to me he asked all kinds of questions, and I answered all of them pretty good, and I didn't see none of them in that article." Weyre, sixty-one, overweight, balding, had been in the village for over thirty-two years. "He asked me, for instance, did I really believe in 'all this stuff,'— that's just the way he said it, too—and I said, 'It's impossible *not* to believe in it if you live it day after day,' which is a pretty good answer, I think. But did he put that in his article? No. He puts in what Andrew"—Andrew Liwush—"said about 'soul travel' and 'reincarnation' and 'astral projection' and all *that* crap—"

Andrew, a couple of seats away, cut in, "Hey,

come on now, that's like a religion to me, Weyre, and you're going pretty far when you insult someone's religion—"

"I agree," said Marcus Breeze, "and I think Weyre should apologize, Sarah."

"I wasn't insulting no one," Weyre said. "Christ sake—"

"Please, Weyre," Sarah cut in angrily, "I want no obscenities here!"

"Yes," Weyre said, "I'm sorry."

Lucius Fairclau died in 1904, his wife a year later. His two daughters left the village and apparently lived uneventful lives. In 1935, Sarah Goode, a then 24-year-old self-professed psychic and medium from Syracuse, New York came to the village and assumed control. Her first order of business was a name change for the village, for obvious reasons. And so, Fairclau Village became Goode's Crossing. Then she quickly ferreted out the most blatant of the village's remaining con artists and "persuaded" them to move their business elsewhere. Then she began placing ads in newspapers, and trade papers, and magazines—one ad even appeared in *The Saturday Evening Post*—which eventually brought new blood into the village of Goode's Crossing, and, for a short time, new life.

Some of those early residents have since moved on, in one sense of the phrase or another, but many still remain:

There is Sarah Goode herself, for instance, who refused to say more to me than, "Goode's Crossing is not a circus sideshow, young man,"—and from her tone and the look on her face it was clear that she felt she was reading my mind—"it is a place

where grief can be assuaged, and loved ones brought
together again."

And there is Francis Eblecker, a very big and very
gentle man of 54 who holds seances in his large,
memorabilia-filled, and gloomy kitchen. "It's where
I concentrate best," he explains.

And Marcus Breeze, also in his fifties, and his wife
Anna, and Sam Pepper, who could have been a
stand-in for Ichabod Crane, and Irene Atwater
Janus, and Stephen Krull and . . .

"We are straying," Sarah said, "somewhat far
afield from the purpose of my question." She
stopped and waited for silence to return to the
room. "Which is, 'Do we want the image—*our*
image, the image of Goode's Crossing itself—to be
as it is put forward in this article?' Not only that
we are, after all, just a pack of fakes and liars, but
that we cannot even keep our homes up, and that
we are just 'having fun' at the expense of those
who come to us for help."

A sudden air of discomfort settled over the
room, as if someone had told a tasteless, off-color
joke, and no one wanted to react to it. At last someone said, "I never really thought about it."

"Who said that, please?" Sarah asked.

Francis Eblecker raised his hand. "I did,
Sarah."

"Would you care to elaborate, Francis?"

He shrugged. "What's to elaborate? I do what I
do—I'm not ashamed of it, I'm not particularly
proud of it. Just like somebody who's a book-
keeper. There's nothing wrong with bookkeeping,
but there's nothing really wonderful about it,

either. The reporter that wrote that article came here expecting to find one thing. He found it, whether it's here or not, and there's nothing any of us can do about it."

"I'm sorry you feel that way, Francis," Sarah announced.

Francis shrugged again; "So am I, I really am."

"Because," Sarah went on, "we *do* serve a purpose, you and I. We bring help and comfort to our fellow human beings, we give them back, if just for a moment, the thing they thought they had lost forever. And speaking for myself, there could be nothing in this world more noble, and more purposeful than that."

She got no response; she expected none. Marjory whispered to Harry, "Jesus, she's really going off the deep end tonight." Harry looked vaguely offended by the remark.

"And if," Sarah continued, her voice rising, "we call upon our 'ingenuity' to aid us in this task, then it is only because we are human, and imperfect, and because Mr. Death was a strong and cold grip and needs *prodding!*"

Several in the group nodded meaningfully at this, as if it were the mirror image of their own thoughts.

"We are . . . caretakers, yes—We are the Caretakers of Eternity."

Marjory rolled her eyes.

Stephen Krull, across the table, looked suddenly ill at ease.

"We usher people back and forth," Sarah went on, and she waved her thin arms over the table, as if sweeping it with an invisible whisk broom, "between our world and the other."

The meeting continued for another hour and a half. There was some talk about sueing *Update* magazine, but it was quickly dropped after Marcus Breeze, who had taken some pre-law courses in his abortive college career, pointed out that waivers had been signed, and agreements made, and that the article had, after all, brought new clients to the village.

But when the meeting was finally adjourned, and people were making their way back to their homes through the unusually warm October night, most of them felt vaguely insulted, as if they'd overheard someone say that they had a collective case of bad breath. It bothered all of them, though to varying degrees, Sarah especially. No one likes to be laughed at, after all. Even if it does bring new clients in.

"I wish I hadn't gone there tonight," Anna Breeze said to her husband Marcus, later, as they lay waiting for sleep to come to them. "It made me feel bad."

"Yes," Marcus agreed.

And at Marjory Gwynne's house, Harry March excused himself early. "I'm sorry, Marjory," he said. "I guess I'm just not up to it, tonight." She said it was okay. And it was.

8

Francis Eblecker couldn't remember a time when he had not been fat. He imagined that there surely should have been such a time, when he was an infant, for instance, or a toddler, but he'd been fat then, too, his mother had told him (she'd used the word "chubby" ... "Babies are 'chubby,' Francis; children and teenagers and adults are 'fat').

He'd gone through all the excuses—it was "glandular," he was nervous and high-strung and so he ate too much (hell, it was better than smoking, wasn't it?), it was the result of a well-meaning but misguided upbringing ("Make sure you eat *every*thing that's put in front of you, Francis. I don't care if you're full!"), until now, at age fifty-four, he'd put all the excuses behind him and had resolved that the fat farms, and the diets, the pills,

78

the counselors, et al, were a thing of the past. He was *fat*, he would die *fat*, and he would be buried *fat*. Pretty soon, too, he supposed—which was okay.

He turned his head and glanced at the chunky Baby Ben alarm clock on a little nightstand near the bed (the nightstand also contained the latest issue of *Alfred Hitchcock's Mystery Magazine*, which helped put him to sleep, a half-empty glass of water, some used Kleenex, a Tensor lamp with blue paint splattered on it): the clock read 7:45. He groaned, reached over, pushed the alarm button to off. The clock was set to ring at 8:00 and he hated the sound of it; he was regularly putting money aside for a new one.

"Goddamn!" he whispered (he began each day with a curse; he imagined that it helped to get his blood circulating), and maneuvered his massive legs to the edge of the bed, pushed himself to a sitting position, swung his feet to the floor. He swore again; "Goddamn!" He also couldn't remember a time when he had not felt lousy in the morning.

He'd come to Goode's Crossing in 1956, after a battery of testing at Duke University proved he possessed, as his testers put it, "paranormal abilities of a precognitive and telepathic nature." It was a phrase he disliked. He was *sensitive*, he maintained, like most of the other people in the village.

He stood, made his way out of the room, down a short, poorly lighted hallway to the bathroom. He used the toilet, splashed cold water on his face, then, feeling a little better, went downstairs to his small kitchen and fixed breakfast—half a dozen eggs, a pound of bacon, six slices of whole wheat toast, a bowl of Cheerios with sliced bananas, several tall glasses of orange juice, and a pot of coffee, light with sugar.

His clients, a middle-aged couple named Weekes, were due to show up at 10:00. He liked them; they were easy to "read" (another popular phrase in the village) and without much effort he'd been able to make them believe that he was just one or two steps down from God Almighty himself.

It was 9:30 and Lester Stanhope was putting on quite a creditable performance. He was using his "double voice" (it had taken him a long time to perfect and involved the vibration of mucous in his throat and in his mouth at different tones; it always hurt him afterwards, but it was very, very convincing), as if—which is that he told the client —two spirits were vying for temporary possession of his vocal cords, both of them speaking at the same time, and both, of course, saying the same thing (which was another trick he'd been trying to perfect—having his "double voice" say two different things at once. He'd had little success with it).

"Mother, no," said his double voice, one apparently the voice of a woman in middle age, the other that of a child, possibly a boy. "Mother, you mustn't!" And he slumped forward, arms and hands flat on the round wooden table, face turned to one side, eyes closed.

The client, a man named Johnston, in his late thirties, thin, fidgety, and blatantly effeminate, gasped audibly and put his hand on Lester's. "Lester, are you all right?"

Lester pushed himself slowly, as if with great effort, back to a sitting position in his hard, ladder-back chair ("Comfort," he told his clients who asked about the chair, "is an enemy of concentration"). He opened his eyes, gathered a look of great weariness about him, sighed: "Oh, they are strong today, Mr. Johnston. They would tear through and into this room if they could."

"Are you all right?" Mr. Johnston repeated.

Lester sighed again, and nodded. "Yes, but I must rest for a moment. You understand, I'm sure."

"Oh, yes, I do, I do understand."

"I believe that your Samuel was one of those trying to break through, Mr. Johnston."

Johnston smiled broadly, with great pleasure. "Oh, I do hope so, Lester. He was such a very strong personality, so very strong, Lester. And *alive!* I loved him, truly I loved him as much as I love myself!" He paused, considered, then hurried on, "And I still do love him, of course. I would have to say"—he held his hands at chest level, spread his palms, and made taffy-pulling motions in the air—"that our love has *broadened*. And it has also become"—he sliced slowly at the air with the edges of his hands—"much more finely delineated. Can you appreciate what I'm saying to you, Lester?"

Lester could not answer immediately. Johnston

was showing a side of himself that he hadn't expected to see and it confused him. He smiled his much-practiced smile of omniscience. "Death," he proclaimed, shooting from the hip, "can be a great teacher to us all, if we let it."

Then Johnston abruptly slipped back into character. "Oh," he cooed, hands fluttering at his mouth, "that is *so* very, very profound." And Lester found himself greatly relieved.

Irene Atwater Janus brought her puffy right thumb and forefinger together at a spot midway down her left forearm. She felt certain she could feel something wriggling there. She grinned, brought the thumb and forefinger up close to her eyes. She grimaced. They were empty. She studied her forearm again, tried hard to find what surely had to be there—she could feel it moving about, sticking its damned *proboscis* in—among the long, coarse, dark hairs. But she saw nothing. She cursed, threw herself back in the large, beige-colored, Queen Anne chair—there were dark areas where her head rested, and at the front of the seat cushion—and thumped the arms of the chair with both fists. "Goddamn raccoons!" she hissed. If someone were to question her about it, she'd have to admit that she hadn't actually seen one in the house, but she sure as hell had heard them, hadn't she? And she sure as hell had lived in the Adirondacks long enough to know when they'd been prowling around.

She threw herself out of the chair suddenly and into the kitchen. She yanked open a drawer, pulled

out a small, .22 caliber pistol, studied it grinningly
a moment, then, sighing, put it back. It wasn't big
enough. The damn raccoons would laugh at it. You
had to take a 12 gauge to raccoons, as her mother
used to! But, of course, a 12 gauge was expensive,
and shells for it were expensive, too, and with a
winter in Thendara only a year away, if air fares
didn't go up too much, she had to watch her
budget like a hawk.

So to hell with the raccoons and with the fleas
they brought into the house!

She glanced at the kitchen clock—a small,
grease-splattered replica of a Franklin stove just
above the sink, between two bare windows—and
saw that her clients were due in less than an hour.
"Christ!" she murmured, uncertain that she could
get everything ready in so short a time. There were
the ropes to connect, first, and the tape recorder
to hook up, which she'd always found difficult,
and the slide projector, and the remote switches to
plug in. She thought briefly of having Sam Pepper,
who lived right next door, come over and help her
but remembered that he'd gone to Merrimac
earlier that morning for firewood. "Damn you,"
she said aloud, and went into her sitting room, a
small dark room next to the kitchen, and set to
work.

Marjory Gwynne had no clients that day, and
she wasn't sure what she was going to do with herself. She was still dressed in her nightclothes—
black panties and a blue-flannel nightgown—and
she wished vaguely that Harry were there because

she imagined she was horny, and an hour or so in the sack would be a nice way to start the day. But then she remembered that Harry was not much of a morning man, that he had considerable trouble getting it up in the morning, and that when he did it usually tended to be unwilling to stay up and they most always finished with mutual apologies and whispered gibberish about "taking a rain check."

She was in the kitchen; it was 9:55. The mailman —an octogenarian named Spaahn who drove an ancient Willys jeep—had already been by, bringing her nothing but junk mail and a utility bill. She'd been hoping for the more-or-less-monthly letter from her son, Josh, who still—at twenty-three years of age—lived with his father in San Diego. Tomorrow, she thought. Because today was a Monday, and if he had mailed his letter Friday, then it would doubtless take four days to get across the country. But, of course, if he had mailed it on Saturday then it wouldn't arrive till Wednesday, and if he mailed it *today*, then . . .

She decided at once that she wouldn't have breakfast that morning. She'd go into Merrimac for a bit of shopping, then take in a movie, then have dinner at the Chung Ho ("Merrimac's Only Authentic Chinese Cuisine"), then take in a movie, and *then* she and Harry could have a nice, steamy evening together.

But, of course, dinner at the Chung Ho always made her nauseous.

And shopping in Merrimac was like stumbling through a bad flea market.

And the theatre there seemed to specialize in biker epics.

And besides, she had no car. Her ten-year-old Pinto, which had never been much good anyway in these mountains, had finally given up the ghost a week before ("Cracked engine block," Harry had told her, with much authority, to which she had answered, "Oh, for Christ's sake, Harry, it is not. It's a busted axle, any fool can see that!" for which she had later apologized).

She could borrow Harry's car, she thought. But then, if he had nothing to do today either, then he'd want to come along and she'd have to think of some way of telling him that she'd prefer to spend the day alone.

She wandered out of the kitchen, started up the stairs, took her nightgown off. "Oh, Pappy," she breathed, "I am so *bored!*"

At 12:30, Stephen Krull came up behind his wife, Lily, who was putting the finishing touches on a small painting of a fir tree with a stylized rabbit peering around it at the trunk, put his hands on her shoulders and announced that lunch was ready, if she was.

She said, "In a minute, Stephen—as soon as I'm done with this."

"It's very nice," he said. "I like the Easter Bunny."

"It's not an Easter Bunny," she protested.

"It looks like one."

"Well it's not supposed to. It's a rabbit, not a bunny."

He said jokingly, "All your rabbits look like bunnies."

And she furiously obliterated the rabbit with a smear of white paint.

"Jesus, Lily, I didn't mean—"

"It looked stupid, anyway."

"It didn't look stupid."

"Your brother always liked my stuff," she reminded him. She was talking about Jim Krull, Stephen's younger brother, dead five years then, the victim of a heart attack.

"And I like your stuff, too," Stephen told her. He coaxed her around so she was facing him. She lowered her eyes. He said, concerned, "Is something wrong, Lily?"

She hesitated, then, "I don't know." She lifted her eyes. "Last night, I guess. I've never seen Sarah like that before and it bothered me. A lot of what she was saying was the truth, Stephan."

"Yes," he answered. "I guess she feels . . . defensive about the village. You can't really blame her —after all, she's been here for what?—fifty years?"

"At least."

"My God—Goode's Crossing is *her*, the same way your painting is you. Shit, that article upset all of us, I'm sure, but especially her, and so she had to get a little . . . philosophical about it. There's no harm in that."

Lily took a deep breath. She said on the exhale, "It's just that I respect her so much, Stephen—"

"We all do, Lily."

She raised an eyebrow at that. "And *because* I respect her, I don't like to think that we're going to . . . disappoint her. Do you know what I mean?"

Stephen thought a moment. "Yes, Lily," he said. "I do."

Sarah lived in a rambling, wood and brick Victorian at the end of Fox Street, a street named, by Sarah herself, after the Fox Sisters of the late nineteenth century, early practitioners of psychic research. She had lived alone in the house ever since coming to the village, as Stephen had guessed, a half century before. She'd never wanted to marry. She had had, in fact, no lasting relationships with anyone. What few relationships she'd fallen into had been short-lived and disappointing, both for herself and for the men involved, and, in fact, had it not been for one strange and painful encounter thirty-five years earlier she would have remained a virgin throughout her life (a fact which would have excited all kinds of Freudian speculation among some of the village's more well-read inhabitants had it been common knowledge. But it was not common knowledge. It was assumed by many—who would swear that it was Sarah herself who had told them; though she had only provided broad hints—that she had once been married but that her husband had been killed in the Second World War).

The house was furnished very nicely, with authentic Victorian and mid-Victorian pieces that Sarah had culled from several trips to New York City and to England, two decades earlier, and

which she kept well-dusted, and polished, and re-
paired. She liked her house, and her furniture,
though she never went so far as to fawn over any
of it, or become obsessed with it. Her obsessions,
she had explained once, were "not for the
material, but for the ethereal." It was a turn of
phrase that had never ceased to please her, and it
was a turn of phrase that she firmly believed was
the truth.

She had money, not lots of it, but enough to keep
her house in order, and the bills paid, and food on
her table for quite a few years. It was money she'd
been able to save over decades of very simple
living, as well as the remainder of a small inheri-
tance which had come to her upon the death of her
Aunt Jessica in 1949, a death she would have
prayed for, she thought, had she been a religious
woman. Like many of the people in the village, she
maintained that her work took the place of
religion. When she was much younger she'd gotten
into several heated arguments about, as she put it
at the time, "the real truth of what I do versus the
stark hypocrisy of organized religion." She had
long since given up such arguments. Those who
chose to see, would see. And those who were blind
would never see.

She was not a marvelously complex woman. She
was persuasive, intelligent, and incisive. But not
complex. She exercised power in Goode's Crossing
as effectively as she did because she felt
supremely comfortable with it, as if it resided in
her as naturally as did her gall bladder. She had
never made a conscious, grasping bid for the

power she possessed, she had merely assumed it, as if it were her destiny to assume it. And because she had never reached for it, because she had never groveled for it, she was not stridently defensive of it, and did not erect elaborate mazes of excuse and rationalization for it. She was comfortable with it. When decisions were to be laid down, and opinions formulated, and pronouncements made, she was right, and others, if they disagreed, were wrong. What could be simpler? It was an idea she believed in as firmly, and unquestioningly as she believed in gravity.

Part Two
THE ACCIDENT

9

October 15

Marian Hauser pushed her front door part way open and peered down Shoemaker Road for the fifth time in an hour. The road was empty. She glanced at her wristwatch; 4:35—the school bus carrying her son, Tod, home was nearly an hour late. Probably the storm, she thought. Freak, mid-autumn snowstorms, even as weak as this one had been, always caught everyone with their pants down.

She closed the front door, crossed her small living room to the kitchen, and stared at the wall phone for a moment. She picked up the receiver, began dialing, hesitated, put the receiver down. What would Terry, her husband, be able to tell her that she didn't already know? She'd just worry him, and there was no need for that, yet.

She shoved her hands into the pockets of her

jeans. Her body stiffened, she grimaced: "Goddamnit all to hell!" she muttered. She didn't need
this . . . aggravation! So what if the bus was late,
what did that prove? If anything had happened, if
there'd been an accident, she'd have been
informed, the police would have called. It would
have been like before, with Jeremy.

("Mrs. Hauser?"

"Yes. Who is this, please?"

"Detective Garner, at the Fifth Street Station.
Could you come down here, please, Mrs. Hauser,
as soon as possible?"

"I don't understand—"

"I'm afraid it's about your son, Mrs. Hauser."

"Jeremy? He's upstairs, studying."

"There's been an accident, Mrs. Hauser—"

"I told you, Jeremy is upstairs, studying. There
is no possible way—"

"Please, listen to me. A boy named Jeremy
Hauser, sixteen years old, was involved in a traffic
accident tonight."

"But that's impossible, I tell you—"

"Mrs. Hauser, please listen to me, I'm sorry, but
the boy is dead.")

That had been seven years ago, in a different
house, in a city a hundred miles away. She'd been
pregnant with Tod, then. And now the school bus
that Tod rode home every weekday on these
narrow, twisting, Adirondack roads was an hour
late.

She went back to the front door, opened it,
stepped out onto the small porch. The snowfall
had started again—wet, and heavy, and very slick.

"Goddamnit!" she whispered. "Goddamnit, Tod!" She went back inside. She'd call Terry, she vowed, in five minutes if the bus still hadn't shown up.

Bill Mann popped another No-Doz into his mouth, swallowed it dry, grimaced, yawned. This, he told himself, was just about the dumbest thing he'd ever done—on the road for twenty hours straight. And why? He didn't need the money all that much. And, hell, it would take more than money to put things right if that load of hydrazine he was hauling decided to let go.

He yawned again, wide, and long. The No-Doz was wreaking havoc on him, he realized. It would probably be a couple of weeks, anyway, before he got back into a normal sleep pattern. He straight-armed the steering wheel and pushed himself back in the seat in an attempt to stretch. His right calf muscle began to cramp up. He massaged it furiously; the cramp dissipated.

He put his foot on the brake pedal and pumped it gently until the rig came to a halt near the narrow soft-shoulder of the road. He grimaced again. "Dumb!" he whispered. "Dumb, stupid!" If they caught wind of this back at the office . . .

He was lost. For the first time in two decades of trucking, he had turned his rig down the wrong road—not just once, he realized, but a couple of times. Because he knew, or thought he knew, these Adirondack roads as well as he knew anything. He'd grown up here, for Christ's sake. He'd once found a couple of lost little kids in these forests. He'd taken a dozen Boy Scout troops, over a dozen years, through this country . . . No way could he be lost! He yanked open his driver's door, stepped down from the cab, and onto the road. "Damn nitwit!" he said aloud. "Damn shit-for-brains nitwit!"

He walked to the back of the truck, swung himself up onto the ladder, and climbed quickly to the top of the bright white tanker. He looked about, hoping he'd recognize some landmark. To his right, a shallow, fog-shrouded valley gave way to a couple-thousand-foot-high chunk of the Adirondack range. It could have been Leslie's Mountain, he supposed. But then again, it could have been Hanson's Mountain, or Bridgely's Mountain, or Mount Everest, for all he knew.

To his left, he saw nothing but pine trees, and darkness. Ahead, the narrow road sloped gently upward, its crest—a half mile off—lost in a creeper of fog.

He swore again. He thought that he might as well be in Oz.

Then he saw, just to the left of the valley, about a mile off, he guessed, chimney smoke rising straight up in several places, and he realized at once where he was—on Shoemaker Road, near Goode's Crossing. Sure. He hadn't been here in years and years, not since he was a teenager—thirteen, he supposed, maybe fourteen—and he and a couple of other guys had decided that Goode's Crossing would be a hell of a place to spend Halloween night. So they had skulked about outside the big Victorian homes for a while, hoping to catch some of the "weirdos" that lived there in a "ritual sacrifice," or worse, but it had all been a bust. Halloween seemed to be pretty much just another night to most of the people who lived in Goode's Crossing; a few poorly carved pumpkins on porches, a cardboard skeleton on someone's front door, some trick-or-treaters from God knew where (because it was common knowledge that there were no children in Goode's Crossing) but no ritual sacrifices. And because the whole thing had been Bill's idea, he'd gotten the blame for the way it had turned out.

He grinned wryly now, remembering, and climbed down from the tanker. His eyes focused momentarily on the words, DANGER: EXPLOSIVE CHEMICALS: STAY 100 FEET BACK in big, bold, red letters on the rear of the tanker.

He went to the cab, climbed in, turned the ignition on.

The snowstorm caught up with him. Within seconds, visibility was reduced to zero. He rolled his eyes in frustration, turned the ignition off. He'd sit this one out, he decided. Mid-autumn storms didn't last very long, but driving in them, especially with this load, and on this piss-poor excuse for a highway, would be a big mistake, and he'd made enough mistakes for one day.

Connie Weeker switched her windshield wipers to HIGH. Nothing happened. She glanced at the switch, turned it to OFF. The wipers stopped moving instantly; they were pointing straight up. She turned the switch to HIGH again. The wipers moved slowly, spastically, to the right, then to the left. They stopped again, at their rest position. She flicked the switch quickly between OFF and HIGH a half dozen times. The wipers stayed put. She cursed. First the sticking door locks, then that stupid knock in the engine, and now *this?!* Well, she deserved it, didn't she, for buying a used car from a dealer. And it wasn't as if her brother, Lou hadn't warned her more than once. By Jesus, he'd sure as hell gloat now ("I warned you, Connie. Didn't I warn you?").

She checked the speedometer. It read 45. "What the . . ." she breathed, surprised at her speed in this storm. She took her foot off the accelerator, the Impala slowed to a crawl almost immediately. She touched the accelerator again, lightly. The back of the car slid to the right; she pulled the wheel hard to the left; the car swung around violently. "Oh, shit!" she muttered, pulled the wheel hard to the right, and took her foot from the accelerator at the same time. The car shuddered to a halt in the middle of the road.

Connie lowered her head to the steering wheel. She was breathing heavily, her eyes were closed, her hands were shaking.

Jesse McMurto had been a schoolbus driver for the last fifteen of his sixty-two years. He was a smiling, good-natured man, and he was very fat. From the back, as he sat in the driver's seat—several of the second-graders in the bus were fond of remarking—he looked like Humpty Dumpty, his ample rear end billowing out this way or that, depending on which way the bus was leaning. They all got a kick out of watching the entire bus lower several inches when he got on, and rise up several inches when he got off. And he, in return, got a kick from knowing they were getting a kick out of him.

Today, he was taking fifteen of them home. Three had already gotten off. On a normal day, the bus would have been nearly full, but, thanks to a recent outbreak of Russian flu, this was not a normal day.

Jesse glanced in his rearview mirror. "You kids all set?" he called.

The children—seven boys ranging in age from six to nine, and five girls, all six or seven years old —had crowded up to the front seats soon after the bus had come to a stop. The children said, almost in unison, "Yeah, Jesse. Let's get goin'." He grinned, "Okay," he called, and turned the ignition on. The engine roared to life.

"Hey, Jesse," Tod Hauser called. "What was wrong with the bus?"

Jesse pulled onto Shoemaker Road and turned the windshield wipers on. This new snowfall, second of the afternoon, seemed even heavier than the first. "Well, I'll tell ya what was wrong with the bus, Tod. It was the Zackafratzamolleycoddler switch is what it was."

"It was the *what*?"

"The Zackafratzamolleycoddler switch, Tod. It controls the Whistlin' Woodsy's in the back end of the bus."

Tod giggled, followed quickly by a couple of the girls, and one of the boys.

Barry White, a very serious, very clear-headed nine-year-old who had purposely seated himself apart from the other kids, said, "There is no Zack-a . . . Zack-afratz-coddly-moddler switch, Jesse. You're just tellin' a story."

Jesse frowned. Between his ears, Barry White had to be ten years older than his real age, and that was a genuine pity, because the poor kid never seemed to get a kick out of anything. "Can you prove there is no Zackafratzamolleycoddler switch, Barry?" Jesse asked.

A slight grin appeared on Barry's face. "I don't need to prove it, Jesse." And his grin broadened just a bit.

Jesse sighed. He glanced in the rearview mirror, caught the eye of most of the children. "Who can count the snowflakes?" he challenged.

Eileen Zelinski, a beautiful, brown-eyed brunette of seven years "going on eight," — the subject of many whispered asides and quick nods of the head among the boys—said, "*No one* can count the snowflakes, Jesse." It seemed, from her tone, to be a fact which awed her immensely.

"You're right, Eileen," Jesse said. "Their numbers are *in*finite!" to which several of the children responded, as one, "Huh?"

"*In*finite!" Jesse repeated, quite mysteriously now.

And Barry White said, as if bored, "'without end,' it means 'without end.'"

"'Without end'?" asked Richie Marlette, a

normally shy and very sensitive nine-year-old with red hair and a splash of freckles across the bridge of his nose. He turned in his seat and looked Barry White squarely in the eye. "What's 'without end' mean, Barry?"

And Barry answered simply, "It means 'infinite,'" to which there was general, high-pitched, childish laughter in the bus.

Jesse McMurto did not laugh. He was worried. It was likely, he thought, that this storm would get a lot worse before it got better, and if it did get worse he'd be forced to pull over to the side of the road and wait it out. If the damned school board, his thoughts continued, had voted to put CB radios in the buses, as he'd suggested, then it wouldn't be much of a problem. He'd be able to call for a snowplow. But there was no CB radio. And, on top of that, the bus wasn't even equipped with snow tires—"They're on order, Jesse. Maybe next week."—and the road was narrow, the shoulder soft, the snow seemed to be piling up higher by the minute . . .

Jesse cursed beneath his breath.

"What's the matter, Jesse?" It was Eileen Zelinski; she was in the seat just behind him. "Why'd you swear, Jesse? Is something wrong?"

"Nothing's wrong, honey. I just have to concentrate on the road, and that's hard to do sometimes. I didn't mean to swear." He chastised himself for letting her overhear him.

She continued, "My daddy says that word, too. He says it all the time, I wish he wouldn't. He seems like someone else when he says it."

"Yeah," agreed Tod Hauser, "mine, too." It was a fact that seemed to make him noticeably glum.

"Uh-huh," Jesse murmured, his attention diverted by something a hundred or so yards ahead, in the middle of the road. He checked his speedometer; 25.

Behind him, Tod Hauser's thermos bottle fell from his open lunch pail and started rolling toward the rear of the bus. "Jees!" he whispered, and got up and went after it.

Jesse began pumping the brakes, lightly. He flicked the lights on. He cursed again. The lights were useless in the heavy snowfall.

"Jesse?" It was Eileen; she sounded upset. "You said that word again."

"I'm sorry," Jesse told her. "I'm sorry, honey."

The right front fender of the bus—an area just below the headlight—barely touched the left front fender of Connie Weeker's Impala. In a similar mid-autumn storm, Jessie had once hit a doe. He thought that what he felt now—a small, spongy thump which he actually heard more than felt—was similar.

Eileen Zelinski said, "Jesse, what was that noise?"

Barry White said, his tone quiet and instructional, "We hit something. A car, I think."

Tod Hauser, halfway to the rear of the bus, said very urgently, "There's something out there, Jesse."

And another of the children, sensing the quick rise of panic in the air, burst into a fit of loud crying.

Jesse said soothingly, "It's okay, kids, it's okay!"

Barry White said very matter-of-factly, "No, it ain't!"

And Tod Hauser glanced back at him. He had never liked Barry too much; he'd always thought Barry was strange, and hard to talk to. But he grinned at him, now—a small, sad grin—and said, "Yeah, Barry—"

The bus hit Bill Mann's hydrazine-loaded tanker broadside, at nearly 25 miles an hour. The tanker ruptured within seconds, spilling hydrazine into the cold, late-afternoon air.

The explosion that followed was white-hot, deafening, and magnificent.

10

In Goode's Crossing

Sarah Goode said to the dowdy, middle-aged woman seated across from her at the small, round, dark oak table, "Yes, there are rooms available, Mrs. Pelcher. Sam Pepper has rooms." She inclined her head to the left. "Number Sixteen Fox Street. Do you know where that is?"

The middle-aged woman sighed, relieved. "Oh, yes, yes, I do. And thank you, Sarah. I have *never* been able to drive in the snow. Not ever. It's very, very *traumatic* for me, Sarah!"

Sarah leaned forward. Her long, thin arm reached across the table; she took the woman's hand gently in her own. "I'm sure it is, Mrs. Pelcher. I'm sure it is." She let go of the woman's hand, straightened, glanced to her right, at a century-old Regulator wall clock that ticked loudly, and comfortingly. It read 4:58. Sarah smiled pleasantly. "Thank you, Mrs. Pelcher. I'm sure our efforts in the future will not be in vain."

The woman looked suddenly flustered. She opened her big, black patent leather purse, stuck a pale hand in.

"No, Mrs. Pelcher," Sarah told her firmly. "I am no longer accepting money for what I do. Your thanks are more than sufficient, as well as the knowledge that I am helping you to bridge the gap that separates you from your brother."

Mrs. Pelcher withdrew a fifty-dollar bill. "Perhaps just a small donation, Sarah."

Sarah's heavily lined face clouded over with quick agitation. "No, Mrs. Pelcher. Only your thanks. Your thanks are sufficient."

Mrs. Pelcher stared incredulously at her a moment, then at the fifty. She stuck it back in her purse. "I don't understand, Sarah."

"I am," Sarah told her, and her tone was one of recitation, "a conduit for knowledge that would normally flow to you from those who have crossed over—"

The phone rang. Sarah answered it immediately. "Yes?" she snapped.

"Sarah?" It was Weyre Goodall.

"Yes, Weyre, what is it?"

"There's been an accident, Sarah. On Shoemaker Road. A very bad one, I think."

"Then I believe that you had better call the sheriff, Weyre. I am not the sheriff!"

"I thought you should know about it, Sarah. I think a schoolbus was involved—that's what John Yount says. He's calling the sheriff now. And the volunteer firemen." He hesitated. Sarah said nothing. "Sarah, are you still there?"

"Yes," she whispered. "How . . ." She cleared her throat. "How does John know that a schoolbus was involved?"

"I'm not sure, Sarah. I guess he was coming back from town and he saw the whole thing happen."

Sarah whispered, "My God!"

Mrs. Pelcher said, "Is something wrong, Sarah?"

Sarah nodded once, briskly. "Yes, Mrs. Pelcher. There's been an accident."

Mrs. Pelcher breathed, "Oh, no." Then, "Was anyone hurt?"

Sarah ignored her. She said to Weyre Goodall, "Drive me up there, Weyre."

"I'm leaving now," he said. "I'll be there in a few moments." And he hung up.

Sarah hung up. "Mrs. Pelcher," she said, "you must excuse me, now."

"Was anyone hurt, Sarah? In this accident?"

"Perhaps." She stood and patted fastidiously at the lap of her long, flower-print housedress; it hung very loosely from her spare frame. "I think there were probably quite a few hurt, Mrs. Pelcher."

"Yes," Mrs. Pelcher whispered, "I see." She looked flustered. "I'll call you, Sarah. Your season ends very soon, doesn't it?"

"Yes," Sarah answered. "In two weeks." She opened a closet door near the wall clock, withdrew a huge, gray wool coat, and put it on. "Call me. We will schedule another session."

"Yes," said Mrs. Pelcher, "I will. You've brought me great, great comfort, Sarah, I want you to know that—"

There was a loud double knock from below, at Sarah's front door. It was Weyre Goodall.

Marjory grasped Harry March's bare shoulders tightly. "Harry, stop. Please."

His body quieted. He sighed.

"I'm sorry, Harry. I'm sorry." She pushed at him; he rolled off her. "Something's wrong, Harry."

"You're telling me?"

"I'm serious, Harry." She sat up on the edge of the bed. Harry turned the bedside lamp on. "I wish I hadn't quit smoking," he said.

Marjory went to a window, parted the curtains slightly.

Harry said, "You're beautiful, you're exquisite!"

"Shhh!" she cut in. "I hear something."

"You're acting very strange, Marjory."

"There's a fire out there, Harry. On Shoemaker Road, I think."

Harry stood, went to the window, peered out. "Where?" he said, because he saw nothing but snow, and the quickly gathering dusk. "Marjory, the light's on."

"So?"

"So, we're standing here *naked*—"

She stepped away from the window, went to the foot of the bed, picked her panties and bra up from the top of a brown wicker chest there.

"What are you doing?" Harry asked.

"I'm going out. Are you coming with me or not?"

"You mean out to Shoemaker Road? In that storm? You're out of your mind!"

"We'll take your jeep, Harry."

"We will?"

She shrugged into a pair of blue jeans. "Yes, we will." She picked her blouse up from the bed, put it on, went to the closet. "I told you, Harry,"—she opened the closet door, took out a heavy, white wool sweater, slipped it over her head—"*something* has happened!" She nodded at his pants on the floor beside the bed. "Are your car keys in your pocket?"

Harry held his hand up as a gesture of submission. "I'll drive, Marjory. Just give me a few moments."

"It happened so fast," John Yount said, as if in awe. "I've never seen anything happen so fast!"

His wife, Judy, beside him—they were standing with their backs to the kitchen counter—took his hand: "Yes," she murmured, and she could think of nothing else to say.

John closed his eyes lightly. "I couldn't even get close, Judy. I tried—Goddamnit, I tried! But I couldn't even get *close!*"

"Yes," she said again.

"I felt helpless. I felt very, very helpless, Judy. I felt . . . impotent!"

"What could you do?" she asked. "Was there anything at all you could do?"

"I don't know. I don't think so. I tried, I *did* try. But it happened so fast, and everything was so hot, everything was so damned hot!"

She squeezed his hand reassuringly. "The sheriff's going to have trouble getting up here in that storm."

"Uh-huh. It'll take him a while." He lowered his head. "It doesn't really matter, though. I can't see that it matters."

"No," she said, and nodded—though his head was still down—at a tall, cream-colored coffee pot on the kitchen table. "Would you like some coffee? It's all ready."

"Yes," he answered, his head still lowered. "Thanks."

She turned around, got two large coffee mugs from the cupboard—one had the words BITCH BITCH BITCH printed on it in big black letters—took them to the table, poured the coffee.

"It's true," John said.

"I know it's true," Judy answered. She gave him the BITCH BITCH BITCH cup. "I know it's true," she repeated.

"It was so damned hot, Judy." He looked pleadingly at her, as if trying in vain to persuade her. "I was . . ." He held his right arm out, elbow bent slight, and clenched his fist. "I was a hundred feet away, and that heat . . . that heat, Judy, it was so incredible, so . . . overpowering!" He unclenched his fist; he stared a moment, blankly, his mouth open a little, at his hand, then back at Judy. His eyes watered. "Judy, *what* could I do?"

"You couldn't do anything, John," she told him,

trying for a tone of finality.

"I couldn't do anything," he said, more to himself than to her. He brought his coffee mug to his lips. He could feel that the coffee was scaldingly hot; the corner of his lips turned upward in a perverse approximation of a smile.

He threw his head back and poured half the cup of coffee down his throat.

"Christ God in heaven!" Judy screeched.

He dropped the cup. It shattered dully on the black-and-gold linoleum. His hand went to his upper chest and clutched it hard. He doubled over and stumbled woodenly about the room, Judy just behind him repeating again and again, "Christ God in heaven, *why* did you do that?!"

At last, he fell face forward to the floor.

Irene Atwater Janus lifted her moist, hazel eyes to the two old people seated with her at the kitchen table and said, "Please, let us join hands." The three of them joined hands. Irene closed her eyes and went on slowly, her tone so low it was almost husky, "Robert is passing quickly through the gate now. He's moving with wonderful purpose, and though he is cold, very, very cold, he is smiling, too." She paused very briefly. A slight, cordial smile appeared on her face. "He tells me that he has missed you both." She squeezed their hands. "He tells me that the pain is gone. He asks that you not worry, that your prayers have done much for him." She shivered noticeably. "He is still cold. He is still very cold. But that is changing, too—with the slow passage of time."

The old woman, Robert's grandmother, pleaded, "May we talk to him, Irene? Is that possible?"

Irene smiled again, more broadly, a smile of assent. The smile faded. Her voice appeared to grow very low and husky; the close approximation of a man's voice. A candle which had been burning at the center of the table went out at once. "How is Max?" the voice said.

The old woman's eyes watered. She lowered her head. "Oh, Robert, my poor Robert! Max . . . is dead."

The old woman's husband explained, "It happened two weeks ago, Robert. He went to sleep. Under the porch. You remember, don't you? —It was his favorite spot."

"He died there, Robert," the old woman cut in. "Peacefully, quite peacefully."

Irene began to cry. "If only," she blurted, still as if in Robert's voice, "he could be here. With me."

The old woman began to weep. "Oh, Robert"— there was the vaguest hint of reprimand in her voice—"you *know* that's not possible. You know you must accept your punishment."

"Yes," said Robert's voice sadly. "I know that." And then Irene's arms shook and she closed her eyes very tightly. "No," said Robert's voice. "No, not so soon!" And Irene flung her arms high above her head and slammed them down hard to the top of the table. A long, breathy sigh escaped her. She paused a beat, opened her eyes. The candle in the center of the table flared to life again. The old woman gasped. Irene looked first at her, then at the old man, then at the table in front of her chest.

"They have taken him back," she said. "The demons of his own creation have taken him back! It will be a long time, a week perhaps, before he can return to us."

The old woman withdrew a handkerchief from her purse and dabbed at her eyes with it. "He understands, Irene. I'm sure of that. Suicide is such a . . . selfish act. He understands."

The old man said, "He's a very smart boy. He used to come to us, Irene, and he used to say, 'I've done something wrong, please punish me!' He actually used to say that." His lips quivered a smile as he remembered. "I always thought that was so . . . so *good*, Irene. Do you know what I mean?"

Irene nodded solemnly. "Yes," she said.

"And so," the old woman began; she was still crying, but she was also making a pronouncement, "he will accept his punishment."

"Yes," whispered the old man.

Irene stood abruptly. "This has been extremely wearing on me," she said.

The old people stood. The old woman took two twenty-dollar bills from her purse and handed them to Irene. Irene accepted them quickly, her eyes averted. She whispered tightly, "I despise the feel of money."

The old people, who had heard the phrase from her before, nodded their agreement.

Lester Stanhope, at Irene's front door, called "Irene?", waited a moment, then knocked, loud. "Irene, it's me, Lester. Open up!" He knocked again. "Irene?"

The door opened; Irene stood stiffly in front of him. She grimaced. "What in hell do you want, Lester?"

"There's been an accident, Irene." He nodded to his left. "On Shoemaker Road. A bunch of kids in a schoolbus."

She hugged herself against the cold. "An accident? What does that have to do with me?"

"Could I come in, Irene?"

She moved to one side. He stepped hurriedly into the house. "Irene, they need a place—"

"They?" She closed the door behind him.

"Sheriff King. He said he'd need a place to take the victims. The survivors, I mean. If there are any. I told him I thought your house would be big enough—"

"Oh, for Christ's sake!" Irene rolled her eyes. "I am *not* going to have my house littered with . . . with *victims*, Lester. You didn't tell the sheriff, anything, did you? You didn't tell him—"

"Is something wrong?" It was the old man. He and his wife had appeared from the adjoining room. "Did I hear something about an accident?"

Lester nodded grimly. "On Shoemaker Road. I'm sorry, it's a bad one, a very bad one—"

"Lester," Irene cut in, "I asked you if you'd said anything to the sheriff."

"I told him I'd ask you first, Irene. That's all."

"Okay, you've asked."

"Are you saying no?"

"I'm saying no." She gestured, with a slight wave of her hand, to the east. "Why don't they use the Dohertys' house?"

"The Dohertys' house?"

"Sure, they're gone for the season . . ."

"It's all locked up, Irene."

"So? Break in. They won't be back until the spring, anyway. They'll never know."

Lester thought a moment, then crossed to the phone, on a small black table near the entrance to the kitchen. He picked up the receiver, dialed:

"Lester," Irene asked, "is that long distance?"

"I'm calling the sheriff's office."

"That's long distance."

"Twenty-two cents, Irene. Twenty-two fucking cents!" He heard little clucking sounds of disapproval from the old woman. He finished dialing, reached into his pocket, pulled out a quarter, laid it on the table near the phone. "I'll trust you for the three cents, Irene."

"Oh, for God's sake . . . " Irene began.

And Lester interrupted, "Maybe you won't have to worry about survivors anyway."

11

Two roads led into and out of Goode's Crossing from Shoemaker Road. One was Pitney Road—so named because a man named John Pitney, an early resident of the village, had built it almost single-handedly late in the nineteenth century; it was made of crushed stone and dirt, was littered with potholes and was all but impassable. The other was Fairclau Close, "Fairclau," after Lucius Fairclau, of course, and "Close" because it was a very narrow road, and tall pine trees crowded it on either side for most of its three-quarters-of-a-mile length.

Weyre Goodall was driving on Fairclau Close now. Sarah was sitting very stiffly in the Jeep CJ-7's passenger seat. She had said very little since Weyre had picked her up at home five minutes earlier. He glanced uncomfortably at her. "Are you warm enough, Sarah?"

She nodded slowly, her gaze fixed on the wind-driven snow dancing crazily in the glare of the headlights. "Yes, I'm warm enough."

"I'd turn on the heat," Weyre apologized, "but it makes the alternator light come on, I don't know why. I guess I'll have to get it fixed one of these days."

"I'm warm enough," she repeated.

He pointed to an area just ahead, barely visible through the snow, where the road forked, and a short, narrow stretch of dirt led east to west to Pitney Road. "That might be quicker, Sarah. Not as smooth, but quicker. Do you think we should take it?"

She said nothing.

"Sarah?"

"You do—" she began and saw that the jeep was drifting off the road because Weyre was watching her instead; she said briskly, "Weyre!"

He looked at the road. "Ooops!" he said, and corrected the drift skillfully.

"You take whatever road you think you should take," Sarah finished.

"Uh-huh," he said, and wondered briefly what her opinion mattered, anyway. She never drove these roads; she never went out, for God's sake. "Uh-huh," he repeated. He slowed the jeep and turned onto the dirt path. "You should probably fasten your seat belt there, Sarah."

She quietly fastened her seat belt.

"Just a precaution," he said, and he attempted a small, apologetic grin. "If it makes you uncomfortable, you can unbuckle it and I'll just drive slower."

"No, I'm fine."

"It's just that some people feel . . . confined by a seat belt . . ."

"I don't, Weyre." Her tone hardened suddenly. "I'm fine."

Weyre fell silent. He became aware that his stomach was fluttering and he realized that he'd never been at the scene of a bad traffic accident before. He wondered how much it would disturb him, if he'd have to try to help at all. He hoped not. He didn't know if he was up to that.

Two thousand gallons of hydrazine will burn at a temperature of nearly four thousand degrees for several hours.

At 5:30 P.M., forty minutes after the first explosion (followed almost instantly by the explosion of the truck's tank of diesel fuel, then by the explosion of the bus's gas tank, and, moments later, by the explosion of the gas tank in Connie Weeker's Impala), Harry March rounded the crest of the hill in his four-wheel-drive AMC Concord and saw the bright, erratic flames. Marjory, in the passenger seat beside him, whispered, "Oh, my God!" He screeched, "Jesus Christ!" at the same time, and hit the brake pedal hard. The car slid a dozen yards, then came to a quick halt on the shoulder of the road.

"It's a schoolbus," Marjory whispered. "It's a goddamned schoolbus, Harry." And her eyes riveted on it. It was swathed in flames, except for the rear end, and a five-foot section extending forward from the bumper—the letters US were visible there. The rear emergency exit had been blown open by the impact. The entire bus stood ten feet from the tanker, where the explosion had thrown it. As Marjory watched, the flames crept over the letters US, and then quickly enveloped the entire back section of the bus. She turned her head away. "No, no!" she whimpered.

Harry switched off the car's ignition and headlights—the flames seventy-five yards away were lighting the whole area around them as brightly as the dawn.

Marjory began, "Harry, do you think anybody's . . ."

"There's nothing we can do here," he cut in, knowing what she was about to ask.

"We've got to tell someone, Harry."

"Yes," he said, "Sarah should know."

"Sarah?"

"She probably knows about it already."

"The *hell* with Sarah!"

He held his hand up to quiet her. "Marjory, do you hear anything?"

"For Christ's sake, Harry—"

"I *hear* something." He nodded solemnly at the bus. "I hear *them!*"

She stared at him, dumbfounded.

Weyre Goodall pulled his CJ-7 up next to the Concord. Harry clambered out and called over the roof of the Concord, "Who knows about this, Weyre? Does Sarah know about it?"

Weyre stepped out of the jeep. "The sheriff's on his way, Harry." He nodded at the jeep. "And Sarah's right here, with me."

Harry moved quickly around the front of the

Concord, then to the jeep's passenger door. He opened it, though only a crack, because the wind had picked up and he wanted to protect Sarah from it. "This is bad, Sarah."

She said, her eyes on the flames, "There are no survivors." It was as much a statement as a question.

"I don't see how there could be, Sarah." He glanced around, at the accident scene, then back at Sarah. A look of great sadness spread over his face. "Sarah," he said, "I heard them—those poor, damned kids. I heard them."

She turned her head very slowly and looked at him the way a teacher might look at a student who's gotten off on the wrong track. "No," she said evenly, "you didn't. You might have thought you did, Harry. But you didn't. It's too soon."

Marjory stuck her head in through the open driver's window. "You two can't be serious. Do you have any idea at all what has happened here?!"

"We *know* what's happened here," Harry answered, and Sarah interrupted him, "I want to get closer." She started to get out of the jeep, saw that Harry was in her way, hesitated; Harry stepped aside.

"Sarah," he said, "it's not safe."

"I must get closer to this," she insisted. She got out of the jeep. She seemed at once very agitated, and at the same time in great control. "We must all get closer," she pronounced, and her gaze went to the three people gathered around her.

"Bullshit!" Marjory hissed.

And Lester Stanhope, in an old, gray Cadillac Fleetwood, pulled up behind the CJ-7. He got out. "Sheriff King is on the way," he called, and moved stiffly toward them, hugging himself for warmth; he was wearing blue jeans, a flannel shirt, and denim jacket.

"You called him?" Harry asked.

"John Yount did," said Weyre Goodall.

Lester said, with a strange enthusiasm, "We're going to be using the Dohertys' place . . ." And then he stopped suddenly and stared in awe at the accident scene. "Lord," he whispered. "Will you look at that!"

The wind shifted. They could hear the continuous, rushing noise of the flames more clearly now, and it fascinated them. Weyre thought the noises were much like the noises a waterfall makes, and Lester, who had spent many of his early years in the midwest, said, "A tornado sounds like that. It sounds just like that."

Marjory thought the whole thing should crackle more, like a campfire.

"Christ," Harry said, "that's really cooking!"

The smells that the wind shift brought with it were the sharp, gaseous smells of burning paint and melting glass, and the cloying, noxious odors of melted plastic, and of rubber tires reduced by the amazing heat to their steel belts. And, overlaying all of it, the smell of the hydrazine.

"You know what that is?" Harry proclaimed, though no one was listening to him. "That's hydrazine! Farmers use it." He sniffed conspicuously; he had worked on a farm for several summers early in his adolescence, and he liked the smell.

Other people from Goode's Crossing began arriving then. Sam Pepper, in an old Ford pickup. Marcus and Anna Breeze, Francis Eblecker, Stephen Krull and his wife, Lily. Andrew Liwush.

They all got slowly from their cars, their eyes fixed and unblinking on the flames, their noses twitching, and their hands shoved hard into their coat pockets, so their arms were straight, and stiff, and their shoulders up. And slowly, inevitably, they moved through the swirling snow toward Weyre's jeep where Sarah waited, and formed a half circle around her.

She said to them, "We are going to get closer to this. We must all get closer to this."

Anna Breeze, at the edges of the circle, called, "But why, Sarah? Isn't it dangerous? Shouldn't we wait?" Her husband, Marcus, put his hand on her arm. "No," he said.

"Death," Sarah began, "has provided us with a very special opportunity—" She quieted suddenly.

The wind had shifted again. The air pressure had risen. And for several seconds the sweet, sickly smell of cooked flesh—Lily Krull, who owned two cats, was reminded of the smell of canned horsemeat catfood that has set uneaten for a long while—mixed with the smell of the molten glass, and melted plastic, and hydrazine, and all of them covered their noses and turned violently away. Some retched. Marjory Gwynne ran to Harry's car, got in, and began to weep.

Then, at once, the air pressure dropped, and the wind shifted again, and in the small half circle there was a general murmur of curses and quick prayers—"God help them! . . . "Jesus, comfort them!"—and within moments all eyes were on Sarah Goode once more.

She lifted her head and closed her eyes. All those around her did the same. She said, "Death has provided us with a very valuable opportunity, a very *special* opportunity. Here. And now. Those who are passing over still linger among us—I can feel it!" And she turned and walked slowly, her head down and her arms folded at her chest against the cold wind, toward the flames. Francis Eblecker was the first to follow her, his head also down, and his arms folded at his chest, then Marcus Breeze, and Harry March, and Weyre Goodall, who limped slightly.

Almost as one, they stopped walking when they heard the wail of sirens behind them.

12

For a quarter of an hour, Marian Hauser had been standing at her side window, holding the curtain open just an inch or so with her right hand, and she had been telling herself that the bright orange glow at the horizon, near Goode's Crossing, meant that one of those big old houses was on fire. She told herself also that she bore no one in Goode's Crossing any malice, and that she hoped whoever owned the house had gotten out safely.

The sheriff's deputy, a young man who seemed to have a speech impediment, had already been over.

("Mrs. Hauser?"

"Yes."

"Mrs. Hauser, there's been . . . I'm afraid there's been . . . an accident. Over there. You can see it. And I'm sorry, Mrs. Hauser, but your son, and a bunch of . . . other kids . . . I'm sorry—"

"That's not possible."

"Mrs. Hauser, please . . ."

"That's simply not possible."

"Mrs. Hauser, the school's bus schedule . . . it says . . .")

But of course he was lying. There was no doubt of that. He was too young, much too young, anyway, to have been a real deputy. He was probably still going to high school, for God's sake, and what he had done had been some kind of cruel prank. Someone had said to him, "Go to Marian Hauser's place and tell her that her son, Tod, has been killed in an accident. Along with a bunch of other kids."

She could see that the glow at the horizon was slowly diminishing. That was good, she thought. They were putting the fire out.

From behind her, she heard, "Honey, is something wrong? Where's Tod? I checked his room."

She turned her head and smiled at her husband, Terry. "You're late," she said.

"Sure I am. It was like a damned blizzard out there." He came over, looked out the window, saw the glow at the horizon. "What's that? It looks like a fire."

"Yes," she said evenly. "A house in Goode's Crossing. Somebody set it on fire. It's been burning for a long time."

"Somebody should torch that whole damned place," he said. "So where's Tod? Is he playing out back? I hope not, Marian, because it's pretty dark out there . . ."

"No," she murmured, her head lowered.

He came over to her, took her by the shoulders

and looked her squarely in the eye. "Marian, what's happened?"

She grinned playfully, reached up, tweaked his nose with her forefinger. "Silly boy—nothing has happened."

He coaxed her firmly away from the window, sat her down on a loveseat nearby, sat next to her, took her hands in his. She continued grinning oddly all the while. "Marian, darling, what has happened to Tod?"

(". . . a bunch of other kids, too, Mrs. Hauser. But it had to have been very quick, it had to have been . . . it was probably"—he snapped his fingers—"like that, just like that.")

Marian stopped grinning abruptly. "We should all go as quickly as that, Terry."

("It was an explosion, Mrs. Hauser. Some kind of truck tanker. Hydrozeele. Hydrogen. Something. I don't know for sure, Mrs. Hauser. They haven't . . . they haven't been able to get real close to it, yet. But it was very quick, it had to have been very . . . quick! They told me to tell you that. That it was very quick.")

Terry said nothing. He had seen that look in his wife's eyes before. Eight years before. When she had told him about Jeremy.

She said now, "But of course, Terry, he was only joking."

13

Lester Stanhope nodded meaningfully at a big, heavily muscled man standing near Connie Weeker's fire-gutted Impala, and said to Weyre Goodall, "The sheriff wants to know why we can't use the old Presbyterian Church, Weyre. For a morgue, I mean. Just for the time being."

"And what did you tell him?"

"I told him it was something I hadn't thought of. I told him I'd have to clear it with Sarah, first."

"So go ahead and clear it with her." He pointed at his jeep. Sarah was sitting stiffly in the passenger seat. "She wants to talk to you, anyway."

Lester looked suddenly ill at ease. "Oh?" he said. "About what?"

"I don't know." Weyre sounded annoyed. Lester was not so much a stupid man as a man who too often overlooked the obvious. "Maybe you should go and find out."

Lester said nothing for a long moment, then, as if he had mustered up some hidden reserve of courage, moved quickly over to the jeep. He got in, sat in the driver's seat, put his hands loosely on the steering wheel. He glanced at Sarah, then out the windshield at the still-burning wreck of the bus and tanker. His grip on the wheel tightened; he was very nervous. "This is awful, Sarah."

"Of course it is," she said, her eyes, unmoving, on the scene of the accident, her tone unnaturally low, and stiff.

Lester glanced at her again, quickly, then looked back at the wreck. "But even here," he began, and he realized that his voice had become high, almost sing-song, "and now, it seems kind of remote. That's odd, isn't it?"

"For the moment," Sarah told him, "it is only a fire."

He nodded his solemn agreement.

She kept her gaze on the wreck. She said, "You should have asked me about using the Dohertys' house, Lester."

He responded immediately, and with gushing sincerity, "Yes, I should have. I'm sorry I didn't, Sarah. I am sorry."

"I prefer being consulted, Lester. You know that."

"Yes. I know that. I think, Sarah, that on the spur of the moment, I . . ."

"In a crisis, we must act together. As one. This, Lester, is a crisis."

He said nothing. She wanted his silence, he realized.

She went on, her tone still low, and stiff, "You

should have consulted all of us, Lester. Because we are all equal participants in this . . . experiment. What affects one affects the group. That should be clear. Those of us who make decisions for the group without consultation, Lester—those who act independently, as Marjory Gwynne often does, and as you have done, now, and as Irene Janus has done in denying that man"—she nodded at the sheriff—"the use of her house without first consulting me, and the group . . ." She hesitated. A slight grin appeared on her lips; it had a chilling effect on Lester because Sarah rarely betrayed humor of any kind. "Well, then," she went on, matter-of-factly, "those people are obviously saying that they wish to be free of the group. Don't you think that that is what those people are saying, Lester?"

He did not answer right away; he was trying desperately to form a correct response.

"Lester?" Sarah coaxed.

He answered, then, haltingly, "I can't . . . speak for anyone else, Sarah, but, speaking for myself I would have to say . . . I would have to say that I have always been very happy in Goode's Crossing—"

She cut in, her tone stiff again, and businesslike, "We will go into this further at the next Group Discussion, Lester."

Lester blubbered a few incoherencies at her, cleared his throat, said, "Yes, thank you, Sarah. If you think there's a need."

"That, of course," she told him, "is the reason we will bring it up. To see if there *is* a need."

He said immediately, "Yes, I understand that."

"Good. Thank you, Lester." She was telling him clearly that the conversation was at an end.

He climbed quickly from the Jeep, took a few steps, stopped, came back, opened the door, stuck his head in: "Sarah?"

"Yes?" She kept her gaze on the accident scene.

"The sheriff wanted to know if he could use the Presbyterian Church."

"As a temporary morgue, you mean?"

"Yes, Sarah. Just for the time being."

"Did you tell him that the roof leaks?"

"I didn't tell him anything. I told him I'd have to ask you, first, Sarah."

"Tell him yes. It's certainly no good to the living." She turned her head, and grinned at Lester again. "Perhaps the dead can make proper use of it."

The Goode's Crossing First Presbyterian Church was built in 1923 and abandoned thirty years later, after the death of the Reverend Michael J. H. Harvey, the only man ever to preach in it. It was an unusually large church, especially for so small a village, and especially because there were so few Presbyterians in the area to pray in it, and when its doors closed at last, and the Presbyterian hierarchy in Albany had all its religious accoutrements taken away, there was talk in the village of turning it into a gym, or a warehouse, or even a Spiritualist Museum of some kind, which would, it was argued, be a good source of revenue for the village. But all of it was only idle talk; it got nowhere, and the building was allowed to lie unused, and to disintegrate slowly.

Its walls were of red brick, its roof of hand-hewn stone tile, its floors of dark oak, and its interior walls of northern white pine. It had had at one time a solid brass altar and cherrywood pews, and huge, leaded stained glass windows which faced west and east to allow for maximum use of morning and afternoon sunlight.

The Reverend Michael J. H. Harvey had been exceedingly proud of the building, even though he preached in it to as few as five parishoners on any given Sunday, and never to any more than twenty.

The church lay just inside the village's eastern boundary, on three acres of flat land which—except for a small, scenic clump of pine trees—had been clear at the time of the church's abandonment. Now, nearly thirty years later, there were young pines everywhere, as well as several maple and black walnut trees. The grounds immediately adjacent to the church were mowed three or four times a year by Marcus Breeze, mostly because he liked to ride around on his aging but still serviceable John Deere mower, but also because his house was closest to the church (no more than a good stone's throw away) and for the sake of business he thought it was best to keep things looking as tidy as possible.

From 10:00 to 10:30 on the evening of the accident, when the third snowstorm of the day was buffeting the village, the remains of the accident victims were brought to the church in black vinyl body bags and laid out in a row, side by side, on the oak floor. Each bag had a white tag pinned to it. One tag read, "Child, possible female." Another, "Adult, possible male." And another, "Possible child." There were nine bags. One had a tag pinned to it which read, "Two victims?"

Most of the winter inhabitants of Goode's Crossing filed into the church minutes later. They stood side by side, very silently, near the church's high, arching front doors, and watched as the sheriff and his men moved about with flashlights in hand and their heads shaking occasionally, each trying very desperately to give the appearance of being at work over the stiff, black bags.

Finally, Lester Stanhope said, his voice low, "It still doesn't seem *real*, does it?"

And someone nearby answered firmly, for them all, "Yes, Lester, it seems very real!"

14

The pews had been removed over the years, some by fly-by-night "antique dealers," others by an auctioneer in the neighboring county, several by residents of Goode's Crossing itself, who thought that with the addition of a few cushions and the liberal application of Old English Furniture Polish the aged pews would make a nice addition to their living rooms or parlors or sitting rooms. In 1960, a scrap dealer dismantled the huge altar and carted it away. In June 1965, the graduating class of the Merrimac Senior High School, twenty miles east, broke into the church (someone in Goode's Crossing—it was never learned who—had put a hefty padlock on the front doors, though obviously not quite hefty enough) and scrawled various obscenities on the white pine walls. The more creative of those obscenities were pointedly directed at the residents of

Goode's Crossing ("Fuck a spook today—it's a very *uplifting* experience").

The body bags were laid out precisely in the center of the church. No one ordered that they be laid out that way, it had merely seemed the most natural and the most respectful way to do it, because shattered stained glass lay all around, except for toward the center of the floor, and there were shallow pools of water here and there, near the sides, where the roof was leaking badly.

But toward the center, the floor was dry and relatively debris-free—a good place to put body bags.

At 11:45, the sheriff and his men prepared to leave. They would take over for several other men who'd been put in charge of directing possible, if unlikely, traffic around the accident scene. Sarah asked that she and the others be allowed to stay at the church a while, "long enough to say goodbye to these departing souls." The sheriff gave her a quick, if confused, okay, and left.

At 12:00, Sarah said to those with her—Sam Pepper, Weyre Goodall, Stephen and Lily Krull, Lester Stanhope, Francis Eblecker, Marcus and Anna Breeze, Harold March, Andrew Liwush— "Let us draw closer," and she moved slowly, her eyes half closed, as if in meditation, from her spot at the back of the church, toward its center. The others followed, at random, several with flashlights in hand. They formed a half circle around her. They drifted slowly toward the body bags. Their booted feet and the rustling of their heavy winter coats echoed sharply in the big, empty room.

Sarah got to the center. She leaned over one of the body bags. She zipped it open.

There was a stifled gasp from one of those behind her—she heard it, noted it mentally, and then she parted the flaps on the body bag.

The smell from within wafted over her. She grimaced, fought it back, peered into the body bag. She saw what looked like a pair of charred, skeletal feet and legs. From behind, one of the men said, "Oh, Jesus, that smell!" and without speaking she zipped the bag fully open. She stood. She held her hand out. "Could someone please give me a flashlight." It was a command. Someone put a flashlight in her hand and she shone it slowly up the length of the blackened, pathetic thing in the body bag. She let the beam linger several moments on the skull. She said to it, soothingly, "Stay here with us, little one." Then she held her arms out, as if in preparation for an embrace. "All of you, stay here with us!"

She heard a heavy, muffled thump from the rear of the half circle. She looked. Anna Breeze had fainted.

Part Three
THE SUMMONING

15

Marjory Gwynne screeched, "We're not witches, for Christ's sake!"

Harry March, standing at the window, turned his head, saw her put a sweater into her suitcase. "You weren't there, Marjory—it wasn't like that at all."

"Damned right I wasn't there, and I'm surprised *you* were, Harry. I assumed that you had better judgment than that."

He raised an eyebrow: "Apparently not. But what kind of judgment are you showing now? Where are you going to go? I know you don't have any relatives who'll take you in, and for sure you don't have any money."

She closed the suitcase, locked it, set it on the floor in front of the bed, went and got another suitcase from the closet.

"Marjory?" Harry coaxed.

She set the new suitcase on the bed, opened it, hesitated. "I don't know," she murmured, and she pursed her lips in self-criticism, and doubt.

Harry smiled. "It'll be okay, you'll see. Sarah just got a little . . . overzealous, that's all. Christ, you can't blame her."

"It was a despicable thing for her to do, Harry."

" 'Despicable'? I don't know if that's the word I'd use." He pretended to think about it a moment. "For myself," he went on, "I'd say it was a very compassionate thing to do."

"Bullshit!"

"Sarah is a lot more sensitive than you or I, Marjory. You can't deny that."

"Sensitivity is not at issue here—"

"It's what we're all about, Marjory." He said the words very slowly, with emphasis on the phrase 'all about.' "It's what Goode's Crossing is all about. And sometimes that sensitivity, that very *special* sensitivity makes us behave . . . makes us do things that might appear . . . strange." He paused a beat, then continued, "I'm sure that Sarah, at this very moment, is having, I don't know, second thoughts about the effect of what she did, on some of the others, I mean."

"Hell, she didn't even apologize to Anna Breeze, Harry. That poor woman—"

"Anna Breeze is stronger than you think," Harry interrupted. "And besides, just this morning Sarah went over to check up on her. I saw her myself."

Marjory pursed her lips again. She stayed quiet.

"Face it, Marge—on this particular matter you are dead wrong."

"Please don't call me 'Marge.' I've asked you not to call me 'Marge' at least ten thousand times, Harry."

He held his hands up, as if she'd pointed a gun at him. "All right, I'm sorry," he said, with an exaggerated tone of apology. "I am heartily sorry for having offended thee—"

"Cut the crap, Harry. Haven't you got a client showing up pretty soon?"

Harry smiled his quick, *Just kidding, sorry!* kind of smile, dropped his hands, and checked his watch: "Yeah, in ten minutes. Somebody named Scranton, says he wants to get in touch with his long lost grandmother because she left a faulty will, or something. I've seen him once before and he's basically a jerk."

"So are you, Harry."

He smiled at her again, his *Just kidding* smile, because she was wearing a poker face and it confused him, then he left the house.

Marcus Breeze put his arm around his wife's shoulders. "It's okay, Anna. It was the accident—it upset her. It upset all of us."

Anna dabbed at her eyes with a lace handkerchief that had the initials AMB embroidered on it in yellow. She was a slight, dark-haired, and pleasant-looking woman in her late forties who had come to Goode's Crossing only ten years earlier, upon marrying Marcus. It was his third marriage, her second. They had a total of seven children and four grandchildren between them.

She looked up at her husband from her chair; he was seated on the armrest. "She doesn't like me, Marcus. She's never liked me. She thinks I'm an outsider. I'm not an outsider, am I?"

He pulled her closer to him and rested the side of his face on the top of her head. He began, "You're . . ." stopped, maneuvered several strands of her hair from his mouth with his tongue, and began again, "You're my wife, Anna. I love you. You know that I love you."

"I love you too, Marcus. I don't want her to kick me out of here."

"She's not going to do that, Anna; she would never *do* that!"

"I think she would, Marcus."

His eyebrows narrowed. "Anna, she's an old woman who is trying to cope with great responsibility, and I believe that sometimes she strains herself just a little too much—"

"You heard what she said to me, Marcus," Anna broke in; she had obviously not been listening. "She said I was weak!" She paused, remembered. "I don't know what she meant by that, Marcus. Do you? I fainted. So what? Does that mean I'm weak?" She waited. Marcus started to respond but she couldn't understand him because his face was still resting on her head and he was speaking in low tones, into her hair. "I can't understand you, Marcus." He quieted suddenly. She thought a moment. "I can't understand *any* of you, sometimes." She waited. Marcus stayed quiet. "I try to understand you, but it's hard from one day to the next." She was on a roll now, letting out what had been churning inside her for several years. "Sometimes I think it's very nice, and that you're lucky, you're all very lucky to be doing this. And I think that maybe you're helping people, and that you're making them happier by telling them the things you tell them, and by pretending—"

"Anna, it's not all *pretense*. I thought you realized that."

"Some of it is, Marcus. Most of it is."

"Occasionally it's necessary, it's a kind of catalyst—Sarah herself said as much a couple of weeks ago, at the meeting. It gets things going."

She ignored him and got back on her train of thought. "And you *are* lucky, Marcus. You know that you are. You like what you do. But then I see you, some of you together, at Fairclau House, and I see you laughing and telling stories, and I listen and I hear that you're laughing about these people, these poor people who come to you for help. I hear you telling stories about them and I'll tell you something, Marcus—it makes me mad at you, it makes me very mad at you. And at all of them, too." She paused. At last, Marcus pushed himself away from her. She leaned forward in the chair, clasped her long, thin hands in front of her. "You confuse me, Marcus. All of you do." She inclined her head sharply to the left. "*She* does not confuse me."

"Sarah?"

"It was a very strange thing for her to do, Marcus—at the church. Very, very strange. But I can understand why she would do it. I do not

understand—maybe I don't *want* to understand—
why the rest of you went along with it."

Marcus had no answer for that.

"Sometimes," Anna continued bitterly, "you are
all like children, like all you are doing is having
fun—"

"Oh, Anna, it's so much more than that." He
sounded genuinely hurt and offended.

She glanced at him. "Yes," she said. "Sometimes I can see that. But not very much, not as
much as I would like."

He stood abruptly, the hurt showing in his eyes.
"Of course we joke and laugh and have fun. You
forget what we have to deal with—you don't know
what it does to us." He pointed at his temple. "In
here." He thumped his chest with his fist. "And in
here."

He paused. Anna couldn't resist saying, "You're
being theatrical, Marcus."

He stared at her as if dumbfounded. He threw
his hands into the air. "I give up!" he proclaimed,
and stalked from the room.

A minute later, Anna heard the engine of his
riding mower start up. She went to the garage,
looked inside. The mower was gone. She went to
the back window, looked out. Most of the snow
from the previous week's storm had melted, but
there still were wide, irregular patches here and
there. Marcus was steering the big red-and-green
riding mower around them; he was on his way to
the church.

It was his way of letting off steam. He had felt his anger building, an argument starting, and he despised arguments, especially with her because he knew that beneath her facade of pleasantness and timidity she was an intelligent and strong woman, fully capable of verbally outmaneuvering him.

He gave the mower a little burst of speed and let it slosh its way through a patch of wet snow. He glanced back at his house, saw Anna looking at him. He stared blankly at her a moment, and turned around. He supposed that he looked like a total fool, and that she was snickering at him, that in a week or so she'd bring the whole thing up— throw it in his face; "You're not a child, Marcus." He brought the mower to a stop. No, he thought, she wouldn't bring it up; he was being unfair.

He glanced back at the house again. Anna was no longer looking at him. He turned, looked at the church, about twenty-five yards away.

He listened, confused. He was hearing something, distantly. From inside the church, he thought. Laughter, he supposed, and talking. It was hard to tell beneath the racket of the power mower. He switched the engine off. He listened again. From far to his left, from one of the dozens of young pines that dotted the land around the church, he heard the shrill call of a bluejay. High overhead, a loose V-formation of geese was pushing its way south and its cacklings were plainly audible.

Ahead, from the church, a squirrel foraged about on a basement window ledge; a sudden, small breeze whined over the sharp edges of stained glass above.

He grinned nervously and realized at once that he did not want to be here. He switched on the mower's engine and did a quick K-turn that took him through a foot-deep patch of drifted, melting snow. He hesitated. He glanced around at the church. *Sarah will have to know all about this!* he thought.

16

October 23rd

Judy Yount shook her head briskly. "No," she said to Irene Janus. "I'm sorry, but no."

Irene sighed. "It's that couple I talked to you about the other day, Judy—the ones whose grandson committed suicide. Jesus, they give me the creeps."

Judy put a hand up, palm out. "As I said, Irene, I'm finished for the season. Besides, I've got John to take care of."

Irene raised an eyebrow. "Oh," she coaxed. "Yes. I see." She paused for effect. "How is he?"

"He's okay."

"That was a very unusual thing for him to do, wasn't it?!"

"Yes," Judy answered stiffly. "It was." She closed the door part way. "I'm sorry I can't help you, Irene."

"It must have hurt like hell. Can he talk yet?"

"Yes, Irene, he can talk."

"I mean, pouring a gallon of boiling hot coffee down your throat has got to be—"

"It wasn't a gallon."

"That's what I heard. I think I heard it from you, in fact. A whole gallon of scalding hot coffee—"

"I never said a gallon, Irene. I said part of a cup. That's all it was, and that's all I said, and he did it because he was upset, very, very upset, we *all* were, some of us still are—"

"You know of course, Judy, that Sarah takes a very dim view of what he did."

"I'm sure she does, Irene. I do, too."

"Have you spoken with Sarah since the accident, Judy? Has she said anything to you? About John, I mean?"

"I haven't had the time, Irene." Judy was becoming annoyed.

Irene grinned knowingly. "Oh, yes, I see. *He* probably takes up most of your time, doesn't he? Pretty much of a child about being . . . sick, I suppose. Isn't that right?"

"No, Irene, that is not right." And she shut the door hard.

Irene stood quietly outside the closed door for a few seconds. Then she grinned again, muttered an obscenity—aimed at many people; Judy, John, the old couple, their dead grandson, and anyone else who might disrupt her life that day—and went home. The Sitting with the old couple was scheduled to begin a half hour later. She had time to make a few phone calls—maybe one of them would pan out.

Fall's Pond lay just inside the northern boundary of the village, several hundred feet behind Sarah's home, and, like many Adirondack lakes and ponds, it was dead. In the summer, the only forms of life supported by it were waterbugs, mosquitoes, and frogs, all within a small patch of reedy marsh at the pond's northeastern edge.

No one in Goode's Crossing had any idea why it was called Fall's Pond. Nobody named Fall had lived in the village; there was apparently no deep, if nebulous, religious significance attached to the word 'Fall.'

It stank of sulfur for several weeks during the summer, and in the winter never froze over completely enough that ice skaters could go safely out on it. "It's fed by deep, subterranean hot springs," Andrew Liwush maintained. "That's why it smells of sulfur." He had briefly thought of having the local Army Corps of Engineers come in and validate his theory, but never saw it through.

The pond was teardrop-shaped. At the point of the tear—the area closest to Sarah Goode's home —someone had built a small boat dock out of red pine. The dock had remained unused for many years and was rotting slowly. At the curve of the teardrop, just behind the thickest part of the stand of pines that crowded up to Fairclau Close for most of its length, a large, four-seated wooden rowboat, gray with age and decay, lay half in and half out of the water. Some people in the village claimed to be able to see the name *Moreau* in very faint, red block letters at the bow of the boat, but only when the light was just right, and only if the eyesight of the person looking was perfect.

Several people had drowned in Fall's Pond. Among others, a teenaged boy skinny-dipping in it early in the 1940s, and a hunter in 1959 who had been shot in the knee by another hunter and had fallen into the pond, unconscious from loss of blood. And so there were stories that the pond was haunted. But the stories had proven to be largely fanciful and were retold only to clients and visiting children and grandchildren, who were warned afterwards to "stay far away from that place," Consequently, there were, several times during the summer, many wide-eyed and trembling children moving with great stealth and self-professed courage around the perimeter of Fall's Pond, all whispering excitedly about "The spook without no clothes on," and "The spook that comes up right outa the middle of the pond and makes you go crazy."

Stephen Krull, walking near the southern edge of the pond, remembered those stories now. They saddened him because it was October 23rd, and the season was over for most of the people in the village—there would be no children in Goode's Crossing for another four months, at least. He liked children. He liked their honesty, and their enthusiasm, and their wonderful naivete. He remembered that several of the children who had prowled the area around the pond were the same children who had died in the accident on Shoemaker Road. That fact made his eyes water. He wondered how any parent could survive the loss of a child. He and his wife, Lily, had remained childless throughout their marriage—and not for lack of trying—but he *knew* beyond doubt that any child of his would have been more important to him than life itself.

It was a brisk morning. The sun still was low in the sky and it cast long, cold, very black shadows —the kind he thought, that looked as if they could shatter like plate glass.

He stopped, leaned over. He saw that the edges of the pond were beginning to ice up. That saddened him, too. He wasn't sure why. He supposed he was just in that sort of mood. He realized at once that he had been in that sort of mood ever since the accident happened.

He saw his face, very diffuse and unrecognizable, reflected in the white ice at the edge of the pond. He said, "You're getting old and tired and weepy, Stephen. You've got to toughen up." But he didn't want to toughen up.

He straightened, shoved his big, bare hands into the pockets of his jeans, hunched his shoulders forward against the cold—Christ, it was going to be one hell of a winter!—and turned.

He stopped at once. The boy standing in front of him was about eight years old, he guessed, maybe nine, and dressed very warmly in a soiled red wool jacket, brown corduroy pants, and black slipover boots.

"Hello," Stephen said. "Where'd you come from?"

The boy turned his head slightly—Stephen saw that some of the boy's hair, around the ears, and at the top of the forehead, appeared to have been poorly cut, as if it had been singed—and nodded in

the direction of Fairclau Close. Stephen looked.
There was a stand of pines where the boy had
nodded. "From in there?" Stephen asked, and
smiled as if the boy was telling him a joke. "Or do
you mean in that direction?"

A look of overpowering sadness came into the
boy's face. "I—" he began, fell silent a moment,
mouthed another word, which Stephen couldn't
make out, and turned his head again, toward the
stand of pines.

Stephen took a cautious step toward him.

The boy looked back. "I—" he said once more,
with great confusion.

Stephen took another step. He held his hands
out to the boy.

The boy bolted off, toward the stand of pines.
Stephen gave chase, but though his legs were long,
and his stride quick, the boy seemed to have a kind
of strange and unnatural energy, and within half a
minute he was gone.

"Mrs. Zelinski?" Irene Janus said into the
phone.

"Yes," Mrs. Zelinski answered.

"Mrs. Zelinski, my name is Irene Atwater Janus.
I live in Goode's Crossing."

"Yes," the woman said again, and there was a
question in her tone, as well as caution.

"I was a witness, Mrs. Zelinski, to the accident
which took your daughter Eileen from you, and I
wanted to tell you how terribly sorry I am and
how terribly sorry all of us in the village are. It
was a tragic, tragic thing—really the most tragic

thing I've ever seen."

"That's very kind of you, Mrs. Janus." The woman's tone said now that she didn't feel like talking.

Irene persisted. "I would have called much sooner, Mrs. Zelinski, but I assumed that you and your husband wanted to be left alone. I'm sure the newspapers and the police and . . . and well-meaning relatives, Mrs. Zelinski, prevented that. I know: I was in a similar situation five years ago. I lost my son." Her voice grew quiet, and strained, as if it were a great burden for her to say what she was saying. "It was an accident, too. A traffic accident." She paused. Mrs. Zelinski said, with the slightest trace of tension:

"I'm sorry to hear that, Mrs. Janus."

"Yes," Irene said. "Yes. But fortunately, oh so fortunately, we have Toby's spirit with us here. In the house." She paused again. There was silence on the other end of the line. "That was his name, Mrs. Zelinski. 'Toby.' After my late husband. He was about your daughter's age when he left us . . ."

"Could you please get to the point, Mrs. Janus."

Irene pursed her lips. This was not going awfully well. Maybe, she mused, she hadn't given the woman enough time. Two weeks—maybe it should have been four. "We miss Toby very much, Mrs. Zelinski. We will always miss him, as I know you will always miss Eileen. I'm sure she was a beautiful child—"

"Yes," the woman cut in. "She was a gorgeous, wonderful child." It was obvious that the woman was crying. "And so bright. She was talking before she was eighteen months old—a brilliant child. She could have made us so very, very proud . . ." She started weeping harder, louder. "We miss her so very much, Mrs. Janus, so very much."

"Toby *did* make us proud, Mrs. Zelinski. Even in his pitifully short time with us, on this earth. And he continues to make us proud, even in spirit, when he communicates with us—"

There was a click on the other end. A dial tone. Mrs. Zelinski had hung up.

"Goddamnit it all to hell!" Irene hissed, and called back immediately: "Mrs. Zelinski, I'm sorry —we were cut off, somehow." Because, she knew, the right kind of persistence usually wore people down, in time.

At the playground, just beyond the southeastern edge of the village, a whisper rose up. It drifted from place to place; it halted, fell to the earth again, rose up. It was a particularly small and insubstantial thing, a memory, a good feeling, and it moved about under the skeleton of the swings, and in circles, slowly, on what remained of the tiny steel merry-go-round.

It disturbed nothing. It was not alive, or dead, and it could not laugh, or ask for love, or plead, "Remember me." That was for others to imagine.

At last, it fell to the earth again. And it stopped.

17

The woman at Marjory's front door was tall, blonde, very attractive. She wore a long, gray cloth coat—unbuttoned because the day was unusually warm—blue jeans, and a red flannel shirt. *Rustic chic*, Marjory thought, and smiled pleasantly. "Hello," she said.

The woman said, "How much is it, please?"

Marjory understood immediately, though she resented the woman's bluntness. She said to her, "I'm afraid the season's over. For me, at least. You might try Mrs. Janus"—she nodded to her left—"just down the street, Number 25."

The woman looked suddenly and deeply disappointed. She said, "Mrs. Janus can't help me today. She told me she's 'all booked up.'"

Marjory recognized that as the kind of phrase Irene used to make herself look busy, and therefore much in demand, and therefore expensive— a come on. She pointed to her right, "Mr. Krull, perhaps—"

"No, please," the woman cut in. "Please, you don't understand: I need someone right now. Please!"

Marjory studied the woman's face. She saw desperation on it, and pleading, and it touched a responsive chord within her. She stepped to one side, opened the door wider. "Please, come in."

The woman looked genuinely relieved. "Thank you," she said, and stepped into the house.

Marjory led her into the small, sparsely outfitted kitchen and nodded at the late-1950s-vintage aluminum and blue vinyl dinette in the middle of the room. "Please, sit down."

The woman put her hand on the back of one of the chairs. She saw the small crystal ball Marjory kept in the center of the table and pursed her lips, as if annoyed. "You don't have a sitting room of some kind? I had assumed—"

"I think this is more natural, and more comfortable," Marjory told her. "Most of us here in the village do it this way." She smiled warmly. "Please, sit down."

The woman pulled the chair out and sat very slowly in it. She looked plainly offended by her surroundings. She nodded at the crystal ball. "Do you really use that?"

"Only as a means of focusing my concentration," Marjory answered. "I don't think I actually 'see' anything in it, if that's what you're asking."

The woman nodded yes.

"Would you like some coffee?" Marjory asked.

The woman shook her head. "No, thank you."

She reached out, put her forefinger on the crystal ball.

Marjory said, not unkindly, "I like to keep the glass as clear as possible—"

The woman withdrew her hand immediately. "I'm sorry," she whispered.

Marjory sat in the chair across from her and summoned up her most professional smile and tone: "What can I do for you?"

The woman answered immediately, her eyes riveted on Marjory's, "You can help me contact my son."

Marjory held the woman's gaze silently for several seconds, then looked away, at the crystal ball. "Do you believe that he wants to be contacted?"

The woman looked confused. "I don't understand."

Marjory looked her in the eye again. "It's understandable that you want to contact him—" She paused very briefly, then went on, "Could you tell me your name, please? Only your last name."

"Yes. It's White. Mrs. White."

Marjory nodded. "It's understandable, Mrs. White, that you would like to contact him. The question we must consider, however, is whether or not *he* wants to be contacted. Do you understand?"

The woman continued to look confused. "No, I'm afraid I don't, Mrs. Gwynne."

"Call me Marjory."

"No, Marjory, I don't understand."

Marjory reached across the table. "Give me your hands, Mrs. White." The woman did as asked.

Marjory held her hands lightly a few seconds, then, "I can feel that you are a very loving woman, Mrs. White. Very caring. I can feel that you wanted only what was good for your son, and that you always had his best interests in your heart. And so I must tell you—" She stopped; her gaze drifted momentarily from Mrs. White. She looked back. "He was a very..." She searched for the correct word. "... a very *mature* child, wasn't he, Mrs. White? I mean very serious, and level-headed. How old was he? Was he about nine, or ten?"

Mrs. White nodded in astonishment. "He was nine, and, yes, he *was* very mature for his age. My husband used to say it was a pity he didn't seem to enjoy his childhood very much."

Marjory squeezed the woman's hand reassuringly. "I think he enjoyed it more than you realized, Mrs. White."

The woman lowered her head. "That would be nice to believe. I loved him so much, Marjory—"

"But, as I was saying," Marjory cut in, "and this may be something that will be hard for you to accept; many of those who have passed over have done so quite willingly—"

The woman withdrew her hands quickly, a sudden look of anger came into her face. "He died on that damned schoolbus, Mrs. Gwynne. He didn't go *willingly*, he didn't slash his wrists, he didn't put a gun to his head, if that's what you're getting at."

Marjory straightened in her chair. She said evenly, soothingly, "No, Mrs. White, that's not what I was getting at, not at all. It has been my experience that many who have passed over, even those who have passed over with great violence— as your son did—do not wish to be contacted by those who have stayed behind. They are at rest, they are happy, and contact with this world, no matter the amount of love we might have here for them, is very painful."

The woman fidgeted in her chair. She was clearly ill at ease. "This was my husband's idea, you know."

"Your husband's idea, Mrs. White? Then you should have brought him with you."

"He wouldn't come. He said it would embarrass him. He asked me to come, and if I had any luck . . ."

"Is that what you're looking for, Mrs. White?— Luck?"

The woman let her hands fall into her lap; she bowed her head slightly, her eyes on her hands. "I want to contact my son," she said, her voice low. "I want to tell him that I love him, and miss him, and that the only thing I want to do—" She looked up, there was a hard, determined look in her eyes. "The *only thing I want to do* is to finish my life and be with him!"

Marjory sighed. She understood the woman clearly, now. Much too clearly. She said, with finality, "I'm afraid I can't help you, Mrs. White. I wish I could, I firmly wish I could. But I can't." And she stood. "I'm sure that Mrs. Janus—"

The woman pushed herself quickly from the chair and began furiously buttoning her coat.

"You people—" she stammered. She finished buttoning the coat, turned, started for the door, looked back. "You people are all a bunch of con artists, anyway!" And she stalked from the house.

Marjory listened to the front door slam shut. She sat slowly, wearily, at the kitchen table. She sighed. "Pappy," she whispered, "this is getting very tiresome."

18

October 26

Marcus Breeze sipped at the strong herbal tea that Sarah had given him; he fought back a grimace. "I've been to the church three times now, Sarah," he said. "First about a week ago. Last Friday. I was on the mower—"

"The mower?" Sarah cut in. "What in heaven's name were you doing on the mower?" She was sitting next to him on a beige, flower-print loveseat. She also had a cup of herbal tea in hand, which she sipped delicately every few seconds.

"I think," Marcus answered nervously; he took a quick sip of his tea, "that it's best to give the grass a final trim before the winter. I've done it for the past few years and it always seems to come up greener in the spring."

"That's very conscientious of you, I'm sure," Sarah told him, without feeling.

"Yes," he whispered. He saw that his cup was almost empty; he set it on a small, darkwood table near the arm of the loveseat. "I have to admit, Sarah," he went on, grasping, in vain, for a tone of self-confidence, "that what I have seen there, at the church, and what I have heard could quite possibly be just—"

She interrupted, "Tell me this, Marcus," and she paused meaningfully, sipped her tea, and lowered her head. When she looked up, Marcus saw something in her small, dark eyes that he had never seen before, something fierce and determined and relentless; it made him uncomfortable, a little apprehensive. "Do you feel, Marcus," she said tightly, her voice almost secretively low, "that the church is being possessed by the spirits of those children? Is that your feeling?"

He answered at once, "I'm not sure, Sarah. I can't say. It could just be . . ." And he paused, considered; it became clear to him what she needed to hear. He said with finality, "Yes, Sarah. Yes, oh God, yes." And he felt very grateful to her for allowing him to sift the wheat from the chaff, to sort out what *could be* from what *was* (because there could really be no other explanation, could there, for what he had seen and what he had heard at the church?).

And she looked so very pleased. It made him suddenly happy. It chased his apprehensions away.

She handed him her cup and nodded at the small table near the arm of the loveseat. "Could you set this there for me, please?" He did it. She stood and moved slowly, as if in contemplation, to a tall window nearby; it was covered by heavily starched, white lace curtains; diffuse sunlight filtering in outlined her small, spare frame sharply. She said, her back to Marcus, "And do you fear what you have encountered at the church, Marcus?"

"No," he answered, too quickly, he realized. He waited a moment. "Yes," he corrected.

She turned her head; he saw the same relentless, fierce determination he had seen in her eyes a minute earlier. She announced, "*I* do not fear it, Marcus! I welcome it. Mr. Death is very big there, he would like to trample us all. So we must grow to understand him. We must fence with him first. Then we must recognize him. Then we must sit down and talk with him. Just as I am talking with you, now. Then we must let him . . . enter us. Each of us in turn. All of us, together. As one." She turned her head and looked questioningly at Marcus. "Do you understand me?"

"No," he answered at once, because, he knew, she'd hear a lie. "I want to, but I don't."

She smiled a pleasant, caring, maternal smile. "Do you sleep very well since the accident, Marcus?"

He inclined his head sadly to one side. He looked down at his knees, then at the floor. "I sleep," he said. "But I dream, too—"

"We all dream, Marcus." She turned her head again. "For decades, I have dreamed. But since the accident, I haven't dreamed at all." She paused, fingered the white lace curtains, parted them. Her gaze settled on the Goode's Crossing First Presbyterian Church, almost a half mile off, and only its roof visible at that distance. "I don't need to dream, anymore," she said, as much to herself as to Marcus. "I sleep very well, indeed."

Marcus left moments later.

And for an hour afterward, Sarah floated aimlessly about her big house, from room to room, the ghost of a smile on her thin, colorless lips, and the phrase *Mother will be very happy; everything will be all right now!* moving about in her brain.

19

Francis Eblecker settled his huge frame into a sturdy captain's chair at his kitchen table and looked up at Weyre Goodall, standing with his back to the side door. "Did you ever pick cherries when you were a kid, Weyre?"

Weyre put his open right hand on his thigh. "I'll tell you, Francis, it's a real chore just climbing stairs with this leg, let alone a ladder."

Francis nodded. "Well," he said, "I picked a million of 'em. Ten million! We had to—the other kids in the family and me. I hated it as much as I ever hated anything because I couldn't get *away* from it. I'd go on home for the day and I'd close my eyes and there they were, right in front of me, bright and big as life—"

"You mean the cherries?" Weyre interrupted.

Francis nodded sullenly. "The cherries. Nice,

163

rounded little clusters of 'em."

"Sounds awful," Weyre said, not really appreciating what Francis was telling him.

Francis nodded again, in affirmation. Then he said, "I see those damned body bags, now. The same way." The body bags had been taken from the church by the authorities in Merrimac two weeks earlier.

Weyre looked suddenly, and deeply pained. He shook his head briskly. "I don't want to talk about that, Francis. Please!"

Francis ignored him. "I see those body bags in my *sleep*, and they're just floatin' there, in the middle of that damned church, right in midair, like a bunch of long, black dirigibles or something. They don't *do* anything. They don't need to *do* anything."

Weyre pulled the side door open. "When you got something better to talk about, Francis, you let me know." And he turned and stalked from the house.

Francis sullenly watched him go. Then he made his way slowly into the living room, hesitated, to catch his breath, and went into his sitting room. He opened the middle drawer of a tall, blonde, and pretty-well-battered armoire, took out a cigar box, set it on the round table in the middle of the room. He sat. He opened the box, took out the small stack of news clippings inside. He thought it was odd that the news clipping about the accident should already be turning yellow with age, as had his clippings about the Kennedy assassinations, and the bombing of Pearl Harbor, and the moon landing, and the several dozen others.

He held the clipping about the accident trem-

blingly between his hands; he'd read it a number
of times. He was amazed that something so terrible and so gut-wrenching could be neatly trans-
ferred to words, and lines, and spaces:

> **FIFTEEN DIE IN TRAGEDY NEAR GOODE'S
> CROSSING**
> (AP) Fifteen people, including twelve children
> ranging from seven to ten years of age, died last
> night in a freak accident near the tiny village of
> Goode's Crossing, twenty miles east of Merrimac,
> New York. Authorities theorize that a truck-tanker
> loaded with hydrazine, a highly volatile chemical
> used by the aerospace industry and in agriculture,
> was rammed broadside in a blinding snowstorm by a
> schoolbus driven by Jesse McMurto, 51, also of
> Merrimac. Authorities believe that . . .

Francis stopped reading. He knew the clipping
by heart—the names of the kids, their ages and ad-
dresses, and he grimaced, now, remembering the
phrase, "Identification was rendered extremely
difficult, and in some cases impossible, by the fact
that most of the bodies were charred beyond easy
recognition." He thought the only body they had
probably had no trouble identifying had been
Jesse's. Big, friendly, smiling Jesse. A good man.
And he sure loved those kids.

Francis had known Jesse for quite a while. They
had met in 1976 at a fat farm outside Albany.
They'd both quit the fat farm after only two weeks
—neither had tried rationalizing the defeat.
"Hey," Jesse proclaimed, "I'm fat. I always will
be. Hell, they'll probably have to bury me in a
damn piano case." Which was an outlook Francis

had liked and so had adopted as his own.

They'd been out of a touch for a while, it was true. But friendships that are, as Jesse put it, "Alliances of imperfection fighting a 'perfect' world," Francis thought, die very hard.

That friendship wasn't dead even now, Francis decided. Because men like Jesse, who had so much love and caring inside them, just didn't die. Like a fat Pied Piper he was doubtless leading those kids back . . .

Francis lowered his head. He set the clipping in the cigar box, with the other clippings. He closed the box.

A fat Pied Piper. It was really a beautiful idea.

"These are portentous events, indeed," Sarah Goode intoned. "I believe . . . I believe with all my heart that Mr. Death is challenging us."

Stephen Krull said, "Sarah, the boy I saw was as real and as tangible as you or I."

She ignored him. He had always been more difficult than the others. "Marcus Breeze has come to me as well, Stephen. He has shared with me a very moving account of things he has seen at the church. He is convinced, as am I, that wonderful forces are at work." She paused briefly, then, "And Irene Janus, of all people, has had several very productive sessions with the mother of one of these children. And now"—another pause, for effect—"you have encountered this boy." She grinned. "Stephen, I couldn't be more pleased."

Stephen leaned forward in the Queen Anne chair, put his elbows on his knees, clasped his hands. Sarah was seated beside him, in a matching chair. "Sarah, that boy could have been anyone."

She nodded, reached over, put her hand on his. He glanced at it—it was very warm, almost hot. "I will concede that possibility," she said. "If he's lost, his parents will have reported it. I'll call Sheriff King directly. In the meantime, perhaps you and some of the other men in the village can mount a small search . . ."

"We've done that. And I've already called Sheriff King."

"Yes?" she coaxed.

"We didn't find anything, of course," Stephen answered. "And the sheriff—"

She interrupted, "Had no knowledge of a missing child?"

He nodded. "That's right."

"So, you see, Stephen, we are all on the edge of something . . . exquisite here." She paused. She got no reaction. "*Do* you see that, Stephen?"

He shook his head; "I'm not sure . . ."

"The evidence is very clear, Stephen," she said, as if it were so painfully obvious that if he didn't see it then his intelligence was somehow in question. "And we, in this village, because of *who* we are, and because of *what* we are, have the means, and the right, and the *duty* to act on it."

He looked quizzically at her. He said nothing.

She nodded solemnly. "Stephen, I have discussed this with several of the others, and I am going to propose it at the next Group Discussion."

"Propose what?" he asked.

She answered simply, "That we merge,

Stephen." She saw him look confusedly at her again; she explained, her voice more animated, now, "All of us—you, I, Marcus, Sam Pepper, Irene, John—we have so much *power*, Stephen. You, especially. I've always sensed it. And we have been using that power, and nurturing it, for a long time. For me, it's been sixty years! Ever since I was a child, ever since my mother passed over. Sixty years! And between all of us, Stephen we have five hundred years!" She was speaking very excitedly, now, her voice rising to a high screech. Stephen had never before heard her speak with such rabid enthusiasm and it confused him; he thought that it might even be frightening him. "One *thousand* years, Stephen! And this chance that Mr. Death is giving us, this opportunity, this challenge he is throwing down, this *responsibility* is not something we can lightly turn aside. Do you see that now, Stephen?"

"What opportunity, Sarah?" He was nearly pleading with her; he wanted desperately to understand. "Please tell me."

She said, a wide smile on her face, as if she were very happy, and her eyes straight ahead, "To bring them back to us, Stephen. To unlock the door, to swing wide the gates, to knock down the wall"— she looked him squarely in the eye, now; he felt a chill settle into his body—"between their world, and ours!"

He could not speak. He understood, at last, what she was saying, and it awed him.

She went on, her head bobbing quickly, "Yes, Stephen, it *is* possible. It's more than possible, it's a certainty, because"—she thumped her chest with her fist—"we are *who* we are, and because" —she thumped her chest again—"we are *what* we are! But we need you, Stephen. *You* are as strong as any of us!"

"My God!" It was all he could manage.

"Soon, Stephen. It will happen very soon."

At the playground, just beyond the southeastern edge of the village, a whisper rose up, then another, and another, and they drifted from place to place, halted, fell to the earth again, rose up.

They were particularly small and insubstantial things, the products of love, and memory, and good feelings. They moved about under the skeleton of the swings, and in circles, at first slowly, then more quickly, then quicker still on what remained of the tiny steel merry-go-round.

They disturbed nothing. They were not alive, or dead. They could not laugh, or ask for love, or plead, "Remember us." That was for others to imagine.

At last, they fell to the earth again, quivered a moment. And stopped.

20

The November Meeting of The Goode's
Crossing Spiritualist Society

Of sixteen in the village that night, thirteen
came to Fairclau House for the monthly meeting.
Without offering an excuse, Marjory Gwynne
stayed home, and so did Anna Breeze: "She's a
little under the weather," Marcus explained to the
group. "A little depressed—the accident, you
know." But no one believed him. It had become
common speculation recently that Marjory and
Anna were going to be asked to leave the village
before winter settled in (one other resident had
been asked to leave—a man named Dunne, eight
years earlier. Sarah had proclaimed him, "The
very worst kind of charlatan," which he had been,
"who makes all of us look bad," which he did, and
so the vote to expel him had been unanimous).

Tonight, Lily Krull served coffee and spice cake

to everyone. She'd been serving coffee and spice cake at the meetings for quite some time. She enjoyed doing it because everyone liked her spice cake, and her coffee, and she looked forward to the compliments she always got—it was the high point of the month for her.

Only at the last moment, and in response to his wife's insistence, and pleadings, did John Yount decide to show up. "Sarah needs you," Judy told him. "You're the Group Secretary" (it had always been a position he took quite seriously). "And besides, John, you don't want her to think you're afraid of something, do you?" which quickly convinced him that he was feeling a lot better than he thought he was feeling.

Stephen Krull was apprehensive. He thought he might even be a little scared, though he wasn't sure of what. Of Sarah, maybe. Or of her power. (His brother, Jim, had once told him, "At heart, Stevey, that woman is a tyrant. Can't you see that?" To which Stephen had answered, "I don't know what I see, Jim. I guess I don't bother to think about it very much. She's always treated me with . . . respect." Stephen thought he knew what Jim would say about what had been going on in the last few weeks, since the accident happened. Something sarcastic, and cutting, of course, but something that was essentially true: "You're all climbing a great big pile of shit," for instance, which had been one of his favorite phrases. And Stephen would respond with something vapid, he knew, like, "*Every*one's climbing a great big pile of shit, Jim," or, "At least it's our own shitpile." Too bad that Jim was dead. He'd have set the world on fire, for sure.)

Francis Eblecker had been losing weight, from 310 pounds the night of the accident to a shade over 276 now. It wasn't because he'd stopped eating. He'd been eating as much as ever—eating was a compulsion with him. And it wasn't entirely because, afraid even to close his eyes for very long, he hadn't been sleeping well, either. It was because *when* he slept he saw the damned black body bags, and the dizzying, wretched odor from within them flowed over him again, and made him sick. He'd vomited a lot since the accident. And that was the main reason he'd been losing weight.

Marcus Breeze had been dreaming. Nasty, brittle, cold dreams that held him tight and wouldn't let him wake because they frightened him and fascinated him at the same time. He wanted to tell Sarah about them because, certainly, she'd be able to help get rid of them. But she seemed very busy lately, and unapproachable, so he thought it was best to wait.

Sam Pepper had spent the last three weeks in a kind of working daze that kept him safely from remembering too clearly what he'd seen the night of the accident.

And as he'd proved upon stalking from Francis's house, Weyre Goodall remembered much too clearly. He could sense the protective bubble that some of the others had put themselves in, and he'd tried it on himself, but it hadn't worked—its skin was too thin, and his memory too strong. He imagined, quite often lately, that Goode's Crossing was in the process of being haunted, and he thought that if it was, that it was Good, and Right, that it should have happened long ago.

At 7:45 that evening, after a nod from Sarah, Lily collected the paper cups and paper plates, put them all in an Alligator Bag, tied the bag up, and set it near the door. It was the signal for the meeting to begin. So, after much quiet shuffling and scraping of chairs as people sat down around the big circular table and made themselves comfortable, Sarah spread her arms wide as a signal that they should all join hands, which they did, and announced, her dark eyes flitting from one person to another rhythmically as she spoke, "Tonight, we will be joined, we will be as one, and those quiet, patient ones standing just outside the door will be released."

Stephen Krull, sitting next to her, watched as she let her hands fall to her lap. After a moment's silence, other hands fell away, and several people lit cigarettes. Sam Pepper lit a cigar and began puffing delightedly on it. He bit it hard, reflexively, when Sarah jumped to her feet, knocking her chair over in the process, and screeched, her body stiff and her face tight with anger, "We are *not* fakes and lairs!"

Stephen got up quickly, righted her chair, then went back to his own chair. He watched, fascinated, as she leaned over the table and glared at each of them, one by one, a drop of spittle at the edge of her lip, her fists clenched on the table top, and her body shaking visibly.

"We are *not* fakes and liars!" she repeated.

Stephen's gaze flitted from person to person at the table. He saw that Irene Janus was twitching nervously, her neck muscles especially, and that Weyre Goodall, wide-eyed, looked for all the world like he was going to faint, and that Marcus Breeze had the slightest trace of a smile on his lips, as if he was about to hear something that would make him very happy. And he saw that Lily, sitting next to him, had folded her hands primly on her lap and looked like a young schoolgirl accepting some deserved punishment.

And then he sensed that Sarah's eyes were on him. He turned his head slowly. He looked at her; for several seconds their eyes locked. At last, he looked away momentarily, and when he looked back she had straightened from her leaning position over the table, and was stepping around and pushing her chair in. She stood with her hands gripping the top edge of the chair as she spoke.

"Sixty years ago," she started, her tone very firm, and instructive, "I called my mother back from the abyss of Death. She had been dead only a few minutes, then, and so her spirit had not yet had a chance to . . . take flight." She smiled a little at this. "And so it was particularly vulnerable. Because Life is stronger than Death." She paused, as if to let this sink in, though it was a phrase she was fond of using, and everyone in the room had heard it from her more than once. John Yount cut in, his voice a deep, scratchy whisper;

"Sarah, do you want me to take minutes of this?"

She did not answer. Her body stiffened.

Stephen closed his eyes lightly; he was suddenly embarrassed for John Yount—the man was obviously in pain, and should not have been there at all: Stephen watched as he pulled his spiral notebook, and a pen out of his briefcase and looked expectantly at Sarah. "No, John," Stephen told him soothingly. "I don't think so." John glanced at him:

"Oh," he said, "Yes. Of course."

"Thank you, Stephen," Sarah said, and when John had finished putting the notebook and pen back in the briefcase she went on, "We called to those children, too, in the same way that I called to my mother—before Death had had a chance to grip them too tightly. And now, my friends, now they are in a kind of . . . anteroom. They are waiting!" Her voice was rising in pitch, and urgency as she spoke. "And Death, which came into this village three weeks ago and sat with us and grinned at us—Death *laughs* at us now because it believes we are fools, it believes we aren't aware of the real and magnificent power we possess, it believes we see ourselves merely as tricksters, and fakes, and liars!" She thumped her chest with her tiny fist. "For myself, I know that I am not, I know that I am *stronger* than Death. And so he does not laugh at me. He fears me!" She pointed suddenly at Marcus Breeze. "It laughs at you, Marcus!"—he looked startled—"And you, Weyre,"—she pointed at him, "and you, Francis, and you, Irene!"—who shook her head very briskly, as if in denial. "It laughs at *all* of you if you do not shout loudly enough that he can hear you"—and she shouted; it was a very shrill, and nerve-shattering noise—"I am stronger than you, Mr. Death! I am not your equal! I am your better!" She stopped shouting. "Because you *are* his better. You know that you are." She sat and spread her arms. Stephen glanced about, from face to face. He saw that there was momentary confusion at the table, and also a kind of hushed, and vibrant expectancy. He took hold of Lily's right hand, Sarah's left. The others followed.

Sarah lowered her head. Stephen heard her inhale deeply, and then exhale very slowly. He felt Lily squeeze his hand hard, and sensed what he supposed was a surge of fear flow into him from her. He wanted to glance at her, and wink at her, as if to say, *It's okay, Lily!* but he knew that Sarah would frown on that.

She intoned, "We are stronger than you, Mr. Death. *We* laugh, at *you!* And together, *together* we will defeat you!"

"Yes," Marcus whispered, and there seemed to be something like elation in his voice. "Lord, yes!"

"Yes," Sam Pepper said aloud.

"Oh, yes," John Yount managed.

"You are nothing, Mr. Death," Sarah continued.

"You are nothing," Lily repeated.

"Nothing at all!" Marcus said.

"Nothing!" Stephen murmured, surprising himself; and suddenly he sensed that an enormous, billowing energy was filling up the room. It was an energy he had sensed before, on a smaller, more personal scale, but now, he thought, it seemed much more tangible, and so very strong.

It was, he knew, the collective energy of them all.

Sarah pushed herself to her feet, lifted her hands slowly, beckoning the others to stand, too. They stood, nearly in unison, except for Irene Janus, who took a moment to scratch her ankle, and Francis Eblecker, who, because of his weight, had always had trouble standing.

She told them, a slight, steady, grateful smile on her lips as she spoke, "Now it is time. We will go to the church, where Mr. Death is waiting for us. We will sit down with him. We will challenge him, as he has challenged us. And we will beat him!"

"Yes, yes," Marcus said, and his voice was trembling with elation.

"Yes," Andrew Liwush said.

"Yes," Stephen said.

21

On Shoemaker Road

Marian Hauser repeated, "I've seen him, Terry."

Terry sighed. "Of course you have, Marian," he said. "And I have, too. Whenever I pass his room at night, I see him sleeping and I whisper to him that I want him to have good dreams. And when I pull the car into the garage and I see his skis hanging up there, I see him. And when I remember hollering at him for no other reason than that I was tired—"

"That's not what I'm talking about. You know that's not what I'm talking about." She was sitting in a bentwood rocker in front of the fireplace. A small fire was crackling delightfully in it. Terry was standing behind her; he had a drink in hand which he nursed very slowly.

"I've seen him, Terry." She inclined her head to the left. "Out where he used to play. I've seen him a couple of times. And he just stands there, look-ing at the house. I even caught his eye, once."

Terry sighed. He could think of nothing to say and he wanted badly to say something.

"And that's why I'm going to go to Goode's Crossing, Terry. I think Tod's trying to tell me something. I think somebody there can help me to find out what."

Terry chose to ignore that, for the moment. He said, "I've given this a lot of thought, Marian, I mean, a *lot* of thought, and I believe it's something we should talk about, anyway. I think it would be best if we sold the house. I think it would be best if we moved away from here."

She glanced around at him, a look of surprise on her face. "Terry, we did that. Because of Jeremy. We came *here*. And it didn't work, did it? The memories came with us. And besides, if we moved now,"—she smiled oddly—"we'd be running away from Tod. We'd be abandoning him when he needs us most. Don't you see that? He *does* need us, Terry. He *still* needs us. He'll *always* need us!"

Terry sipped his drink. He decided that he wouldn't try to rationalize with irrationality, that it would be like hugging a porcupine to stop it from biting. "You really believe that, don't you?" he said, not in surprise, or criticism—he was usu-ally a very reasonable man—but merely as an observation.

She turned her head back, eyes on the fire. "You'll see him, too, Terry. It's just a matter of time, but you'll see him, too."

"Yes," he whispered sadly. She didn't hear him. "I probably will."

22

From her bedroom window, Marjory faintly saw the little group leave Fairclau House and start for the church. Sarah, easily recognizable even at night, and even at that distance, was out in front a few steps.

Marjory said to herself, "The damned fools!" and realized at once that she ached to know what exactly they were doing. There had been rumors in the last week that Sarah was planning something for tonight. "Something magnificent," Marcus Breeze had said.

Marjory sighed. "Oh, Pappy, tell me what to do, Pappy!" She didn't expect an answer from him. She never had. He was where he was, and she was where she was, and to believe otherwise (Pappy himself would have said) was just wishful thinking. But still she talked to him.

She wished there were a snowfall tonight—she thought the occasion deserved it. But the sky was clear, and crowded with stars, so the air was very cold, and the only snow remaining from the storms of a couple of weeks earlier were dismal gray patches at the bases of trees, and on the leading edges of roofs. Above the little group, a diffuse cloud of carbon dioxide hung like chimney smoke.

Marjory knew what she was going to do even before she decided to do it. "Thank you, Pappy," she said. She got her coat from the closet, put it on, and hurried from the house.

Andrew Liwush said, through clenched teeth, "Damn, but it's cold," and Sarah, several yards ahead, glanced back. "You are being touched by the fingers of Death, Andrew," she told him.

Stephen, to her left just behind her, murmured, "Yes," and sensed that the energy he had felt at Fairclau House was growing stronger by the second, as if he—all of them—were drawing inexorably closer to some great fire.

Lily, beside him, slipped her hand gently into his and murmured, "Yes," as if she'd been reading his thoughts. She squeezed his hand again and, from her touch, he knew that her fear was dissipating; it made him happy.

Marcus, at the back of the group, said loudly, "The Fingers of Death!" as if the phrase had some deep religious significance. "Oh, the Fingers of Death!"

Stephen saw Sarah wince at that.

John Yount coughed weakly. Once. Then again. *John*, Stephen wanted to say, *why don't you go on home?* But he knew that that was something for

Sarah to decide.

She began to step over a long, thick branch that had been ripped from a nearby maple tree by a summer windstorm. He reached out to help her. "No, thank you, Stephen," she said tightly. "I can manage." And she did.

When Irene Janus got to the branch she cursed and made a show of having to step over it. Francis Eblecker executed a wide, slow detour around it.

Fifty yards ahead, the Goode's Crossing First Presbyterian church looked, Stephen mused, very lumpish and black, like a mound of coal with an arched doorway at its middle. A good place for Death to be waiting, he thought.

But as he drew closer he could see colors bleed from it—the dark red of the brick, the soft blues and greens and yellows of what remained of the stained glass, the muted orange of the roofing tiles.

He heard Sam Pepper say, "It almost looks warm," and glanced at him, saw him clench his fists and shove them into his coat pockets to shelter them from the cold air.

"It is a tomb!" Sarah proclaimed.

"Yes," Lily whispered, "A tomb."

"A tomb!" Marcus shouted, and Stephen saw Sarah wince again.

Weyre Goodall's ample belly started aching then, and a knot formed in his chest. He imagined that he was going to have a heart attack, and he reached out, put his hand on Stephen's shoulder: "What's wrong, Weyre?"

Weyre shook his head, let go of Stephen's

shoulder and drifted away, to the right of the group. Stephen watched as he kept pace with effort.

Down the garden path, Stevey. That's where she's leading you.

She's not leading us anywhere, Jim. It just looks that way because we're all going in the same direction.

That's very profound, Stevey.

He shook his head. He supposed that his mind cleared.

They got to the bottom of the wide and badly age-pitted church steps by ones and twos—first Sarah, and then Stephen and Lily, walking hand in hand. Then Marcus, Harry March, and Lester Stanhope. Then Sam Pepper, John and Judy Yount, and Irene Atwater Janus. And finally Andrew Liwush and Francis Eblecker, followed by Weyre Goodall, who was moving very slowly.

Then, as if by instinct, they formed a circle around Sarah, who closed her eyes and grinned very slightly and breathed the words, "Mr. Death is exceedingly quiet tonight, isn't he?"

And indeed he was.

"We will go in now," she said.

And they did.

Anna Breeze opened her cellar door wide and called down the stairs, "Who's there, please? Is someone there?" She waited. She got no answer. She reached into the cellarway and flicked the

light on. She began tapping her foot nervously—
God, but she didn't want to go down there! "Is
someone in the cellar?" She waited a moment.
Again nothing.

She knew too well how an intruder would get in
—through the poorly latched double doors at the
base of the house's south wall (which Marcus had
been promising to fix for a long, long time). It had
happened once before, a couple years ago. Just a
wretched bum trying to get in out of the cold—
what he was doing in Goode's Crossing no one ever
knew because he'd died of exposure at the Merrimac Hospital the following morning.

"I have a gun," Anna shouted, and decided
immediately that it was probably a stupid thing to
say, even if it had been true. She chewed on her lip
in exasperation. "Damnit to hell," she breathed,
and easily convinced herself in the next few
seconds that what she had heard a couple minutes
earlier had probably been just a squirrel foraging
about in the root cellar, or maybe a raccoon, and
that the chances that it was anything more sinister
than that were very low. She grabbed the edge of
the door, hesitated a moment, and slammed it
shut. She bolted it hurriedly, as if whatever was in
the cellar—if anything *was* in the cellar—knew
what she was doing and didn't want to get locked
out of the house.

"Goddamn you, Marcus!" she muttered. "Goddamn your perverted little games! Why aren't you
home? You should be home!"

Sarah looked benignly at Marcus. "Marcus," she
said, "could you get us some candles, please?"

"Candles?" he said, confused.

"That's right, Marcus. Do you have any? We need thirteen of them—one for each of us."

"I think so, Sarah," he answered, still confused. "I'm not sure. I guess I'd have to go and look."

"I think we need more light in here, Marcus," she explained. There was a diffuse, yellowish light filtering into the church from the lights of the village; it was barely enough to see by. "And our flashlights simply will not do. You understand that, I'm sure." Sam Pepper and Lester Stanhope had their flashlights turned on and aimed at the floor. "Your house is close by, isn't it, Marcus?" Sarah went on. "If I'm not mistaken, it's just behind the church."

"Yes, it is," Marcus answered glumly.

"Good. Then it won't take you long." Her tone was almost cloyingly benign, now. "One candle for each of us, Marcus, as I said. And thank you very much."

Marcus hesitated, on the verge of a protest, then left resignedly by the church's side entrance, which was closest to his house. He hadn't wanted to leave. He supposed that if anyone but Sarah had asked him to leave, he would have said no.

He found that walking in the near pitch darkness behind the church was difficult, at best. Cold-hardened clods of earth had been tossed up here and there—by gophers, he supposed—and every once in a while his foot connected with one and he stumbled, which made him feel foolish and clumsy.

(He tried hard, and in vain, to avoid the sinking feeling that, for some reason of her own, some *good* reason of her own, Sarah had banished him from the church. If it were true, he realized, she'd share the reason with him later. Much later.)

The lights of his house came quickly into view. He quickened his gait. He'd left only a minute or so earlier, he guessed, so if he hurried he could be back within five or ten minutes.

Marjory slipped quietly into the church by the same side entrance that Marcus had used and made her way cautiously over the shattered stained glass that littered the floor around her to the dark northeast corner. She stood very stiffly, and quietly, there, watching. She felt immediately as if she were playing a perverse game of hide and seek, and the dozen people huddled together in the center of the church hadn't yet been told about it.

She looked forward to the amusement she felt certain Sarah was going to provide. She despised Sarah. It was a fact she had come to realize long ago, shortly after coming to Goode's Crossing. And she also feared her, which was a fact she had only recently come to realize. Sarah had power, and Sarah had wisdom—or at least she professed to, which seemed to be good enough for most of the others in the village—and if she told everyone clustered around her now to walk naked into Fall's Pond in the dead of winter, some of them probably would.

And so, Marjory thought, it would be very, very good to laugh at her, if only in silence.

At Sarah's bidding, the eleven people left in the

church with her quietly formed a circle. Sarah,
her back to the spot where the altar had once
been, was at its apparent head. Stephen was on
her right, and Francis, who wanted desperately to
relieve himself outside somewhere—but stayed
quiet about it because he knew Sarah wanted no
such interruptions—was on her left. Lily stood
close to Stephen; they were still holding hands.
Sam Pepper, fighting an urge to light up another
cigar, stood next to Lily, his big, skeletal hands
folded across his narrow chest.

Weyre Goodall, whose belly still ached, had
placed himself at the opposite end of the circle
from Sarah, with his back to the church's front
doors. He'd convinced himself that he wasn't
going to have a heart attack, because the knot in
his chest had cleared. He had shoved his hands
hard into his coat pockets; he was shivering a
little.

John and Judy Yount stood next to Weyre, their
arms hanging loosely at their sides. John was in
pain. Every few moments, Judy heard a small
groan escape him and she glanced nervously about
to see if anyone else could hear it. Apparently no
one else could.

Viewed from above, the circle would have
looked pretty ragged. Lester Stanhope and
Andrew Liwush, across from the Younts, Lester
with flashlight in hand, were a yard further in
than they should have been, and Harry March,
who was developing quite a severe headache because he hadn't eaten since noon, was a little too
close to Irene Janus. She, in turn, was a step

further away from Francis than she otherwise
would have been, because she itched badly, and
felt unclean because of it. She mused that if someone were going to mete out punishment to her for
all the misdeeds of her life, the damned itching she
was going through now was perfect.

But beneath their unspoken pains and com-
plaints, and beneath their private, momentary
needs, Sarah knew they all shared one thing:
power. Whether any of them realized it or not was
hardly important, because she could so easily
make their doubts go away. It was merely a matter
of suggestion, a matter of her own power. And her
own faith.

She raised her hands to the level of her shoulders, palms out. She became aware that in a
corner of the church, water was dripping slowly
and rhythmically from one of the holes in the roof.
With a tiny mental effort, she blocked the noise.

"We will begin now," she said, and her voice
was silky-smooth, almost sensuous; it took
Stephen, standing next to her, by surprise:

"Sarah?" he whispered, "what about Marcus?"

She answered, in the same, silky-smooth tone,
"Marcus is very . . . impressionable, isn't he,
Stephen?!" And it was clear to him that she
thought the words were explanation enough. He
merely nodded.

"We will begin now," she repeated. "Let us join
hands." They joined hands. She went on, very
slowly, her tone now one of deep and measured
incantation, "We have come to challenge you in
your own house, Mr. Death! You have taken our

children into your vile bosom, and you have offered to feed them there, and you have laughed at their quick and awful starvation." She paused. Stephen glanced briefly at her, saw her teeth clench, and the muscles of her small face go taut, and her tiny, dark eyes close tightly—a profusion of crow's feet appeared at their outside edges. Her voice lowered a full octave: "We spit on you, Mr. Death! And oh, we do despise you!"

In the northeast corner of the church, Marjory began to chuckle softly, nervously.

Stephen said, in much the way that Sarah had, "We spit on you, Mr. Death! And oh, we do despise you!" He glanced at Sarah. "Again," she whispered. He repeated—Lester, and Andrew, and Francis in unison with him—"We spit on you, Mr. Death! And oh, we do despise you!"

"Again!" Sarah demanded fiercely of them all.

And they said together, "We spit on you, Mr. Death! And oh, we do despise you!"

Sarah lowered her head so her gaze was on the tips of her transparent slipover boots. The corners of her lips turned upward in an approximation of a grin. She thought, *They are falling into place, Mother. It is going to work!*

She raised her head quickly, and opened her eyes very wide, as if she were in shock. She began shivering violently. And then she called, with great anger, into the cold, still air of the church, "*Your* children, Mr. Death—your wraiths, and your demons, and your blood-sucking fiends—do not frighten us! They are images which are gray, and flat. They are images of putrefaction!"

Stephen felt Lily begin to shiver next to him, as if in response to what Sarah was saying. He squeezed her hand in reassurance. He looked at her; her eyes were moist, she was obviously on the verge of tears.

When she saw the thing's hand, she saw it unclearly, because it was nearly the same color as the refrigerator, and because the rain was cutting off her vision . . .

"Lily?" Stephen whispered. She made no response.

"They are images of decay!" Sarah screeched. "They are images that fade, and are gone! You are *nothing*, Mr. Death, and we do not fear you!"

She took another step up the gully's slope. It was enough. She saw the head, then, and the body— doubled up into a fetal position, its arms high and bent hard at the elbows. It looked, she decided, like a big, wrinkled, naked, gray doll made of papier-mâché.

"You are nothing, Mr. Death!" Stephen shouted. "And we do not fear you!" and he heard, as he shouted it, that Lily was shouting it, too, at the same time, but as if in desperation, or pleading.

"Again!" Sarah demanded. "He does not believe you!"

And, as one, the group responded, "You are *nothing*, Mr. Death, and we do not fear you!"

Marjory Gwynne had stopped chuckling. She

sensed something strange in the air. Something still, and dark, and very cold.

Once more, Sarah lowered her head. "Please," she said, and the others in the ragged little circle lowered their heads, too. She looked up, set her gaze on a bare spot just above the front doors of the church. "Focus," she breathed. "We must all focus. We must call up our power and bring it together and hone it into something fierce, and then we must hurl it very, very hard at Mr. Death!" She paused, then; "But first, we must *recognize* him!"

"Oh, yes," Lily whispered, "I do." And her thoughts still were racing back more than thirty years, to her childhood, and a hot day in July, when she'd gone looking for whatever it was that her brother and his friends found so appealing in the gully behind her house.

"We must *recognize* him," Sarah repeated. It was clearly an invitation to them all. "Go back, my dear, dear friends! Go back!"

An so they did.

"I'm sorry, Stephen, but Jim passed on five minutes ago. At least we expected it."
"Christ, Doc—that's no help!"

"Why were you running, Weyre?"
"Because of Red, Dad."
"Red? Who's he?"
"My friend, my new friend. He fell, Dad. He's . . . dead!"

"Go back, my friends. *Focus. Recognize* him!"

A big, wrinkled, gray doll made of papier-maché . . .

And what Harry March was hearing now, in these barracks—the belches, the farts, the squeaking bed springs, the snoring—was, he guessed, a carbon copy of other nights here, in the years just passed . . .

"We do not fear you, Mr. Death!"
"We do not fear you, Mr. Death!"

Weyre wasn't sure what he was seeing, at first. He supposed momentarily that Red's body was at a different angle on the stairs than he'd first thought, or that maybe there had been a subtle change in the light . . .

"Not as smart as a pig, Marjory, it's true, but lots smarter than the average horse, or the average cow, and tons smarter than the average insurance salesman."

. . . because Red's left arm looked as if it were hanging backward, or inside out, from the shoulder, and his right hip seemed to jut queerly several inches above where it should have been, and for one quiet moment . . .

For a moment, there was silence in the barn. Dead silence. As if all the cows, and the chickens,

*and geese, and horses had somehow gotten
together and agreed that, if only for that moment,
they would give Marjory the quiet that she
wanted . . .*

"Do you recognize him, my friends? Do you
recognize him?"

"Yes," Stephen whispered.

"Oh, yes," Lily said.

"Yes," Harry March told her.

"God, yes," Weyre Goodall managed.

*. . . and deep within that silence, as if from deep
within a well, from deep within the mud and the
debris at the bottom of that well, she heard Pappy.*

*And even at that great distance, and for that brief
moment, she could tell that he was enjoying himself immensely.*

Marjory was trembling; the thing she had
sensed before—the strange, cold, still thing set-
tling into the church—seemed very strong now.

*. . . and this place, inside these barracks, within
these walls, had been their jumping-off point. From
here, they'd all gone out to meet eternity. Harry
smiled to himself. These are indeed corny times, he
thought. And he became aware that someone was
standing very quietly beside his bed . . .*

*. . . a big, wrinkled, gray doll made of papier-
mâché . . .*

... Sarah watched the dark figure climb gracefully out of the lake and up, onto the pier. She watched the figure stand on the pier quietly. She listened to the small, dull plopping sounds of water dripping on old wood.

Sarah lowered her head. "Please," she said. The others lowered their heads. "And so we recognize you, Mr. Death," she said.

"And so we recognize you, Mr. Death!" the group repeated.

... a big, wrinkled, gray doll made of papier-maché ...

... the figure sat quietly below the attic window. Its eyes found Sarah's, then its head turned and its eyes found the lake ...

Sarah grinned very slightly. She threw her arms high into the air; her body began shivering violently; her eyes opened wide; she called shrilly, "Come into this village, Mr. Death. Walk its streets with us, and enter our houses, and sit down with us! We do not fear you! You are nothing! And you beget nothing, and so you cannot hold *our* children! And so we demand that you give them back. We demand it!"

"We demand it!" the others shouted in unison, with much the same frenzy that was gripping Sarah.

... "Mother is alive, Aunt Jessica. Mother is alive!"

"Oh, my child, my poor child!"

And then Marjory Gwynne found, all at once, that she couldn't see, and she guessed, frantically, that the beam of one of the flashlights had caught her momentarily, that her eyes hadn't readjusted, and so were not letting in enough light—like coming in from bright sunlight to a dark room.

But through her blindness, she heard Lester Stanhope murmur, "Where's . . . the light gone?"

And Irene Janus screech, "What's happening here, what's happening here?!"

And a quick silence settled into the church.

In hushed tones, Anna said to Marcus, "I think there was someone here, Marcus. Down in the root cellar."

"Why? Is something missing?"

"I didn't check."

He harrumphed. "Raccoons, Anna. They like to get in out of the cold, like anything else." He looked around the dining room. "I need some candles, Sarah sent me for some candles. Don't we have any?" He opened a drawer of the buffet and pulled out two long, white, tapering candles. "Don't we have more than this?" He rummaged in the drawer. Anna opened the drawer beside it and pulled out a box of eight utility candles. "Here," she said, and she handed him the box.

"I need some more, Anna. We've got to have another box somewhere around here."

"I don't think so," she said, and added, "Could you at least look down there before you go, Marcus? Just to make me feel better."

"Look where? In the root cellar?"

She nodded. "I *did* hear something, Marcus. And I don't think it was a raccoon."

"Sure it was, Anna. What else could it have been?" He shoved the candles into his big coat pockets. "I guess this will have to do," he said, and paused. He looked sharply at Anna, as if in reprimand. "Anna, you should come with me. This is a very important thing we're doing tonight. Sarah would like you to be there, I'm sure."

"No," Anna told him. "I don't think so."

"She would . . ." He paused, considered, then went on, "She would feel better about you, Anna. About both of us, I think."

Anna looked up at him, a tinge of anger in her face. "No," she said tightly. "I'll stay here. You go. Take your candles and go!"

He sighed. Saying nothing, he left the house quickly.

If he had turned his head to the right when he came in through the church's side entrance, he would have seen Marjory, about fifteen feet away, as an elongated, grayish swell in the darkness. But he did not turn his head. It had been more than five minutes since he'd left, closer to fifteen, he guessed, and he was in a hurry because people were probably getting bored and cold, and they were depending on him.

He approached the circle with his left hand out and the candles clutched in it. "I could get only ten of them," he said. He got no response. He shouldered his way in between Irene Janus and Francis

Eblecker. "Sarah?" he said. He looked quickly from one face to another. From Sarah, to Harry, to John and Judy Yount, and Sam Pepper, who had a flashlight in his hand. Marcus took it and shone it into Stephen's face. "Good Christ!" Marcus whispered. And in the next moment, he let go of the flashlight, because he did not have the strength to hold on to it, and heard it clatter to the floor.

He felt as if he was being wrapped from head to foot in a blanket. But it was a blanket without substance or warmth. As if the cold, still air around him had begun to solidify. And though he still could breathe it, he could not move in it, or cry out, as he so desperately wanted, and he knew that his face, like the faces of all those around him, was frozen in a tight and awful grimace of panic and fear.

We spit on you, Mr. Death!
And we loathe you!
Your children—your wraiths, and your demons, and your blood-sucking fiends do not frighten us! They are images which are gray, and flat. They are images of putrefaction. They are images of decay. They are images which fade, and are gone! You are nothing, Mr. Death, and we do not fear you! Come into this village. Walk its streets with us, and enter our houses, and sit down with us.

"You know what, Terry?" Marian Hauser said. She was sitting in her chair in front of the fireplace, her gaze on the soft dance of a fire going out.

"No, what?" Terry answered; he'd just come

into the living room from the kitchen where he had fixed himself a sandwich and a glass of milk.

"My mother told me something once and I've been sitting here trying to get some comfort from it." She paused. Terry waited for her to continue. In a moment, she did. "She told me that the only thing we have is Life—with a capital L. And then she told me, 'How can we have Death? How can we have Nothing—with a capital N?' which I thought was interesting."

Terry had come over and was standing next to the chair. "Yes, it is interesting," he said. "But does it give you any comfort?"

"No," she answered immediately. "It doesn't. I mean ... there has to be *something*, doesn't there?"

Terry shrugged. "I don't know, Marian. I guess we're all graffiti artists at heart."

"Sorry?"

"Graffiti artists—you know; we see a blank wall, and we just have to fill it up." He grinned.

"Oh," she said. "Yes, I see." A short pause, then she nodded at his sandwich. "What is that? It looks awful."

"It's peanut butter and Marshmallow Fluff," he answered. "Tod used to eat them. I thought I'd give it a try. It's not too bad."

Marian raised an eyebrow. "Uh-huh," she said.

In the Goode's Crossing First Presbyterian Church, Stephen Krull fell slowly to his knees, lowered his head, closed his eyes. "Oh, dear God," he murmured.

Distantly, as if she were in another room, he heard Lily weeping softly. With effort, he turned his head; she still was standing beside him; she had her face buried in her hands. He reached for her, touched her; she recoiled. "Lily..." he managed, and then he struggled to his feet, and gathered her almost violently into his arms. He felt her trembling, heard her weeping grow louder, and more frantic.

Around him, he sensed movement beginning, heard someone—Harry March, he thought—murmur, "Kenny?" and Weyre Goodall whisper, "I don't want to do that, Red."

Judy Yount pleaded, "Sarah, help me, Sarah!"

He glanced at Sarah. He thought at first that she was in pain, but then he saw that what he had supposed was a grimace wasn't that at all but something closer to a look of overwhelming ecstasy, as if—he shuddered—she were in the throes of an orgasm.

"Stephen," he heard Lily say into his chest. "Oh, Stephen, what have we done?" He patted her back in reassurance. "It's all right, Lily. It's all right."

Out of the corner of his eye, he could see that Irene Janus was in an agony of itching, and that John Yount, near her, was frantically rubbing his eyes and yelling, "My eyes—I can't see! My eyes!" And then, as Stephen watched, John quieted and his sight apparently came back to him.

Stephen glanced at his watch.

"My friends!" Sarah called suddenly.

It was 8:45.

"My friends!" Sarah called again. And Stephen

watched as, very slowly, over the space of several minutes, the others in the group shifted their attention to her.

She smiled tightly, as if in pain. "My friends," she said again. "He has come to us. And he has filled us up."

"But Sarah, it hurts," Weyre Goodall said.

"I feel so . . . empty, Sarah," Francis Eblecker said.

Sarah's grin grew softer, more soothing. "We must remember that we are *stronger* than he is. And so we have no need to fear him—we must not fear him!"

There was no response.

"We are stronger than him!" she coaxed. "And we must not fear him!"

"We are stronger than him," Stephen managed.

"We are stronger than him," Francis repeated.

"And we must not fear him!" Lester finished.

"We do not fear you, Mr. Death!" Sarah called.

"We do not fear you, Mr. Death!" Stephen, and Francis, and Weyre, and Harry March called, followed, moments later, by Lily.

"*Your* children, Mr. Death," Sarah called, "your wraiths, and your demons, and your blood-sucking fiends, do not frighten us! They are images which are gray, and flat. They are images of putrefaction!"

All but Irene Janus repeated it.

"And so now that you have filled us up," Sarah called, "we will *beat* you!"

Everyone repeated it.

"Because we are Life, and Life is stronger than Death."

Everyone repeated it.

Sarah held her arms wide. "My friends," she told them, "it has begun." She closed her eyes lightly; "And now," she finished, "we must rest for the great battle that is about to unfold." She moved slowly, as if in pain, to the front doors of the church. The group —led by Stephen and Lily—followed. They clustered around her. She turned her head, looked at them. "Soon," she told them, and, with much effort, she pulled the doors open. Without hesitation, all of them made their way down the wide, crumbling steps, through the chilly November night, to their homes.

At the playground, just beyond the southeastern edge of the village, the whispers rose up. They drifted from place to place, halted, fell to the earth again, rose up.

They were small and insubstantial things—the products of love, and memory, and good feelings. They moved about under the skeleton of the swings, and in circles, quickly, on what remained of the tiny steel merry-go-round. And, like hands clutching, they curled over tree limbs.

They disturbed very little. They were not alive, or dead, and they could not laugh aloud, or ask for love, and they did not want to plead, "Remember us." That was for others to imagine.

They moved like tiny, swirling currents of air around the things in the playground, and, at last, they fell to the earth again, quivered, rose up, fell.

And stopped.

Part Four
OUT OF THE MIRROR

23

"Marian?" Terry Hauser called from the kitchen window. "What are you doing, Marian?"

She turned her head, looked at him. She was standing in back of the house, near the property line—a boundary marked by a short white picket fence in need of some repair. "Nothing," she called back. "Looking," she added. "I'm just looking."

But she hadn't said it loud enough. "I can't hear you," Terry called, and moments later he left the house by its rear door. His long legs and quick stride carried him across the yard to his wife in seconds. He put his hands on her shoulders. "Did you say you were looking for something, Marian? For what?" His tone was quiet and soothing.

She looked around at him, put her hand on his. "For Tod, of course." She looked back at the tall weeds behind the picket fence.

"Uh-huh," Terry said, not wanting to strain the obvious.

"I know he's dead, Terry, if that's what you wanted to say."

"It's what I wanted to say."

She patted his hand again. She said, "But you see, Terry—*I'm* still alive!"

It was a drab morning, the feel and color of slate, and very quiet.

"We're both alive," Terry said.

Again she patted his hand; the gesture was beginning to annoy him. "I don't think you understand, Terry." She turned her head and smiled sadly at him. "And I don't think I can explain it."

"I miss him, too, Marian." His lower lip trembled as he said it.

"I know you miss him. Do you think I'm questioning that?"

"No."

She studied his eyes a moment, then told him, "I went to Goode's Crossing yesterday."

"Oh?"

"That doesn't upset you?"

"Of course it upsets me." He said the words matter-of-factly, without anger.

"But if it made me feel better? . . ."

"Did it?"

"No, it didn't. I just drove in and drove out. I didn't talk to anyone." She grimaced. "It smells bad there, Terry. Do you know that?"

"I've never been there, Marian."

"It smells like sulfur. That's perfect, isn't it?"

She paused. Terry said, "Uh-huh," without conviction. She went on, her voice a coarse whisper, "I do miss him, Terry. I miss him quite a lot, more than I thought I would. I used to think about that—about how much I'd miss him if anything happened. Maybe because of Jeremy, I don't know. But I used to sit there and wonder how long it would take me to stop missing him if something ever happened to him. And I'd guess, oh, maybe it'll take a month or two. Maybe it'll take a year. And then I'd think that of course I'd never stop missing him, that I'd always have some little place in my heart for him, some little corner where he'd go on living forever. But I've found out something, Terry—I've found out that it's much, much more than a little corner. It's everything. I think about him almost constantly. That's why I see him out here, I think. And that's why I come looking for him. Because I want to bring him back inside. I want to talk to him. I want to give him something to eat. I want to tuck him into bed." She turned her head and smiled sadly again. "And then, Terry, I want to . . . look in on him. Like we used to do. Remember? When he was still a baby? We used to look in on him every half hour, I think, just to be sure he was okay."

"I remember."

"He was such a good little kid, Terry. So bright, and sensitive, and affectionate. Remember we used to say how lucky we were? Remember that?"

"Yes, I do." This was becoming very difficult, Terry thought.

She scratched idly at her ear lobe and looked

back at the weeds beyond the picket fence. "He and I used to talk a lot. He'd come home from school and he'd look up at me and he wouldn't have to say anything. I knew that he wanted to talk. So we'd sit down in the living room. He'd sit in your chair, and I'd sit on the ottoman, and he'd take a while to get comfortable, and then we'd talk. We talked about lots of things. About his schoolwork, and his teachers—he had a crush on Mrs. Simone,"—she grinned—"—and about his friends. He had lots of friends. And we even talked about death. She glanced at Terry again for some reaction to that. He looked surprised. "You didn't know that, did you?" she said. "That he thought about death, I mean."

Terry shook his head. "No," he said.

She nodded solemnly. "He used to ask me about Jeremy. If Jeremy looked like him, or talked like him, and who I thought was smarter, and which one I loved more. And how much I missed Jeremy. And if he could ever take Jeremy's place."

"What did you tell him?"

"I told him 'no,' of course. I told him that no one can take the place of anyone else. That it was foolish even to try. I told him that Jeremy could never have taken *his* place. I think he understood that. He was a smart boy."

"Yes," Terry said, "he was."

"One day he came home . . . he came home and told me about some little friend of his. At school. He told me that this friend of his had died. Just like that. He said, 'Is that the way it happens, Mommy?' I told him that it happens that way sometimes. I told him that when it happened to me that that's the way I'd want it to happen. He didn't like that at all. He didn't like the idea that his mommy was going to die. It took me a long, long time that day to calm him down. I told him that death happens to everyone. That when it happened, they went back to the earth, they were put back *into* the earth, because that's where they came from—he liked that—and that they became, you know, flowers, and trees, and even other people, maybe. He liked that, too. I think *I* liked that." She paused and lowered her head. "It doesn't help at all now, Terry. I almost wish—no, not almost, I *wish* I had some religion to cling to. That would be a great help. I think that would pull me through all this."

Terry gently turned her around to face him. He looked silently at her a moment. Then he pulled her close, into a long, warm embrace, and they went back into the house.

Who is she?

She's someone you know, I think. Do you remember her?

She's very pretty. I don't remember her. I wish I did, but I don't. How do I remember her?

That'll take time, I think. We have lots and lots of time, though. Do you remember him?

I don't remember him, either.

Do you remember this house?

No, but I want to. I want to very bad.

I think I'm hungry again.

Yeah, me too.

*I remember that—being hungry. I don't like
butter beans, I think. And I don't like squash. But I
like summer squash and squash pie because it
tastes like pumpkin pie. And peanut butter and
marshmallow sandwiches, too. And blueberries are
nice.*

*I had them smeared all over my face once. And in
my ears. She had to take me to the doctor.*

Who had to take you to the doctor?

*And I don't like Muenster cheese, either. He had
to take them out with a probe. He said it was a
"probe." And he said I shouldn't put anything in
my ear that would fit in it. If something fit in it
then it shouldn't go in there. He said I would go
deaf.*

Like before?

Uh-huh.

*But it don't hurt no more, anyway. It hurt bad. It
hurt badder than anything. Badder than when I
broke my ankle!*

I remember that. I remember I cried.

"Worse." She says "worse," not "badder."

Who says "worse"?

She does.

*I remember I cried till I couldn't cry no more
and then I went to sleep and when I woke up I was
in the hospital.*

Yeah, with the sick people.

And the dead people.

I seen them.

Seen who?—The dead people?

*Lots of 'em, all laid out in a row and not even
bleedin' no more.*

Dead people gotta get buried.

I know, yeah, I know.

That's what she says.

She says you bury 'em and they come back up into the flowers. Maybe they will.

I'm still hungry, you still hungry?

I could even eat butter beans I'm so hungry.

I could eat squash.

Yeah, but peanut-butter-and-marshmallow sandwiches would be great.

You cold?

I'm freezin'!

Let's go back, then, before it gets real cold.

Yeah, it's gonna get real cold. I know it is. It always does.

24

Stephen Krull toed the thin white ice at the shoreline of Fall's Pond. The ice broke; frigid water heaved up over the edge of the hole, and quickly receded. He remembered doing the same thing—but on a more time-consuming, and physically larger scale, with rocks instead of his toe—when he was a kid. It had always seemed odd that the water beneath the ice should heave up the way it did, as if it were constantly moving underneath, or as if it were breathing, and alive. It still seemed strange, and that pleased him because it was a mystery from childhood that growing up hadn't pushed aside and made trivial, and there were damned few of those.

He realized at once that he was actively trying not to think of the events of Sunday night. It was why he'd come here, he admitted, to be away from Lily and her incessant babbling about it ("She did it, by God, Stephen—she really did it! I'd never have believed it. Do you believe it? They were there, Stephen. I could feel that they were there. I still feel it! What a wonderful, marvelous thing!").

Because he could feel it, too. And it felt wonderful, just as Lily had said. But there was something in back of that feeling, too. Like the water beneath the ice, only in reverse—ice moving beneath the water, waiting to rise up and quiet them all.

Marjory didn't know what she would do with the dead mole cradled in her hand. If the ground wasn't frozen she would bury it, she thought. But doubtless the ground was frozen, to a depth of a couple inches, and all she had was a flat-bladed coal shovel, anyway, so what she'd probably do with the mole, she supposed, was toss it in the garbage can.

"How'd you get in?" she whispered at it, and she gently stroked its short, close gray fur. She kept her eyes away from its face—moles were ugly enough, anyway, and this one, with its mouth drawn back into a kind of rigid grin, was a tiny horror. "You shouldn't have come in. Balboa probably scared you to death, didn't he?" Balboa was her cat—a huge, rangy, black-and-white Tom with only one-and-a-half-ears who spent most of his time prowling Leslie's Mountain. Only on very cold nights, as the previous night had been, did he come meowing for warmth. Marjory didn't so much think of him as "her cat," as merely some wild creature who occasionally ate her food and accepted her affection. And killed small intruders. Like this mole.

It was a little strange that Balboa hadn't eaten it. He never passed up a meal.

She carried the mole downstairs, to the kitchen, got a Baggie, dropped the mole into it, and dropped the Baggie into her pop-up garbage pail. She reminded herself mentally to empty it that morning.

She washed her hands. "Balboa?" she called. "Here, kitty!"

She glanced around the kitchen. He was not in his wicker basket, where he usually spent his time indoors, and he was not underfoot, begging for a handout.

"Balboa? Here, kitty-kitty!"

She remembered letting him in the night before, around eight o'clock. "Balboa?" she called again. He appeared in the kitchen doorway. She smiled at him, leaned over, patted her thighs: "Well, come here," she coaxed.

The cat meowed pathetically at her, turned around, and wandered back into the living room.

Marjory told herself that it was no wonder she didn't like cats all that much; they had no loyalty at all, or gratitude.

She got some coffee out of the cupboard. She'd make it strong, and drink it black, she decided. It had been a long, strange night with Harry, his "swan song," he told her ("It's middle-age, Marjory," he said, as an excuse for the exhausting sexual athletics he'd put them through. "It's the realization that you're approaching that final bend in the road, you know? And what better way to avoid it than to turn around and go back." It was as good an excuse as any, she supposed). And she was very tired. She thought that she had never before been so tired.

"I don't know what she did," Marcus Breeze told his wife, and he sounded genuinely, and deeply, confused.

"She tricked you," Anna said.

Marcus shook his head. "No, Anna. There was no trick. I know there was no trick."

"She hypnotized you, then. It was probably very easy for her. She worked you all up into a frenzy—"

"'A frenzy'? My God, Anna, you make it sound like we were all running around naked and shouting at the devil."

"You were there, Marcus." She was not chastising him, merely reminding. "I wasn't."

Again Marcus shook his head. "I'm not sure where I was, Anna, or of what happened. I know I was scared. I was terrified!"

"Of what?"

"I don't know that, either. Of what we tried to do, maybe." He shivered suddenly. "Jesus, it's cold in here, Anna." He nodded at the thermostat. "Turn the heat up a little, would you?"

She did it. "I saw something near the church," she said. "Early this morning, before you woke up."

"Oh?" he said, without much interest.

"Uh-huh. A little boy, I think. It was hard to tell.

I saw him from the bedroom window."

"There aren't any little boys in Goode's Crossing, Anna."

"I know that. But I did see him. He was carrying a shovel."

"A shovel?"

"That's what it looked like. It could have been anything, I guess." She grinned in mock playfulness. "Maybe he was one of yours and Sarah's ghosts."

He grimaced. "That's in poor taste, Anna."

She laughed hollowly. "*You* are in poor taste, Marcus. You and your friends. What you did the other night—"

Marcus threw his hands into the air in exasperation: "This is pointless!"

She stood abruptly. "I'd say a lot of things are pointless. I've thought so for a long time."

He looked up at her, puzzled. "What's that supposed to mean?"

"You know what it means."

He sighed. "Oh, for Christ's sake . . ."

She turned quickly and left the room. He leaned over and turned the thermostat up another two degrees. Damn, but it was cold!

Irene Atwater Janus thought that maybe it was psoriasis she was coming down with, or eczema, or hives, or scabies (she shuddered at the word).

She scratched her left elbow angrily. "Goddamnit!" she hissed. This was agony. It was worse than a toothache, because you could take stuff for a toothache. Aspirin, or codeine. Maybe you could go to sleep. But it sure wouldn't help this damned itching.

She scratched her right elbow. Then her forehead, and her thighs, and crotch. She felt suddenly unclean, and it bothered her immensely. She rushed into the bathroom, turned the shower on, tested it, tore her clothes off and got under the spray.

She jumped out, shivering violently. The water was icy cold.

She began itching again. Under her arms, at her ankles, on her chin. She clawed at herself for relief. She opened long, thin wounds everywhere.

And, at last, the itching stopped.

Francis Eblecker's house was almost precisely at the junction of Fairclau Close and Main Street, and since the village was in a valley between Leslie's Mountain and Shoemaker Road, the Close angled upward out of the village at a fairly steep angle. So, from his west-facing window, the view Francis got was nothing less than fantastic. He had often wished he had the money for "one of those expensive Japanese cameras," so he could capture forever the view from that window. And, at any rate, he did have a painting which Lily Krull had done for him, though he privately thought the painting was much "prettier" than it should have been. Because, after all, the dark, narrow road cresting so steeply and suddenly a hundred yards away, and the tall pines crowding it on either side, and the stiff black shadows leaning across wasn't so much pretty as breathtakingly stark, and it was that quality that he wanted to capture.

He had been spending much of his time in the last few days seated at that west-facing window, his eyes on the Close, precisely as if he were waiting for something to appear suddenly, at the crest of the hill, and march down it, into the village.

He was waiting for Jesse McMurto to appear, he knew. The Fat Pied Piper, and his kids that he loved so much dancing close behind. Because Sarah had called them, hadn't she? And no one disobeyed Sarah.

At 2:34 P.M., with his eyes on the Close, Francis saw a big, dark figure appear at the crest of the hill. He pushed himself mightily to his feet. He breathed, "My God!" and a huge, happy smile spread over his face.

And then, as he watched, another, much smaller figure appeared, at the crest of the hill, and then another behind it, and another, and another, and Francis fell backward into his chair, suddenly exhausted by his quick and immense elation.

They would come here, Stephen thought sadly. *This is a place for children.* He was still at Fall's Pond. *This is where I would come.* He smiled at that. Beneath his thoughts he was remembering his own childhood on a small farm deep in the Maine woods, where he'd had the benefit of a pond similar to this one. It had been alive, though, and Fall's Pond was not.

Leslie's Mountain, outlined in deep blue just east of the village, was reflected from the quiet, flat surface of the pond. The air was still, and very cold. Nothing moved around him. He had spent more than a few winters in Goode's Crossing and he knew what the air was telling him now. It wasn't a guess or a prediction, it was knowledge. A storm was on the way.

He heard music rise up suddenly behind him. A flute, he guessed, and it was playing something lilting, and whimsical, at a good distance—from Fairclau Close a couple hundred yards south, he realized. He wondered who in the village could play like that, and who indeed could play the flute at all. He turned his head. He listened a moment. A slight, glad smile came to him and he thought that nothing could have been more out of place, and more pleasant, in the village today than that music.

And then it stopped at once.

At the playground, just beyond the southeastern edge of the village, where children played once, and laughter rang out, and shins got scraped, and memories got started, the whispers rose up. They drifted from place to place. They halted, rose up, fell to the earth again, though for just a moment, and rose up again. Higher. And louder, so a field mouse háppening by looked up briefly, and wonderingly, then hurried on its way.

The whispers were small and insubstantial things, the products of love, and memory, and good feelings, which constitutes the real stuff of life, and they moved about under the skeleton of the swings, and in circles, quickly, on what remained of the tiny steel merry-go-round. And, like hands clutching, they curled over tree limbs, and held on tight to the big metal replicas of Donald Duck and Mickey Mouse that someone had brought to the playground decades before.

The whispers disturbed very little. They were not alive or dead and they could not laugh loudly, and did not want to ask for love, or plead, "Remember us!"

They moved like tiny, swirling currents of air around the things in the playground and, at last, they fell to the earth again, quivered, rose up, fell.

And lay asleep, and quiet.

25

That Evening

Marcus was very confused. "Anna," he pleaded, "why are you doing this?"

She looked up at him from her chair. She was surrounded by suitcases and overnight bags. She said simply, "I've had enough, Marcus. I love you, but I have had enough."

He was standing near the fireplace. He had started a roaring fire in it and was keeping himself warm. "We never talked about it, Anna."

"We talked. *I* talked, anyway. You just never listened." She paused, then, "It's too hot in here, Marcus. You're going to make yourself sick."

He ignored the remark. "Twelve *years*, Anna. You're going to forget that?"

"No, I'm not going to forget."

"And where are you going to go? Have you thought about where you're going to go?"

"I've thought about it, Marcus. My brother will take me in."

Marcus said nothing; his face screwed up a little, as if he were in pain.

"It's noisy there, I know," Anna conceded, "and it's crowded. But at least I'll be away from here. I *want* to be away from here, Marcus."

He looked quizzically at her: "And me . . ."

"I'm leaving this village as much as I am leaving you. I'm scared, Marcus." A car horn sounded from the street. Anna stood, gathered up her suitcases. Marcus came forward, extended his hand to help. "No, I can manage, thank you, Marcus." He backed off. The horn sounded again. Anna sighed. "Goodbye, Marcus." She was clearly saddened by what she was doing.

He was standing with his back to the fireplace, again. "I don't want you to go, Anna," he said, his voice low and weak.

She started for the door, stopped, looked back. The horn sounded from outside, again. "Marcus," she said, "you should be scared, too." And she left.

Marcus listened a moment. He heard the taxi door slam shut. He listened closer. He couldn't hear the taxi driving off because the fire in the fireplace behind him was too loud. He whispered, "I *am* scared, Anna."

The difference, Judy Yount realized, was in its colors. They'd gone tepid, flat, and lifeless, as if the painting had been put out in the sun for too long.

She'd always considered it one of Lily's best—a

cheery, impressionistic view of Goode's Crossing
done three years before, as seen from midway up
Leslie's Mountain. The village itself took up half
the painting, its center; around the edges, in the
foreground, there were the intruding, bright green
branches of fir trees. That happy, bright green
now was closer to olive drab. And the various
colors of the village itself were apparently
changing to gray—gray-red, gray-blue, gray-
orange. The whole scene was very stridently
spooky, something that might be put on the covers
of a gothic horror novel, she thought, which upset
her essentially happy view of things.

She blamed the color change first on the oils.
Then she decided that that was improbable. Oils
changed their color over time, of course, but certainly not so much as this, and not so soon.

She took the painting down from where it had
hung for the past three years, on the south wall of
her parlor, near a tall, narrow window covered
only by a yellowing shade. She held the painting at
arm's length. At once she felt a small, bothersome
kind of sadness come into her, as if from the
venom of a tiny, poisonous insect.

She rehung the painting. The sadness stayed
with her. She stepped away from the painting.

Your *children, Mr. Death, your wraiths, and your
demons, and your blood-sucking fiends do not
frighten us! They are images of decay, they are
images . . .*

She turned, as if from the words themselves,

and her memory of them, and hurried into the kitchen to busy herself with dinner preparations. Tuna casserole tonight, she'd decided. It was one of John's favorites. She hoped his appetite—which seemed to have left him entirely in the last few days—had come back to him; she decided it probably had. His winter job in Merrimac, as a fork-lift operator for an electronics part warehouse—today was his first day back—always made him ravenous.

She took a saucepan from the cupboard, carried it to the sink, ran water into it.

Your images are gray and flat. They are images of putrefaction. They are images of decay. They are images that fade, and are gone. You are nothing, Mr. Death, and we do not fear you!

She wanted desperately to shake that memory, but it was very hard, like trying to shake a particularly annoying piece of music—the harder you try the more tenaciously it sticks.

And the sadness still was with her, like a hunger that can not be appeased because it is a hunger of the spirit.

She believed with all her heart in the spirit. It was a part of her, as breathing is.

And so she wanted to shake the memory of Sarah's words. And of what Sarah had done. What they had all done.

She closed her eyes tightly. She felt the sadness growing in her, like the dull ache that precedes sickness. She shook her head quickly, again and again and again. She whispered harshly, her teeth clenched, "No! No!" The saucepan fell into the sink; the water in it splashed over her apron. She clutched the hard, cold edge of the sink—it was something to cling to. She said again, "No!" She opened her eyes wide. She screeched the word, "No!"

She lowered her head and closed her eyes lightly. She felt very weak.

At last she looked up, through the window over the sink. It was night and she saw that Fox Street was empty, except for something large, and slow-moving—a dog, she supposed—fifty yards off, which was apparently trying to keep well away from the glare of the street's only street lamp.

She strained to see what the thing was, exactly. Because no one in Goode's Crossing owned a big dog, if it was a dog, and she wasn't at all sure of that.

She turned off the fluorescent light near the sink. She saw the thing outside stop moving at once. She imagined that it turned its body toward her and then that she saw it rise up, and stand, as a man would. And even at that distance, in that darkness, she saw that its small, round eyes were on her, and that they were a deep red, like the last moments of sunlight, and that its body was trembling visibly, as if with the cold, or in need.

It covered the space between itself and the house as quickly as light. It slammed sideways into the outside of the house, below the window, and the house shook. The fluorescent tube winked on, then off. A can of tuna near the edge of the counter clattered to the floor.

The thing backed off. Only a few yards, but it stayed in darkness. It stood very quietly a long moment. It got down on all fours again. It kept its head lowered and rolled its eyes up; they caught Judy's eyes and held them.

She imagined that a wide sneer spread over its snout.

Then, as smoothly and as quietly as ice moving on ice, it loped back, across Fox Street, from where it had come. In moments, it was gone.

Judy stood weeping at the sink for a long time.

"Sarah? This is Francis."

"Yes, Francis?"

"They're coming, Sarah."

"Who, Francis? The children?"

"Yes. I've seen them. On the Close. But they fade very quickly, Sarah. They need our help."

"Mr. Death has a very strong and cold grip, Francis. We must all be as strong."

"Yes. I see that."

"And we must not let fear overcome us; fear will destroy us if we succumb to it."

"I'm not afraid, Sarah."

"That's good, because I believe that this has only begun, Francis. Do you understand?"

"Yes, Sarah."

"Many, many doors are opening, now. I can feel it. And all we need is patience, and strength."

"Yes. Thank you, Sarah. I see that. I understand that."

"Goodbye, Francis."

"Goodbye, Sarah. Thank you, Sarah."

Marcus Breeze had no idea what he was doing here now. He supposed that if anyone saw him—which was, thankfully, not very likely—they'd tell Sarah and Sarah would believe he was a fool.

He wanted to keep the mower's engine at a steady, low hum, but that was impossible because the air was cold, and the engine out of tune, so he had to gun it often to keep it running.

He told himself many things as he drew closer to the church. He told himself that he missed Anna already, which was true. And he told himself that he was really a child at heart, that he had never grown up, and didn't want to, which was why he'd come to Goode's Crossing in the first place, and that he was out here because he was going to try to scare himself, and what better place was there for that than in that God-forsaken church?!

The mower's engine died abruptly a hundred feet from it. He cursed and tried several times to restart the engine—muttering little obscenities all the while—but in vain.

He got down from the mower, kicked it, began cursing again, louder, more viciously, as if finally releasing some long pent-up hostility.

He saw a light inside the church. He fell silent at once.

It was a feeble light, a dull blue-green in color, and very diffuse, like a bunch of Christmas tree lights seen through a thick evening fog. And it was moving slowly, from the basement of the church, as he watched, up, into the center.

His first impulse was to call out, "Who's in

there?" because he felt suddenly very protective of the church, he wasn't sure why. Then he thought that at · this distance whoever it was wouldn't hear him, anyway. His second impulse, which overlapped the first, was to turn and run back to the house. Not that there was anything very frightening about the light itself—it could easily be some kind of flashlight, he supposed— but because it seemed so out-of-place and so strange that it wasn't difficult to imagine that it had nothing to do with him, that it was none of his business and that, for his own sake, it should stay that way.

His final impulse, which stood quivering and bashful behind the first two, like a schoolboy trying to gather up courage to ask for a date, was the hero impulse, and it told him that all things strange and out-of-place had to be dealt with quickly, and forcefully.

But he was not a hero.

He tried the engine of the mower one more time, in vain, cursed, and started back for his house.

When he looked around at the church a moment later, the light was gone. In its place, at the bottom of the smashed stained glass windows, and at the basement windows, and even around the tiny arched windows in the rear door of the church, like an odd kind of ornamentation, he saw the staring, silent, slack-mouthed faces of the children.

"Sarah? John Yount."
"Yes, John?"

"Sarah, Judy has . . . She has seen something."

"What has she seen?"

"A dog, she says. Some kind of large dog."

Judy whispered, "It *looked* like a dog. It wasn't a dog."

"She says, Sarah, that it only looked like a dog. She doesn't know what it was."

Silence.

"Sarah?"

"Tell her not to fear it, John."

"I don't know if that's possible."

"Fear will destroy us all, if we succumb to it."

"I understand that, Sarah."

"And many, many doors are opening. I can hear them opening."

"This thing scared the shit out of her, Sarah!"

"Then we will exorcise it when it is time."

"Exorcise it?"

"Yes. When it is time. Goodbye, John."

It was the smell that Lily Krull noticed first. It made her nose screw up, and her stomach turn over. "Jesus Christ!" she whispered. And she began taking very shallow breaths because the smell seemed weaker that way.

She glanced around the bedroom. It was large and cluttered with furniture—a huge fourposter bed, an antique chiffarobe in need of repair, a floor-standing oval mirror, a tall chest of drawers, two mahogany nightstands—and was poorly lighted by a badly tarnished brass ceiling fixture which contained only one working bulb out of four installed in it.

She supposed the obvious, that something had crawled into the house and died in a corner of this room. Under the chest of drawers, perhaps. Or behind the headboard. It had happened before ("It's one of the blessings of life in a small country town," Stephen had once told her).

Then she wondered why she hadn't noticed the smell earlier, why it hadn't crept up on her over a period of a couple of days as the thing—whatever it might be—slowly decayed.

She had no answer for that.

She noticed, then a high-pitched, and intermittent, hissing noise, like a radiator hissing, and she glanced confusedly around the room again.

Her gaze settled on the open door which led into the adjoining bathroom. She imagined that the hissing noise was coming from near it, or from behind it, and the image that came to her in that moment was of a cat that had dragged its kill into the house and was warning her to stay away. That had also happened before. But this was not the same kind of hissing. This was lower in pitch, and breathier, as much a wheeze as a hiss. And then she heard that a small, shuffling, scraping noise accompanied it, not unlike heavily starched or heavily soiled cloth rubbing against itself.

"Is someone there?" she whispered, and suddenly her breathing grew heavier with fear and the awful smell in the room assaulted her, and she put her hand to her stomach because the smell was rapidly making her nauseous: "Jesus Christ!" she said again, and at the same moment that she turned quickly to leave the room, the bathroom door pushed slowly open.

She turned her head, then. She heard the hissing noise grow louder. She looked.

She saw the thing's mouth first. It was open very wide, and its small, bright red tongue was pulled tightly back so its tip pointed straight up. She realized at once that it was where the hideous smell in the room was coming from because she could see bits of clotted blood and little pools of saliva around the lips, and gums: The teeth were yellow, and largely blackened by decay, and the canines were hideously prominent.

The small, roughly oval face was the color of old barnwood, and so very deeply and heavily lined that the eyes and the nose—which seemed to have receded far into the skull—were tightly pinched between folds of gray skin and only barely recognizable.

Dirty swatches of black cloth clung to the skin here and there, but except for that the thing was naked—its penis shriveled, its testicles apparently pulled all the way up into its pelvic cavity.

The thing had been crouching behind the door. It slowly rose, now. Its skeletal gray arms went up so its forearms were against the sides of its ears, as if it were making itself deaf. It continued hissing. It was telling her to stay away.

She wanted desperately to scream, to call out to Stephen, who was down in the living room. But she could not speak. And she could not move. She was trembling, and her eyes were watering with fear, and a sudden, thick sweat had started under her arms and under her chin.

Then, from behind her, in the hallway, she heard Stephen gasp, "My God, what in hell is that?!"

And she turned her head and blubbered at him, "Stephen . . . I . . ." And when she looked back, the thing near the bathroom door was gone. Its awful smell lingered in the room for a long while.

26

On Shoemaker Road

"I've seen him again, Terry," Marian Hauser said. "In the same place." She inclined her head to the left. "Out back. He was just standing there, staring at the house."

Terry had gotten home only minutes earlier. It had been a long, dreary day for him. He thought he was not up to merely listening to Marian delude herself. He went to the liquor cabinet, opened it. "Can I get you something?"

She lifted a glass from the end table near her chair. "No, thanks, I'm all set."

He raised an eyebrow. "That's not like you, Marian."

"What's not like me? Drinking all alone?" She sipped the drink, straight Scotch. "I guess I'm blazing new frontiers," she announced, grinning humorlessly. She took another sip. "You don't want to talk about it, do you?"

"About drinking alone?"

"No. About Tod."

Terry began to mix himself a gin and tonic. "Tod's dead, Marian."

"No, Terry—he's alive." She thumped her chest. "And not just in here, either."

Terry stayed quiet.

"*I* think he's trying to tell me something." She sounded almost petulant.

"Marian, for Christ's sake—"

She turned in the chair and stared into her nearly empty glass a moment. "It was this morning, just after you left, Terry. That's when I saw him."

Terry said nothing.

Marian kept her eyes on her glass and fingered it distractedly. "Let me tell you something, Terry," she said. "And I mean this—I'm very sincere about this." She turned her head suddenly and caught Terry's eye. "The next time I see him I'm going after him! I'm going to follow him wherever he wants to take me." She had a look of fierce, and unyielding determination about her. "He's my *son*, Terry. I love him. I will *not* abandon him!"

27

November 10

Wednesday, November 10th, was Sarah's birthday. She was seventy-two years old, a fact she noted only obliquely because she despised birthdays (she had once maintained that they were designed primarily to keep greeting card manufacturers in business. It was a comment which had caused some to believe she was possessed of a charming, hard-bitten, W.C. Fields-type sense of humor when, in fact, she was one of those very rare persons who has almost no sense of humor at all.)

At just about 5:30 that morning she climbed out of her big, spindle bed, used the bathroom, splashed water on her face from a century-old white porcelain washbasin she kept filled near the sink, and made her way down the wide spiral staircase to the first floor, and then to her well-appointed kitchen to fix breakfast.

The thought came to her as she moved about in the semi-darkness that everything about the house seemed very outsized, very much bigger than life. She thought, *Old ladies shrink!* It was an unsettling idea and it made her grimace, as if in reaction to sour milk. Then, strangely, the idea became more palatable and she grinned at it. "Old ladies shrink," she whispered, and, still grinning, she put her hand to her stomach. In the next few moments she did something she hadn't done in decades, ever since she was a child and had been forced by her Aunt Jessica to swallow several raw eggs (a kind of punishment, she remembered): she vomited. And when she was done, and could feel that her stomach was nicely hollowed out and the momentary sickness that had spread over her was all but gone, she cleaned the mess up and made herself her usual breakfast of black tea, Cream of Wheat, and plain, white-bread toast.

Before she sat down to eat, she raised her head, closed her eyes, and whispered, "Mother, we have done it."

And then she sat down. She ate ravenously. She was very happy.

Stephen said, "She'll probably be awake now, Lily. She'll know how to deal with this."

He and Lily had spent the night in their kitchen, at the table, draining one cup of coffee after another and trying to convince themselves that the thing they had seen crouching behind the bathroom door—Stephen for only the briefest moment

—was nothing more than the hideous results of exhaustion and bad lighting and a draft snaking through the house, and imaginations made vivid by the events of the past month. They were convenient explanations, and comfortable, and as the hours passed they became more and more acceptable.

But there was still doubt, of course, which was stronger than rationalization, and so they had stayed in the kitchen the entire night ("I like sitting in the kitchen, Lily. We should do it more often.").

He repeated, "She'll know how to deal with this."

Lily said, "I hope so. I'm scared, Stephen. I'm very scared."

He reached across the table and patted her hand. "So was I, Lily." He considered a moment. "I still am," he added, in a quick and offhanded way that tried to imply that it didn't really matter. He pushed himself to his feet, nodded at the kitchen window: "The sun's up, Lily. Let's go."

She got slowly, as if with effort, out of the chair. She pushed it back to the table, fussed around with arranging it for a moment. She sighed. "Something's wrong, Stephen. I can feel that something's very wrong."

He let the words sink in, then came quickly around the table and embraced her. "Yes," he whispered. "But we'll go to Sarah now. She'll set things right." The words surprised him. He had never before realized how very much trust and confidence he had in Sarah. It was something he'd never thought about.

They put their coats on and left the house.

Andrew Liwush had his tree picked out—a towering Fraiser fir, at least one hundred years old, he guessed, which stood just inside the tree-line on Leslie's Mountain, within shouting distance of Fox Street.

He'd brought along a stout chainsaw. He could fell the tree in minutes with it, he knew, then, maybe tomorrow, maybe Friday—when he felt better, anyway—he'd come back and begin slicing the tree up into face cords. And besides, his thoughts continued, he didn't like messing around with chainsaws—zip, there goes a finger. Zip, zip, there goes a hand. Zip, zip, zip, there goes an arm, a leg. And visions of his brother-in-law, Winston, dead five years then, came to him. Poor, stupid Winston chuckling that the very chainsaw Andrew carried now was just "a toy," then, moments later, letting it get fatally away from him. He had only himself to blame, of course.

Andrew grimaced and shook his head violently, in an effort to shake the memory away. It was impossible. He'd had to lug Winston's body back, and he'd had to stare into Winston's dead face all the while, a face that had a look of stark fear and surprise and confusion frozen on it, and Andrew thought now, as he approached the towering Fraiser fir, that what he had seen on Winston's face then had been what Death was really all about.

Strangely, the idea gave him a kind of cold and

brittle comfort. He imagined Winston prowling Eternity, chainsaw in hand, that grotesque look on his face, and blood layered on him like bits of old wallpaper, and mumbling to himself, "Why did I do that? That was dumb!"

Andrew laughed aloud. He stopped abruptly. The laughter hurt.

When he got to the Fraiser fir he sized it up visually, in an effort to estimate where it would fall. Then, suddenly exhausted, he set the chainsaw down and sat with his back against the fir's trunk, and his legs out straight—his heels in a small patch of gray snow—and breathed, "God-damnit!" because he thought he had never before been so totally and completely and utterly exhausted as he was at this moment.

He heard someone whistling behind him, from deeper in the woods. He remembered that Winston liked to whistle. The same tune, in fact, that he was hearing now—"Melancholy Baby." He remembered telling Winston a thousand times, "Shut up, would you?" because Winston couldn't whistle worth a damn, it always came out scratchy, and off-key, and from time to time made the hair on the back of Andrew's arms and neck stand up.

Just as this man's whistling was doing.

"Shut up, would you?" Andrew growled.

The whistling stopped at once.

Andrew's brow furrowed: "What in the hell?" he murmured. He leaned over, turned his head, looked around at where the whistling had come from.

And there, just behind and to the left of the Fraiser fir, was Winston, chainsaw in hand, a stark look of fear and surprise and confusion on his face, and blood clotted all over him like bits of old wallpaper.

"It's been a couple of days, Marjory," Harry said, and he nodded to indicate the inside of her house. She was holding her front door halfway open, and was dressed only in slippers and her blue flannel nightgown. It was 9:00. "Can I come in?" Harry went on, grinning as if in apology for some unknown misdeed that would explain why they'd been apart for so long.

"No," she answered. "I'm tired, Harry. I'm very tired. Let's make it some other time, okay?" She began to close the door. He put his hand on it:

"Marjory, what's wrong?" His concern surprised her. She let the pressure of his hand open the door a few inches. She was about to answer, "Nothing's wrong," but thought better of it, because he'd immediately see through the lie, and repeated, "I'm tired, Harry. I really am very tired." It was the truth; he could see it around her eyes, in her stance, and even in the way she held the door open, as if she were using it for support.

"Let me come in, Marge. We've got to talk."

"About what? And please don't call me 'Marge.'"

He liked that. "About everything, I guess," he said. "About us, about last week. At the church. You were there, weren't you?"

"Yes." She nodded once, gravely, as if the

memory gave her pain.

"It was a bad scene, wasn't it?"

"I don't know if that's the phrase I'd use."

He grinned again. "I miss you."

She raised an eyebrow. "Uh-huh," she managed. "I've got to go now, Harry. You're letting the cold air in. I've got to go." And she closed the door.

Harry raised his hand as if to knock again, then, sighing, turned and started for his house.

Marjory stood quietly in the kitchen doorway, her eyes on Balboa's wicker basket. She'd never known exactly how old Balboa was. He'd come to her one amazingly cold winter night several years before and had looked to be fully grown at the time.

She supposed now, as she leaned over and stroked his matted black fur, that he had no doubt been pretty old as cats go, that he'd probably spent at least ten or fifteen years prowling Leslie's Mountain—and that was a fine life for any cat. He had died sometime during the night, she guessed. In his sleep, mercifully, as the old often do. She felt honored and strangely comforted that he'd chosen her house, and the small wicker basket she'd given him, as a place to spend his last hours.

She covered him with a yellow pillowcase she'd brought down from the bedroom. "Goodbye, cat," she murmured. She straightened.

It came to her suddenly that she was seeing things, in the last few days, with much greater clarity than she ever had before, as if, for some reason, she had taken blinders off. She really did

love Harry March, for instance. He was a chauvin-
ist, and arrogant, yes. But she loved him nonethe-
less. She could think of no concrete reason for
loving him (he was very strong, for instance, or
heroic, but he was neither of those things). She
thought that people often loved other people
without apparent reason—that was the nature of
love. But the fact that she loved him was something she'd never really been able to admit before.
And she admitted also, and at last, that she had
come to Goode's Crossing ten years earlier not because she had some burning desire to help others
—because she was "sensitive" and caring and
could help—but because she thought it would be
the easiest thing to do, that Goode's Crossing
would be a place to hide, and play kid's games, and
forget.

She wondered where this great honesty had
come from. She thought it was like someone clean-
ing her house up before turning on the gas; death-
bed confessions; self-imposed last rites (And
Harry, she remembered, had been the same way
several nights earlier: "I have a confession to
make, Marjory."

"Oh?"

"Uh-huh."

"You're gay!"

"No. I don't think so. I'm a fake."

"Really?"

"I came here under false pretenses."

"Where—to my bedroom?"

"No. Here. To Goode's Crossing."

"I don't understand."

"Neither did I. Not at first, anyway. It's a long story."

"Real long?"

"A couple of minutes. No longer than that."

"Okay, shoot."

"Did you know I was in the army?"

"I've never given it much thought, Harry."

"Well, I was. Not for long, though. Just three-and-a-half short weeks. I got booted out. A Section Eight discharge. Know what that is?"

"It means you're not playing with a full deck, doesn't it?"

"More or less. I was 'hallucinating.' That was the official ruling."

"Oh? What were you hallucinating?"

"A ghost."

"Someone you knew?"

"I didn't think so at the time. At the time I thought it was some poor slob who'd come back to haunt the barracks from overseas. You know— someone who got killed in the war and thought it would be a good idea to get even with the place that sent him there."

"Sounds reasonable."

"Sure it does. But I didn't realize until quite a few years later, and quite a few sleepless nights, that my ghostly GI was really my cousin—Jesus, I can't even remember his damned name, now— who blew *himself* away, right in front of me, when I was just a wee sprat."

"My God, Harry—"

"I just barely remember it. I think I was three, maybe four years old. It's the same old story. My father kept some guns in the house, I got hold of one—a big one, I think—and poor Cousin What's-His-Name came in and caught me with it and decided he was going to have some fun. So he points it at me, and pulls the trigger: 'Bang!' he says, and then puts it in his shirt. And then *it* says 'Bang!'—kind of a delayed reaction; old powder—and poor Cousin-What's-His-Name gets a four-inch-wide hole blown in his chest. Nice story, huh?''

"No, Christ, Harry, why in hell would you want to tell me something like that? Especially now?''

"I don't know. Confession's good for the soul, I guess. Because *I* was the one who found the damned gun. And because I've seen Cousin What's-His-Name again, in my house. Just here and there—in mirrors, around corners. I even saw him reflected in my coffee the other morning.")

She went to the stairway, stood quietly at the bottom, her hand on the railing for support. She was barely able to hold herself up, she realized, let alone climb the stairs to her bedroom. "Oh, Pappy," she whispered. "Pappy, what did she *do* to us?''

From one of the upstairs rooms she heard a low, earthy chuckle.

"Pappy?" she said tentatively.

She heard another chuckle, as if Pappy were sharing some private joke with her, as he often had.

"Pappy, are you there?" She heard a quick laugh, from near the corner of the landing, she guessed. "Pappy?" she said again, and started up the stairs.

"Marjory?" she heard. She stopped. She did not recognize the voice. It was low, and harsh, and gurgling, like the voice of a drunk, and Pappy never drank ("It's the devil's brew, Marjory!").

"Come here, Marjory!"

"Who are you?" she whispered, and took a step backward, down the stairs.

"Come here, Marjory. We'll have a little fun, you and I. We'll have lots of fun!"

She took another step down, and another.

She imagined that she saw movement at the top of the stairs, where the wall joined the landing, as if someone had very quickly stepped onto the landing, then back again.

"Pappy?" she said, her voice trembling.

"We'll play a game, Marjory. You like games, don't you?"

It was a quiet morning, and Lester Stanhope, whose house was next door to Marjory's, heard her front door slam shut and sensed immediately that something was wrong. He went to his bedroom window, and looked out. He saw her run across her front lawn, her arms high and her head shaking violently from side to side. He pushed his window open, leaned out.

"Marjory!" he called. "Are you all right?"

She did not look back.

"Marjory?" he called again. She disappeared behind a short line of trees.

He moved as quickly as he could down the stairs and out of the house to the street. He saw her, then, a hundred yards off.

"Marjory?" he called. She turned to her left,

toward Harry March's house.

"Something wrong?" he heard. He glanced around. Weyre Goodall, who lived close by, was standing on his porch and wrapping a robe around himself.

Lester pointed toward Harry's house. "I don't know," he said, and shrugged. "No," he said. "I guess not." He went back inside.

It's very cold.

I told you it would get cold. I bet you're gonna say you're hungry, too. Go ahead, say it!

I'm hungry.

I knew you'd say it.

And I don't wanta be here.

So let's go somewhere's else.

Where we gonna go? It's cold all over.

We'll go someplace that's not so cold as this.

You wanta know why it's so cold here? It's because this is where they *were, that's why it's so cold here.*

They made it cold?

Sure they did.

How'd they do that?

You know how they did it. Don't ask stupid questions.

He used to say that.

Who used to say that?

He used to say, "Why do you ask so many stupid questions?"

He never said "stupid."

Sure he did. He said, "Why do you ask so many stupid questions?"

*He didn't say "stupid," he said "dumb." There's a
real big difference between "stupid" and "dumb."*

Yeah, well I'm still awful cold!

And stupid, too.

*That ain't nice. Mom'll put you in your room for
sayin' that and not let you watch "Sesame Street"!*

Who?

"Sesame Street."

*Naw, she won't let you watch "Baretta"! She says
he don't talk right.*

Who?

*"Baretta." He don't talk right. Hey, I'm awful
cold here.*

Yeah, and hungry, too.

Yeah, and scared. You scared?

I'm awful scared.

"You know, of course," Sarah was saying, "that
these are in all likelihood only temporary manifestations."

Stephen, next to her on the flower-print loveseat
—Lily sat nearby in a matching chair—shook his
head sadly. "We had convinced ourselves,
Sarah—"

"That the manifestation wasn't real?" she interrupted.

He nodded.

"In a sense," she told him, "it wasn't."

"In what sense?" he asked.

"I would say . . ." she began, stopped, and appeared to search for the right words. "I would
say," she went on after several moments, "in the

sense that the entity which came into your house found itself loosed upon the world..." She stopped again; she held her hands up, fingers wide, near her face; she lifted her head slightly and let her gaze rise, to the ceiling. Despite himself, Stephen got the clear impression that she was having trouble getting her thoughts in order, and it made him ill at ease. Finally, her gaze fell and caught Stephen's again, and she dropped her hands to her lap. She seemed to be in control again; it made Stephen feel better. "It found itself loosed upon the world," she continued, "without warning! Like a dog that has been straining at its leash for a long time and finally the leash snaps and the dog is propelled forward by its own desperation, and for a few minutes the dog is frightened, and confused, and wants only to get back to its cage, because that is where real comfort and security lie." She grinned, it was close to a smirk —she was obviously very pleased with her analogy. "I believe, Stephen, that we have the same sort of thing here. Except there is a difference, a very important difference, and that is that the entity which came into your house"—she paused for effect—"is a creature of Eternity." She smirked again; again Stephen felt ill at ease. "Do you understand me, Stephen?" she asked.

"Yes," he answered quickly, though he wasn't at all sure he did. "Oh God, yes."

And Lily said, "Yes, Sarah," in the same grateful, sure tone that her husband had used.

Sarah took hold of Stephen's hand—he nearly recoiled; her hand was icy cold—and stroked it, an obviously maternal gesture. "Stephen," she soothed, then looked over at Lily. "Lily. There are others we have loosed upon our village, too, of course." She hesitated; Stephen and Lily glanced at each other quickly, then back at Sarah. "Others?" Stephen asked.

"Yes," Sarah answered matter-of-factly. "And though they are only temporary manifestations, and we have, I believe, begun to free the children as well, perhaps we have opened the door too quickly."

"I don't . . ." Lily began, and lowered her head. "I don't know," she murmured. "This is very strange, Sarah." She looked up; her eyes were watering. "This is all very, very strange. It scares me."

"My child," Sarah told her, "if we let fear overwhelm us, we are doomed. We will send this creature back that has come into your house. But we must not fear him!"

Lily smiled gratefully. "Thank you, Sarah." She got out of her chair, came over, hesitated very briefly, then leaned down and embraced Sarah. "Thank you so much."

And Stephen, looking on, felt his own eyes mist over with gratitude.

Sarah stood. "You must go now. There are preparations I must make."

Stephen and Lily left at once.

At the playground, just beyond the southeastern edge of the village, where children played once, and laughter rang out, and shins got scraped, and memories got started, the whispers rose up. They drifted from place to place. They halted, rose up, fell to the earth again, though for just a moment, and rose up, higher, and louder, so a great horned owl happening by in search of food looked over briefly, and wonderingly, then hurried on its way.

The whispers were small, and insubstantial things, the products of love, and memory, and good feelings, which constitutes the real stuff of life, and they moved about under the skeleton of the swings, and in circles, quickly, on what remained of the tiny steel merry-go-round. And, like hands clutching, they curled over tree limbs and held on tight to the big metal replicas of Donald Duck and Mickey Mouse that someone had brought to the playground decades before.

The whispers disturbed very little. They were not alive, or dead, and they could not laugh loudly, and did not want to ask for love, or plead, "Remember us!" That was for others to imagine.

They moved like tiny, swirling currents of air around the things in the playground and, at last, they fell to the earth again, quivered, rose up, fell.

And lay asleep, and quiet.

28

Afternoon

Harry climbed into the bed with Marjory and put his hand on her shoulder. "Marjory?" he whispered. "Are you awake?" He got no answer; he hadn't expected one. She was clearly exhausted ("Please, Harry—I don't want to talk. I just want to lie down, I need to lie down. We'll talk later, okay." "Sure, of course. But what's wrong? Jesus, I've never seen you like this." "Nothing's wrong, Harry. No. That's not true. Everything's wrong! But I don't want to talk about it, now. I just want to lie down. I'm very, very tired. Please try and understand").

He slipped his arm around her stomach. "I'm glad you came here, Marjory," he whispered, and his hand drifted idly up, to her breasts, and he thought happily that there was probably nothing in the world more pleasant to touch. "Thank you for needing me," he whispered.

She whispered, in her sleep, "Pappy?" and he heard more than question in the word; he heard confusion as well, and fear.

"Marjory?" he said, though he knew she wasn't awake.

There was a knock at the front door. He glanced in its direction. He looked back at Marjory. "Marjory?" he said again.

"Don't do that, Pappy," she whimpered. "Please don't do that."

He took his hand from her breasts. He had heard something strange in her tone, and it made him feel somehow unclean. "I'm sorry," he said aloud. He leaned over so he could see the side of her face.

He saw her eyes open wide.

There was another, more urgent knock at the front door. He glanced toward it again, thought of yelling that he'd be there in a moment, decided against it, for Marjory's sake, because he didn't want to wake her too abruptly.

"Marjory?" he said.

He saw her mouth the word, "Pappy" again.

"Are you awake, Marjory?"

She screamed, then. Deeply. And shrilly. As if something were trying to burrow its way out of her skull from deep within.

The knocking at the door grew very loud, and very urgent. "Jesus," Harry screeched, "hold on!"

Marjory continued screaming until he scrambled from the bed, came around to her side, sat her up, and slapped her, hard.

She stared at him in stark disbelief. "My God!" she breathed. "My God, Harry—that was *me*, wasn't it?"

It took him a moment to understand her question. When he did, he began gently massaging her face where he'd hit it, and said, "Yes, it was."

From below he heard, "Harry, it's Sarah! Let me in, please!"

"Is she coming?" Lily asked. "Can you see her?"

Stephen, holding the dark curtains open with his hand, answered, "No. Not yet. She's probably got a million things to do, Lily. She'll get here before long."

"Yes," Lily murmured. "I know that." A brief pause. "Stephen, do you *have* to go to Merrimac?"

He sighed and glanced around at her. "Yes, I do. I have to get that pump today. If I don't get it today we won't be able to get it for another week, at least—"

She held her hand up; he stopped talking. "Okay, Stephen. I just think it's a hell of a time . . ." She shook her head slowly. "No. I'm sorry. I'll be okay."

"Sarah will be here real soon, Lily. Everything will be fine."

"Can you at least wait until she does get here, Stephen?"

He answered at once, "Sure," and glanced out the window again. "I think that might be her now, Lily." It was a cold, clear afternoon, the shadows were crisp and very black, and the sunlight was almost white against the tall pines and the stiff, gray-green grass, and the old houses. "No," he said a moment later. "I guess not." And he wasn't sure who it could have been that had appeared so briefly on the street, a hundred yards off. "Pretty soon, Lily."

"I hope so," she answered. "You want some coffee, Stephen? I'm going to have a cup. I need it."

"Thanks," he answered. "I will. Brew up a whole pot, why don't you, then we'll have some for Sarah when she gets here."

"Yes," Lily said. She got up from her chair. She went into the kitchen.

She stopped. "No," she pleaded.

It was the smell she noticed first.

"You wanta know how long I've been here, Francis?" Weyre asked. "In Goode's Crossing. You wanta know how long?"

Francis, seated in his big, green, Naugahyde La-Z-Boy near the west-facing window, the window that looked out on Fairclau Close, said, without much interest, "Sure, Weyre."

"Close to thirty-five years," Weyre answered. "And I've never been haunted till now."

Francis didn't acknowledge that.

"I don't know what we did the other night, Francis. At the church. I'm sure Sarah knows, but I don't think she's gonna tell us till she thinks we're ready to know."

And Francis said, as if to himself, "Right up there. That's where I saw them."

"Saw who?" Weyre asked.

"My friend Jesse, from the fat farm," Francis

answered. "And those kids of his." He turned his head and smiled his huge, bloated smile. "It's a beautiful, beautiful thing to see, Weyre."

Weyre wasn't listening. "Thirty-five years," he said. "I had a friend named 'Red.' You ever have a friend named 'Red,' Francis? I guess most people have."

"They came right down there," Francis was saying at the same time, and he pointed limply at the Close. "Right down there. He had his flute—he played the flute pretty good—and those kids of his were right behind him, dancin' this little soft-shoe."

"I can't remember his real name, Francis. Just that nickname. 'Red.' No one ever gave *me* a nickname. And you wanta know what happened to Red? I'll tell you what happened to Red. He fell ten stories off of a building while he was jerking off and splattered himself all over the street. Fell on some little dog, I found out later. Killed it, too, of course. I guess when you fall ten stories you get goin' pretty damned fast—"

"And they'll be back," Francis declared. "Sarah says so. 'Watch for them, Francis,' she says, so that's what I'm doin'. I'm watching for 'em."

Irene Atwater Janus was sure of it, now. The raccoons *were* in the house—she'd seen them, at last. And as she'd expected, they were huge. And so were the fleas they carried. And if she allowed it, they would certainly take her home away from her.

She pulled her .22 caliber pistol from the

kitchen drawer, slammed the drawer closed, studied the pistol grinningly a moment.

She stalked from the kitchen and into the Sitting Room. She jerked her head from side to side in a vain search for the raccoons. Of course, she realized at last, they'd gone upstairs!

She left the sitting room, went to the stairs, started up. "You miserable bastards!" she hissed, and she leveled the gun at a point just above the railing at the top of the stairs. She squeezed the trigger. The hammer fell on an empty chamber. She squeezed the trigger again. Again the chamber was empty. She continued up the stairs; she was still grinning. She squeezed the trigger again, and again. "Miserable bastards!" she hissed. "I'll get you, I'll get you!"

"I would like to speak with Mrs. Gwynne," Sarah said to Harry.

Harry looked confusedly at her. He moved to one side. Sarah stepped into the house. "How did you know she was here, Sarah?"

"It is my business to know such things," she said, without looking at him, and she shrugged out of her big, gray wool coat.

Harry took the coat from her. "She's upstairs, Sarah. She's very tired. You couldn't make it some other time, could you?"

"We are all tired, Harry—she no more than any of us."

He hung the coat in a closet. He smiled. "You're looking very fit, Sarah." He realized immediately that it was not something she wanted to hear, because they both knew it was untrue. He looked momentarily embarassed; he gestured toward the stairs: "I'll go get her right away, Sarah, please" —he gestured expansively at the living room— "make yourself comfortable."

She sat in a nearby armchair. "I have very little time to waste, Harry."

"Yes," he said, and went upstairs to fetch Marjory.

"Stephen . . ." Lily whispered. "Stephen . . ." She had backed away from the thing in the cellar-way and was now standing near the side door, her hands pressed hard into the jamb. "Stephen . . ." She could not speak above a whisper, and she knew that Stephen could not possibly hear her.

The thing in the cellarway had its mouth open very wide; she could see the faintest suggestion of eyes within the gray folds of skin, and she knew that they were watching her.

The thing was down on its haunches, facing her, and now, as she watched, its forearms went up suddenly, to block its ears. A short, breathy hiss escaped it, and it began waddling slowly, and ob-scenely toward her, its thin and shriveled penis moving woodenly from side to side between its bare, skeletal legs.

"Stephen, please—" she managed. Tears came to her. She backed further into the door, she groped for the knob, found it, turned it: the door was locked.

The thing waddled into the kitchen table; the table slid a couple of inches to one side. The thing hesitated. Another breathy hiss, longer than the first, escaped it.

It began to rise. Its thick, bright red lips pulled back, and the canines—long, and white, and hideously prominent, thrust forward.

"Mrs. Gwynne," Sarah said, "I must ask you to leave Goode's Crossing."

Marjory had just come into the living room from upstairs. She stopped in the entranceway, gathered her blue flannel nightgown together at the front: "I think that's something the group should decide," she said.

"We do not have the time for that ... luxury, Mrs. Gwynne. And so I am speaking for the group."

"I see." She came slowly, meditatively, into the room. "Well, you always have spoken for the group, haven't you?"

Sarah did not answer.

"And if I choose to stay, Sarah?"

"If you choose to stay, Mrs. Gwynne"—she looked directly into Marjory's eyes; Marjory saw her grin ever so slightly—"against my wishes, and the wishes of the group—"

Harry, standing in the doorway, interrupted, "Sarah, I really believe—"

Sarah snapped her head toward him. "Stay out of this, Harry. And be glad I do not include you in it."

Harry quieted.

Sarah turned back to Marjory. Her grin seemed broadened. "As I was saying, Mrs. Gwynne—if you choose, against my wishes, and the wishes of the group, to stay, then it will be at your own peril."

Marjory smiled. "That sounds very much like a threat, Sarah."

Sarah snapped back, "It *is* a threat, Mrs. Gwynne. You are not wanted here. I do not want you. The group does not want you. *They* do not want you!"

"They?"

"And so I very strongly suggest, Mrs. Gwynne, that you leave. And at once." She stood.

Marjory watched her silently.

She went to the closet where Harry had put her coat, got it, put it on.

Harry said, "Sarah, perhaps we can discuss this—"

"Did I imply that there was room for discussion, Harry?"

Harry thought a moment; then, "No," he whispered, "I'm sorry."

Marjory said, "Harry, did I ever tell you that you're made of jello. *Jello*, Harry!"

He lowered his head, ashamed.

Sarah glared at her. "Now, Mrs. Gwynne! Today! This instant! Do I make myself very clear?!" And she left the house before Marjory had a chance to answer.

"It's my sensitized kneecap," Lester Stanhope said to Andrew Liwush. "And it's never wrong, Andrew."

"I don't give a damn about your 'sensitized kneecap,' Lester. I came here to tell you about Winston.

My brother-in-law. He's in my house right this very minute, Lester."

"So what am I supposed to do about it? He's *your* brother-in-law."

"He's *dead*, Lester. He's *been* dead for five years. He sliced himself up with a chainsaw, for Christ's sake!"

"Jesus, Andrew, you're beginning to believe your own con game."

"I'm serious, Lester—"

"Sure you are. It's what we're all about—"

"And, like I said, I need to stay here, Lester. Until he goes away. Can I stay?"

" 'Course you can." Lester laughed a quick, this-is-really-great-bullshit kind of laugh. "Stay as long as you want, Lester. Just tell me this: How do you know your brother-in-law—what's his name . . ."

"Winston."

"How do you know Winston's not going to come over here looking for you?" And he laughed again, harder, and longer.

Andrew felt himself sit heavily on the couch. He supposed his mouth was open. At last he said, "Jesus, I don't know, Lester. Jesus, I don't know."

"Lily?" Stephen called. "She's on her way. Sarah's on her way." He glanced toward the kitchen. "Lily?" He got no answer. He glanced once more at Sarah, fifty yards down the street and moving stiffly, quickly, toward the house, then he stepped away from the window and toward the kitchen. "Lily?" he called again.

She appeared in the kitchen doorway. She was

bent over; her hand was on her stomach; her face was as pale as snow; she was weeping. "Oh, Stephen, My God, Stephen . . ."

He ran to her, helped her to the sofa, sat next to her on it. "Lily, what in the—"

"It was that . . . thing, Stephen—God help me . . ."

"Jesus, Lily, where?"

She pointed stiffly at the kitchen. Stephen pushed himself to his feet, ran to the kitchen, glanced quickly about. He noticed, very faintly, the odor of the thing. The odor quickly dissipated. "Lily," he called, "there's nothing here."

"The cellar!" she called back frantically.

He looked at the cellar door. It was bolted. He went to the doorway. "No, Lily," he began, "I don't think so . . ." The doorbell rang. He moved quickly to the door, put his hand on the knob, glanced back at Lily. "It's Sarah, Lily. She'll know what to do." He opened the door. Sarah glanced at him.

"Hello, Stephen," she said, and stepped into the house.

"It's out there, John," Judy Yount said. "I saw it." They were in the bedroom. John was getting ready to go to his winter job as a fork-lift operator in Merrimac. He had a pair of blue work pants and a blue work shirt laid out on the bed, a pair of steel-toed, black shoes in front of it, white crew socks folded inside them. He was dressed in green boxer shorts, and a clean white T-shirt. "Sarah's on her way," he told Judy. "She'll stay with you, I'm sure."

She looked confused, and hurt. "John, I *did* see it, I am not imagining things."

He picked up the pair of pants, stuck one leg in. "I never said you were imagining things, Judy. Of course you saw it. You saw a dog. And if you stay inside, there's absolutely nothing it can do to you."

"John, Sarah herself said that it was *not* a dog. And *I* know it wasn't a dog."

"Sarah never said that, Judy." He stuck the other leg in, pulled the pants up to his waist, zippered them. "If she had said it, it would be a different story, but—" He buttoned the pants, slid the belt in.

"I'm begging you, John—stay home today . . ."

He looked wearily at her. "Don't you think I would if I could, Judy? Don't you think that all I want to do is shuck out of these clothes and into that bed and sleep till next year? I am very, very tired, Judy. And so are you. And that's why you're turning dogs into . . . into God knows what."

She stared incredulously at him. Then she turned abruptly and went to a window. She looked out. After a minute, she announced, "I see it, John. It's out there, right now. Come here and look."

He came over, slowly, as if in resignation. He looked. "I don't see anything, Judy."

She pointed stiffly at a growth of three fairly young pine trees with a lone maple to one side: "There, for Christ's sake. There!"

John strained to see. Clouds had moved in over the course of an hour, cutting off the sunlight. "I'm sorry, Judy. I really am."

"And my sensitized kneecap," Lester concluded, "says that we got one hell of a storm coming in. Tonight, maybe. Maybe tomorrow."

Andrew Liwush said, "You're right, Lester. He could come looking for me here. There's no reason he wouldn't."

"You got your firewood laid by, Andrew? If you don't I'd say you're in a heapa trouble!"

"That's why I went out there in the first place. To get firewood. And that's where I saw him. Right around in back of the tree." He was speaking in low, secretive tones—as if in awe. "He was whistling, Lester. I told him to shut up because he really can't whistle for shit—it drives me up a wall. Like chalk scraped on a blackboard, you know? And when I told him to shut up, he shut up all right, but then he followed me home. He's sitting in my favorite chair right now, Lester. He's sittin' there with that damned chainsaw in his lap, and his feet up on the ottoman. Jesus, he's bleedin' all over everything. So you can see why I had to come here, can't you? But you're right, of course."

"I'm always right, Andrew. Tonight, tomorrow, maybe. But it's coming, no doubt about that."

"There's no reason he won't come over here. There's no reason he won't go anywhere."

"It was sure nice while it lasted, Harry," Marjory said to herself, and she stuffed a bra and a tube of toothpaste into her overnight bag. She'd come back in the morning for the rest of her stuff, she had decided. For now, just getting away from

Goode's Crossing was enough. "And if you ever wriggle out from under *her* thumb, Harry . . ." She sighed, put a skirt and white blouse into the overnight bag, glanced around the room to see if there was anything else she needed. No, she decided, and she closed the bag.

She started to leave the room. "Oh, Pappy," she murmured, out of habit. Then, "Goddamn you!" she hissed.

"And so he has," she heard, from the other end of the upstairs hallway.

"No," she whimpered. "No, Pappy!"

"Oh, yes, Marjory. You call, I come. It's like a game, isn't it? You like games. We both know you like games!"

She heard him get out of a chair. She stood stiffly, one hand clutching the overnight bag, the other clenched into a tight fist. She stayed quiet. She listened to Pappy move down the hallway. She imagined he was moving very slowly, and very deliberately, much as he did in a game he'd played once—'Detective,' he called it.

She imagined he was playing that same game, now. And it was a game she didn't want to play.

She pleaded with him, "Go away, Pappy!"

"'Where does it hurt, Marjory?'" she heard. "You want to play that? That was a good game, too, wasn't it?—You like that game especially."

"Go away now, Pappy. Oh, please go away."

"Or how about, 'Out of the Mirror.'" She guessed that he was halfway down the hallway, now. "'Oh, who is that in the mirror?' Remember that game, Marjory. 'Can it be me?' I liked that one. I liked that one a lot."

"Oh, Pappy!"

"I'm out of the mirror now, Marjory." It was a screech, loud, and harsh, and powerful, like a screech of conquest. *"I'm out of the mirror now!"*

"You have nothing at all to fear, Lily," Sarah soothed. She had seated herself next to Lily on the sofa. Stephen had taken up a position in his armchair nearby. He looked very concerned.

"Tell us what to do, Sarah," he said.

She glanced sternly at him. "The most important thing, Stephen, is to be strong. I've told you that. I've told you what fear can do to us if we let it. And you see what can happen, what *has* happened, when you let your strength ebb."

"But Sarah," Lily protested weakly, "it was waiting for me—"

"It was waiting for you, Lily, because you were afraid of it, and it feeds on fear, all of them do. They smell it, like a dog does. And if we do not fear them, they will go away."

"But it was so . . . hideous, Sarah!"

"It was a reflection of your fears," Sarah told her. "Merely a reflection of your fears. Do you understand that?"

"I don't know . . . Yes, I think so."

"And if you want to rid yourselves of it, you must *challenge* it, just as we—all of us—challenged its father a week ago. We are stronger than they are, Lily. You must believe that!"

"Yes," she said at once. "I believe it."

Sarah got up, with effort because she was very

tired, from the couch. "I think you do," she said. "It is your only defense." She started for the door. Stephen followed her.

"And if it does return, Sarah?"

She stopped, turned her head, and grinned at him: "If it returns, Stephen," she said, "ignore it." And she left the house.

"You're really going to go, aren't you, John?"

"Yes," he answered wearily. "Yes, I have to, Judy." They were in the kitchen. He picked a black lunch pail up from the table, hefted it, thought of asking Judy what she'd made for him, decided not to. "Nothing has changed, Judy."

"That's a stupid thing to say," Judy shot back, with emphasis on the word "stupid."

He thought a moment. "Maybe," he said. "But we still have to eat." He went to the back door, opened it.

"And if that thing gets into the house, John?"

"I don't think it will," he told her, with a sad and strange kind of certainty. "I really don't think that it can."

And Sarah appeared at the back door.

Judy came forward immediately, extended her hand. Sarah took it. "Judy," she said briskly, in greeting, then nodded at John. "John."

She stepped into the house. Judy, behind her, prepared to take her coat. "No," Sarah said. "I'm staying only a moment."

"But, Sarah," Judy began, "that thing is out there. It's out there right now."

Sarah ignored this. She nodded at John's lunch

pail. "Please don't go into work today, John. I need you."

He hesitated only a moment, then closed the door, stepped over to the table and set the lunch pail on it. "Yes," he murmured. "Of course."

Sarah put her hand on his. His fingers tightened up—her hand was very cold. She held her other hand out; Judy took it. "My dear, dear friends," she intoned, "I'm afraid we have done our job much too well. And now we must undo it."

"I don't understand," Judy said.

"Tonight I believe that you will," Sarah told her.

The truth sat leadenly at the back of Marcus' brain, and so avoiding it was all but impossible. But he did avoid it. He thought about Anna, instead, and about his life in the village and how really unsatisfying it had all been, and that there were several very descriptive words for the role he had played, to Sarah's lead, and none of them were terribly nice words. But he was not quite to the point where he could blame anyone but himself, especially Sarah.

("Marcus, this is Sarah."

"Sarah? I'm so happy it's you. I've been trying to call you all morning and afternoon. I have . . . wonderful news." He could feel himself smile, the kind of smile that had come to him only once before in his life—at the birth of his first child. "Sarah, I've seen them again. I've seen the children again. I've seen them at the church. And they need us, I can *feel* that they need us."

Silence.

"Are you there, Sarah? Is something wrong?"

"Marcus, I'm sorry that I have to ask this, but you must understand, it's quite necessary. It is imperative, in fact."

"Ask me what? Sarah did you hear what I just said to you."

"Marcus, I must ask that Anna leave Goode's Crossing. She is not one of us. She can never *be* one of us."

"My God, Sarah—"

"It is not, of course, a matter of personal dislike. I have always liked Anna, whatever can be said for that. It is a matter of strength. And of loyalty."

"Sarah, please—"

"We're like a chain in this village, Marcus. And so we are only as strong as our weakest links. Especially now."

"Sarah, Anna has—"

"Anna is one of those weak links, and Marjory Gwynne is another. I have already told Mrs. Gwynne to leave. You must understand that something . . . historic is happening in this village. You must understand that."

"She left me, Sarah. Last night. I assumed you'd know."

Silence.

"Sarah?"

"No, Marcus, I didn't know. How was I to know?" She was clearly upset. "Why was I not informed of this when it happened?"

"I didn't think it was—"

"Any of my concern?"

"No, of course it concerns you, Sarah. I was just . . . upset."

Silence.

"And because I was upset, Sarah, my responsibility to you—"

"Your responsibility, Marcus, is to this village as much as it is to me." A momentary pause, then, "Be at Fairclau House at 7:30, tonight." And she hung up.)

Marcus wasn't sure that he'd be there. He thought that, a week ago, under similar circumstances, there would have been absolutely no question of it.

But now there was the truth gnawing at him, and he was avoiding it, yes. But it was also making him weak, bone-tired, exhausted, so fighting it was a real chore. He realized that before long it would leap on him, hungrily, and devour him.

"I miss you so much, Anna," he whispered, and he wished it were the only truth he had to deal with.

Part Five
THE PLAYGROUND

29

Marian thought she really couldn't blame Terry for taking off ("I'll be back . . . I don't know—after twelve, I guess, as soon as I've made some kind of dent in that workload."), because she couldn't deny that she'd become a real drag to live with since Tod's death. And she convinced herself she didn't expect Terry to believe what she'd told him, that she didn't even want him to *pretend*—and he didn't—that he believed her.

But, Lord God in Heaven, it was lonely here and he really was wrong, inconsiderate, unfeeling to leave that way, and if he didn't believe her why couldn't he keep it to himself and at least let her babble a little bit? She deserved it for Christ's sake!

She sighed. Nothing, she decided, was more pathetic and self-defeating than crying all alone, as she was doing now. Crying should be a shared thing, of course. It was a form of communication, and if no one was there to see it and react to it . . .

She glanced at the telephone, at the other end of the living room. Maybe she should call him. Apologize. Promise she'd never mention it again, even if there were reason to mention it. Tell him she was adjusting, at last, as he (Goddamn him!) had, and that all she needed, and wanted, was his patience, and his love, and understanding. It would be a simple thing to do. Really just a physical act. Get up. Dial the phone. Say the things he wanted to hear.

As, she thought, *a prostitute would!*

She sipped her Scotch and let it slide over her tongue and down her throat without tasting it. "Unfair," she whispered, not caring much if it was or wasn't.

She stood suddenly, spilling what was left of the Scotch onto her jeans. She realized that she was very angry. And not just at Terry, but at herself, too, for her weakness. And at Tod, for not staying where chance and fate and accident had put him.

"Oh Christ, it *is* unfair!" she hissed, her fists clenched at her side, her muscles tense, her breathing quick and shallow, and an extraordinary sadness coursing through her.

And beneath it all she was glad Terry wasn't here, because she would, without a doubt, start throwing curses at him, and acting like a crazy woman, and then, later on, would fall into his waiting, patient embrace and blubber incoherent apologies into his chest. She'd done it before.

More than once. And she did not want to do it again. This time she wanted resolution.

With effort she calmed herself.

The next time I see him, Terry, she remembered, *I'm going after him,* and she wondered what sense there was in waiting for Tod to come to her, what difference it really made. If he was out there, somewhere, she'd find him. Her love for him would lead her to him.

She got into her warm wool coat, and boots, and gloves—frost starting on the windows told her the night would be bitterly cold—and left the house by the rear door. She did not hesitate. She crossed the backyard quickly, made a slight detour around the picket fence, pushed her way through the tall grass beyond, and, within minutes, despite the gathering darkness, found the narrow path that she and Tod had used once, a year before, to go on a little nature hike.

She stopped. She cupped her hands around her mouth. She called, "Tod?" and smiled. She remembered that she used to call him in that same way to come home for dinner, or to come in out of the dark, or because it was time for him to do his homework. "Come home now, Tod."

She listened. The air was very still and she could hear small rustlings occasionally in the tall, dark grass that flanked the path—field mice, she supposed, and quail, maybe even a fox ("Look at this, Mom. It's still alive. I found it out there. I think it fell out of its nest. Can I keep it, Mom? Huh? Can I keep it?").

She looked back at the house, a hundred yards

off. She thought she couldn't remember leaving so many lights on, and she chastised herself for it.

It was 7:05.

"Tod?" she called again. She heard in response only the small rustlings of the night creatures, and she began walking north on the path, quickly, with her hands jammed into her pockets and her head down against the cold. A slight breeze lifted up from the valley just ahead, where Goode's Crossing was. Snow began swirling around her like dust.

This is home!
Home? Whose home?
Her home. And his. Their home. They live here.
Yeah? With who?
With nobody no more. Not no more.
Not anymore.
That's what she says. Not anymore.
I like it here. It's warm.
Yeah, warmer than that other place.
And it ain't so dirty, and it ain't so dark, and there ain't no spiders.
Ain't any spiders.
Except in the corners, maybe. Course that's where they belong. Up in the corners so they can catch flies. That's what he says.
She says if they're crawlin' around on the ceiling it's okay 'cuz it's good luck.
He says that's just a stupid-stition.
Well, he ain't always right. Just mosta the time.
He says she's fulla stupid-stitions. Chock full of 'em.

Yeah?—Well, there ain't no harm in it, that's what she says.

Ain't any harm in it.

Yeah, that's what she says.

And he doesn't know everything. Just most things. He don't know what I know.

Like what don't he know?

Doesn't he know. Like about ghosts and such.

There ain't no ghosts and such. That's what he says. He says ghosts and such are people's imaginations running crazy with them and making them see things 'cuz they wanta see things, 'cuz it ain't so bad to die then if there's ghosts and such, 'cuz then you can go on livin' forever. That's what he says.

And she says he don't know everything.

Just most things.

He don't know what I know.

Doesn't know what I know.

He sure don't.

Where is he, you think?

Workin'. He's always workin'. She says workin's gonna drive him into an early grave.

Yeah. Like Jeremy.

Jeremy didn't do no work. All he did was he died.

Everybody dies, that's what I say.

Yeah. Like going to sleep and not havin' no dreams. That's what he says.

Yeah, but he don't know everything.

Just most things.

Yeah, but he don't know what I know.

Hey, you think we're dead?

No, we ain't dead. How can we be dead?

Yeah, and be hungry at the same time?

7:25: In Goode's Crossing

"I'm sorry," the man on the other end of the line said, "but we can't get nobody out there tonight. In the morning, maybe, but not tonight."

Marjory took a couple of quick, shallow breaths; she hadn't expected this kind of complication, and it annoyed her. "What time in the morning?" she asked.

"I don't know. Depends on a couple things," the man said. "Depends on how long the storm lasts—"

"What storm?"

"Maybe you ain't got one over there yet, but we sure as hell got one here in Merrimac, and like I was saying, it depends—"

"Forget it!" Marjory snapped. "I'll call back in the morning. Thank you." And she hung up. She stared glumly at the phone. She could try the other cab company in Merrimac, she supposed, but if there was a storm—she glanced out a nearby window and saw a couple random snowflakes hit it—then they'd tell her the same thing. Goddamnit, why hadn't Harry listened to her? ("Harry, you have no idea what's happening here."

"And you do?"

"Yes, I do. At least I think I do. And if I'm right, then you've got to leave with me, now!"

"I'm sorry, Marjory, but Sarah needs me there, tonight."

"Of course she needs you, Harry. She needs *all* of us, except for me, and Anna—because we see her for what she really is. My God, Harry, the people in this village *feed* her, they *nourish* her—"

"That's dumb. You're trying to make her sound like some kind of three-headed beast, or something, God knows why, but she simply does not deserve it. I'm going to Fairclau House tonight. What you do is entirely your business!")

Asshole! she thought now, and immediately felt lousy for it. "Jesus, Harry," she whispered.

She had come to his house several hours earlier, one poorly packed bag in hand. She'd told him nothing about Pappy. Pappy was an embarrassment now—a grotesque *faux pas* littering her past. She hoped that someday she'd be able to exorcise him from the corner of her brain where, at that very moment, he sat leering at her. And she thought it was ironic that, somehow, Sarah had called him down from the mountaintop, where he used to reside, and had put him there, in that corner. Without a doubt, Sarah had no idea that she'd done it. Without a doubt she had no real idea that she'd done anything. Because, like all who come to power unquestioned, and unquestioningly, she saw no need at all to justify her actions, or explain them, to anyone, not even to herself. Power shapes. And power creates. And power leads. It's more than a fact of life—life depends on it.

Marjory whispered again, "Jesus, Harry!" because, Lord!—he really was made of jello, wasn't he! And most of the others were, too—Marcus, especially, and Lester Stanhope, and the Younts. Even Stephen Krull, who had always seemed to possess a pliant, good-natured strength. Inside he was made of jello!

"Damnit, Harry! Can't you see what she's done —can't you see what all of you have called into this village?!" And she realized, suddenly, that yes, they *could* see it—how could they help but see it, it was so obscenely clear:

They had called Death in!

And it was wrapping itself around them. Smothering them! Filling them up and pushing out whatever was inside—all the dreams, and the memories, and the fears sleeping inside!

Because Death takes and takes and takes, but does not keep, and so can not give back.

"I love you, Harry," Marjory whispered desperately. "I will not lose you!"

7:30 P.M.—Fairclau House

Sarah smiled, the kind of smile that none at the big round table had seen on her before—a smile of gratitude and love and good feeling. Then she closed her eyes lightly. Weyre Goodall, sitting beside her, could see her eyes moving beneath the lids, as if her gaze were falling on each of them as she spoke: She said their names, first, slowly, as if with reference:

"Weyre," she said, and turned her head, eyes still closed, toward him, "Sam," she continued, "John, Judy, Stephen, Harry, Irene, Lester, Francis, Marcus, Lily, Andrew."

And then she paused. Her smile stuck on her face, her eyes popped open, and for a moment she looked like a strange and aged mannequin that had been put there as an odd joke.

She spread her arms.

All those at the table joined hands:

She told them joyfully, "We are pioneers, you and I. We have looked Mr. Death squarely in the face. We have challenged him to enter our village, our homes, and our hearts. And he has." She squeezed Weyre's hand, and Lily's hand, who was on her right side. She repeated, with great, quivering emotion, "And he has!" She closed her eyes lightly again. "And we have been lifted up by him, transformed by him, made stronger by him. Even his minions are fearful of us, we are so strong. Like dogs suddenly unleashed they are confused, and fearful, and they see *life* around them, and are made into cringing, cowering things by it!"

Lily felt Stephen squeeze her hand, as if in reaction to what Sarah had just said.

"But it is not those whom we have called," Sarah continued. "Death's minions have come to us only by chance. We have merely to command them to go, and they will have no choice. They are not . . . comfortable here." She said the word "comfortable" almost sneeringly, as if she found humor in it. "They move about us, in our village and in our homes, quivering and snarling and hissing because they feel pain here. Because this is where *life* is!"

She opened her eyes. She looked from one face to another at the table. Finally she said, "And so we will command them to go. And they will! And we will tell Mr. Death to set loose those children. And he will! And we will make a place for them forever, here, in our little village." She let go, suddenly, of Weyre's hand, and Lily's hand, and pushed herself to her feet.

And, with varying degrees of quickness—in his haste to follow Sarah's lead, Francis Eblecker knocked his chair over and thudded to the floor; Marcus Breeze helped him to his feet—the others stood, as well.

"And now," Sarah told them gravely, "we will go where Death still waits, where he still clutches those children to his vile bosom."

She turned around, started for the door, stopped at once.

Weyre Goodall, close by, saw her hand go to her stomach, saw her lean forward very slightly, heard her whisper, as if in pain, "No!"

"Sarah?" he said, concerned. "Is something wrong?"

She straightened immediately, and took her hand from her stomach. She turned her head so her gaze settled first on Weyre, then on the others in the group. She said, her voice suddenly very strong and commanding:

"He waits! We will go now!"

30

On Shoemaker Road

Terry Hauser was not a man who could not admit his mistakes, and that is why he'd come back, because he thought he'd made a big mistake in leaving when he had, when it was painfully obvious that Marian needed him—perhaps not as someone to reason with, or even as a shoulder to cry on, he supposed, but only because—simply enough—she should not have been left alone tonight.

He was glad he'd come back. He liked himself for it. He planted a big, apologetic smile on his face, shoved the key into the lock, opened the door, stepped into the house. "Marian?" he called. "I'm a fool, Marian. I'm a big, stupid fool!" and he liked himself even more. He waited for her answering call—"Keep going," or "Big, maybe, but not stupid"—which would be the old Marian, the Marian that had oh-so-slowly, but inexorably, emerged from her grief over Jeremy's death, but was wallowing in that same kind of grief now, and plainly did not want to rise above it.

"Marian?" he called, concerned because she hadn't answered immediately, as she usually did. "Answer me, Marian," he said playfully, and stuck his head around the corner of the archway and looked into the living room. "Marian?" Her chair was facing away from him, toward the big fireplace at the other end of the living room—there was a fire burning in it—and he wanted to see her get out of the chair and come over to him and put her arms around him . . .

But he knew instinctively that the living room was empty, and so he passed quickly through it and into the kitchen. When she was upset, and she was surely upset tonight, she liked to bake things —cookies, coffee cakes, an occasional pie. He liked that. He thought it was "pleasantly domestic." But he knew even before he got there that the kitchen was empty, too.

He stepped around the counter which separated the dining area from the kitchen and stood, quietly confused, in the center of the kitchen for a few moments.

He saw an open jar of Skippy on the counter, some Marshmallow Fluff and a dirtied knife nearby. "Hey, Marian," he called, "are you pregnant or something?" He decided instantly that it was a stupid thing to say, that it was even vaguely cruel, and he was happy that, quite plainly, she was not in the house to hear it.

He went to the back door, pulled it open, looked out into the darkness. He flicked on the spotlamp. He saw big, heavy, quickly moving snowflakes dancing crazily in the light. "Marian?" he called. He listened. He heard the wind whining around the edges of the opened door. He cursed. He didn't want to go out looking for her—he disliked darkness, and he despised the cold, and deep inside himself he resented Marian for what had obviously been a fit of childishness.

He still had his boots and coat on, and his gloves. He'd need them. He glanced around again, at the kitchen, and especially at the open jar of Skippy, and the Marshmallow Fluff, then, cursing once more, he left the house.

He's gonna be mad.

Yeah, he's gonna holler.

He's gonna holler loud!

Real loud! I don't like it when he hollers like that —he scares me, bad.

I can't get to sleep when he hollers like that.

She says don't worry about it. She says he don't mean nothin'. She says we gotta love him just the same.

You love him?

Yeah, I love him. I don't know.

You think maybe we should go away now? So he won't holler?

Yeah, but it's warm here, ain't it, and comfortable, and maybe he won't holler too much.

You think he saw the fire?

Naw, he didn't see the fire.

Or the peanut butter, either?

Maybe he saw that. I don't know.

You think we should go away, now? You think we should go back?

You wanta go back?

I don't wanta go back, but maybe we should. I don't know.

It's real comfortable here.

It's real warm here. I like it here.

But we gotta go. I know we gotta go.

Yeah, we gotta go.

Before he comes back, I mean. I mean we gotta go before he comes back.

I love her, too. She smells nice.

Yeah, she smells nice.

31

Judy Yount didn't call the group's attention to the thing that was following them, at a distance, to the church because she was embarrassed by it, as if it were something inside her—something loathesome—that had slipped out and taken shape and wanted desperately to go back to where it had come from.

At one point, she nudged John, walking beside her, and nodded at the thing. But he didn't look, or acknowledge her, although she'd nudged him very sharply, and so she merely continued watching as the creature slipped behind trees, and buildings, and reappeared briefly—moving fast, and low to the ground, on all fours—its huge, dark, misshapen head down, as if it were some grotesque, kind of bloodhound following a scent. And every once in a while it looked up at her, and

287

caught her gaze momentarily, then hurried on.

And when the little group was about halfway to the church from Fairclau House, a distance of about a third of a mile, and the church was visible as a huge, dark red, geometrical swelling in the blackness, Francis Eblecker stopped walking abruptly (so Harry March, just behind him, stepped on his heel; "Jesus, I'm sorry, Francis!" But Francis seemed not to notice), and smiled a big, happy smile, and pointed quiveringly to his left, at a dark section of Fairclau Close that was just visible through a break in the pines. He saw Jesse there, holding his shiny flute to his lips, and dressed gaily in a red vest, and white, frocked shirt, and blue knickers, and brass-buckled shoes. And the children, all of them, were just behind him, doing the same, charming, tippy-toe dance that he was doing.

"Sarah?" Francis called, trembling with happiness. But she did not acknowledge him. "Sarah?" he called again. Still, she did not acknowledge him. A look of mammoth disappointment came over him. He watched Jesse and the children vanish into the darkness. "Jesse?" Francis called. "Don't go."

"C'mon, Francis," Harry March said. "Let's get a move on." And very reluctantly, Francis began walking again, very slowly, so his feet dragged on the hard, frozen earth.

"You do not scare us, Mr. Death!" Sarah called every now and then, and Weyre Goodall—just behind her and to her left—saw that she was clutching her stomach hard now, and knew that if he

could see her face he would see that she was becoming nauseated. "Sarah?" he said several times,
concerned, as earlier, but she didn't acknowledge
him so he kept silent.

The words, *I told you so!—My kneecap's never
wrong!* were on the tip of Lester Stanhope's
tongue, because a light, erratic snowfall had
started and he knew, having spent more than a few
winters in Goode's Crossing, that it would soon
strengthen and a storm would roll into the village.
But, like Weyre, he kept his silence. It was what
Sarah wanted, after all, and needed. And he sensed
that there was something very big happening here.
Bigger than his sensitized kneecap. Bigger than
himself, in fact. Bigger even than the storm. And
he felt a kind of painful ecstasy that he was being
allowed to be a part of it.

"We are not afraid of you, Mr. Death!" Sarah
called out suddenly, startling a few of those in the
group, and she threw her arms high into the air, as
if in victory, and held them there just a moment.
Then she clutched at her belly again.

Stephen Krull, at the back of the group, glanced
at Lily, beside him. He saw from her expression,
that she was thinking what he was thinking and he
whispered, "No, Lily. No, it's all right!" and he
slipped his arm around her waist and kissed her
lightly on the cheek—it was the kind of
comforting, affectionate geseture they hadn't
shared in a long time, and Lily felt glad for it. But
she knew deep inside herself that he was wrong.

When the little group arrived at last at the

Goode's Crossing First Presbyterian Church, most of them were very cold, and tired; some of them were nauseous—Francis Eblecker, for one, and Andrew Liwush, who supposed it was due to some canned vichysoisse he'd had for supper—and Irene Atwater Janus was in an agony of itching, though she had clenched her teeth and tightened her muscles and tried to will herself to ignore it (which she found impossible), because Sarah would certainly not like it if she began furiously scratching herself.

All of them made their way slowly up the wide steps to the tall, arched front doors of the church. They stopped there and Sarah held her arms wide and gathered them into a tight circle—which some of them found comforting because it sheltered them from the cold—and they put their heads down. Sarah told them, in low, joyful tones— small, gray clouds of carbon dioxide rising up over her face as she spoke—"Oh, my dear friends, my dear, dear friends, we are embarking on a great . . ." She paused, took a breath. " . . . voyage. We have become the messengers of life, we *are* the messengers of Life." She stopped. She heard someone in the group moan, as if in pain. She went on, "We are needed here! In this place of death we are needed by those too small and weak to challenge . . ." She paused again, longer. Her hand went to her stomach; most of those near her saw her cringe. She straightened suddenly, her eyes opened very wide, her body stiffened.

"Sarah?" Weyre said.

The snowfall, light and erratic minutes before,

suddenly grew much heavier.

"Sarah," Weyre said, "can I help?" and he put his hand on her arm, not tightly, but as if he were merely letting her know he was there.

She said one word, "We . . ." and Weyre recoiled at once, because her voice was deep, and hard, and unrecognizable. "We challenge you, Mr. Death!" she finished. And she collapsed.

At the playground, just beyond the southeastern edge of the village, the whispers rose up. They drifted from place to place, halted, fell to the earth again, rose up.

They were small and insubstantial things, the products of love, and memory, and good feelings. They moved about under the skeleton of the swings, and in circles, quickly, on what remained of the tiny steel merry-go-round. And, like hands clutching, they curled over tree limbs.

They disturbed very little. They were not alive, or dead, and they could not laugh aloud, or ask for love, and they did not want to plead, "Remember us." That was for others to imagine.

They moved like tiny, swirling currents of air around the things in the playground and, at last, they fell to the earth again, quivered, rose up, fell.

And stopped.

32

Weyre caught Sarah before she fell to the steps and the first thought that came to him was that she was very light, as light as a feather, and it surprised him. He supposed she should have been more solid than that, as solid as a rock perhaps. But her eyes fluttered open almost immediately, and her body stiffened up again, and she hissed at him, "No, you must *not* touch me, you must *not* touch me!" And he let go of her.

With obvious effort, she held herself erect. She said to the group, in a tone of enormous urgency, "We must rid ourselves"—she took a quick, deep breath—"of these entities we have set loose"—another deep breath—"upon our village. They are . . . draining us, and we must send them . . . back!" Then she turned slowly, and rigidly, and faced the church doors. She reached out. She took the doorknobs in both hands. She went stiff for a moment. Then, with all the strength she had gathered in that moment, she threw the doors open wide.

She went in immediately, swaying a little from side to side (almost like a drunk, Stephen Krull thought). She did not beckon the others to follow. Most of them followed as if by instinct. Francis Eblecker stumbled slightly on the steps, but did not fall. Irene Atwater Janus began scratching at her wrists, quickly opening a small wound; the sight of her own blood seemed to help the itching. And Judy Yount glanced back and saw, through the darkness and the swirling snow, just inside the perimeter of what little light there was near the church, that something was moving very swiftly and low to the ground, and raising its head every few seconds to look at her. She whispered at it, "Go away!" though she knew well enough that it was not about to. Then she went into the church.

The last one in was Andrew Liwush, who turned his body around, took hold of the doors, and closed them, as an usher might.

They gravitated to the center of the church. They formed a circle again. They joined hands.

Here and there—above the spot where the altar had once been, and in areas near the north wall —the snow came in through holes in the roof and wafted slowly through the still air to the floor. Little pointed mounds of snow had begun forming at these spots.

Marcus Breeze imagined, as the group waited in silence for Sarah to speak, that a barely unnoticeable undercurrent of the awful smell of that night almost four weeks ago still lingered in the church. He thought it was fitting.

Lily Krull, whose eyes, like everyone else's, were on Sarah, snapped her head to the left suddenly: "What was that?" she whispered. "Did you hear that?" No one answered. She peered over Lester Stanhope's shoulder, toward the source of the noise—a little alcove that led out of the church —and saw, dimly, that something was squatting in it, and shuffling back and forth as if in agitation, so its bare feet scraped on the floor, and that its arms, apparently, were up, covering its ears, and that a slight, breathy, hissing noise was coming from it. And she, like Judy Yount, whispered "Go away!" at it, though she also knew that it was not about to. Then she turned back, and focused on Sarah, who lifted her head, and closed her eyes, and pronounced:

"We, Mr. Death, are the means of your *destruction!*" And then she let her head drop, so her chin touched her chest, and she groaned, "We have come for these children." She lifted her head again. Her eyes opened wide. A smile—like the smile she had used on the group an hour before, at Fairclau House, a smile of gratitude, and love, and good feeling—spread across her face. She screeched into the still, cold air of the church, startling some of those in the group, "We are the *Messengers* of *Life*, and we have come for these children that you hold clutched to your desolate bosom."

And Marjory Gwynne, who had been standing, watching, from the dark northeast corner of the

church, stepped forward and said, "It is *you* that
Death holds!"

Sarah's gaze fell on her; the smile stuck on her
face. She held her arms out, palms flat, and curled
her fingers up. "Come here, Marjory." It was a
chilling gesture. And, one by one, the others
turned their heads to look at Marjory, and some of
them repeated, "Come here, Marjory," and Harry
March smiled, in the same way Sarah had: "It's
good that you've come, Marjory," he said. He let
go of Lester's hand, and Lily's hand, and took a
few cautious steps toward her.

Marjory pleaded with him; "Harry, you've *got* to
come with me!" She reached tentatively for him.
"Please, Harry! You have *got* to leave this place!"
She let her hands drop.

He took several more steps toward her, more
quickly. "Marjory, I'm not going anywhere." She
heard a vague, implied threat in his tone. "I *can't*
go anywhere, Marjory."

"I'm leaving now, Harry, and I'm taking your
jeep, and I want you to come with me! Please come
with me!" She was still pleading with him, but
with less a sense of urgency, now, and more a
sense of resignation. "Will you come with me?"

He was halfway across the floor to her. "We
need you, Marjory. Sarah needs you. I need you!"

"For Christ's sake—" Stephen Krull began and
fell into a stunned silence when he saw Harry
lunge across the several yards remaining between
himself and Marjory and grab her by the ankles.
She fell backwards immediately; Harry crawled
over her. "Please, Marjory, oh please stay here,

don't leave me, please don't leave me!" Then he too fell silent because he could see that Marjory was not fighting him, or responding to him. He pushed himself up off her to a crouching position. He studied her face in the dim light. "Marjory?" he whimpered.

He saw a dark smear behind her head, and looked above it, on the stone wall. He saw another dark smear. "Oh, my God!" he breathed. He pushed himself to his feet. "Oh, my God!" he repeated, and he looked around at the group still clustered in the center of the church. "I didn't . . ." he stammered. "I didn't mean . . . My God, I love her . . . " He felt movement at his feet. He looked. Marjory was sitting up, her hand on the back of her head. He stepped away from her, he heard her curse sharply.

"Marjory," he said, "I'm so sorry, I'm so sorry . . ." He continued stepping away from her. "I love you, Marjory." He was still moving away from her, toward the little group at the center of the church.

She looked up at him. He thought he saw something close to pity in her eyes. "I'm sorry, too," she said, and, using the wall for support, got to her feet and stumbled wordlessly out of the church, through the front doors.

Harry made his way quickly back to his place in the circle and joined hands again with Lester Stanhope and Lily Krull.

A long, dull silence followed. Until, at last, Sarah—who had been smiling all the while—told them, her voice quivering with ecstasy, "Oh my dear friends, my dear, dear friends; it is being done. He is releasing them." She began to weep.

And they saw that she was staring at something near the church's just-opened front doors.

They looked.

Tod Hauser was there, staring in.

33

He was afraid of many things—of vampires, and werewolves, and drowned people reaching out to him for a frigid embrace, and fireworks, and yelling, and wild dogs.

He was afraid, now. More afraid, he knew, than when the accident happened, and the flames shot up around him, and nibbled at him, and he saw that the others in the bus were screaming, and their faces were twisted up in pain, but he couldn't hear them because the terrible noise of the explosion had made him deaf.

And more afraid, even, than when he had leaped from the bus's open rear door and had stumbled into the village, and then into the church, and had watched the big, black plastic bags being brought in. *Which one is mine?*, he wondered then, because if all his friends were in those bags then surely so was he.

And if they were dead, then they had to be buried—that's what she said. If only just parts of them. And if only in very shallow holes.

And he was more afraid, much, much more afraid, than when he had spent night after cold night in that root cellar, with the field mice, and the darkness, and the jars of tomatoes, and pickles, and raspberry preserves to eat.

It was *their* faces that he was most afraid of!— The faces turned toward him from the center of the church. The tiny, round eyes, and the open mouths, and the gray skin sagging in on itself. He had planned to plead with them, *Take me home now. I want to go home!* But he knew they wouldn't hear him. And he was afraid of that, too. Because he wanted desperately to go back home, even though *he* would yell, and *she* would cry. He'd spent long enough in the cold, and long enough among the dead. He wanted to go home now!

"I want to go home now!" he whimpered, despite himself.

And distantly, as if someone was whispering to him through a heavy, closed door, he heard, "Yes, my dear. Oh, yes. You *are* home. You're with us. You will stay with us forever!"

And he looked quickly, desperately, from one face to another for the source of the voice. He saw that one mouth was moving slowly, like the mouth of a fish. He heard from it, "My poor child, you *will* stay with us—you have no place else to go."

And then he began screaming for his mother.

34

It was a beeline west to north from Marian's house to the spot where Pitney Road joined Fairclau Close, and from there only a hundred yards south to Marcus' house. It was the first house that Marian saw, though she saw only a vague suggestion of it because the storm was churning fiercely around her now, cutting off her vision. Her feet and hands and forehead were numb, her speech slurred—"Where are you, Tod? Tod, I've come to take you home." She moved woodenly down Pitney Road, toward Marcus' house, her head down against the wind and her shoulders up, her hands shoved into the pockets of her coat. She whispered into the little hollow of calm air near her face, "Come home, Tod. It's time to come home." She had been weeping, because she knew, after all, the futility of what she was doing and the tears had frozen to her cheeks. She thought she looked wretched, and pathetic, like a crazy woman. She thought it was not an altogether unpleasant image, that it was better, certainly, than the image Terry ached to have of her again, the image of a Strong, Intelligent and Rational Woman Bearing Up Marvelously Under Enormous Suffering and Loss. She'd already played that part, after Jeremy's death. And this was better. Fantasy was better. She even thought that if she tried hard enough she could bring Jeremy back, too.

She lifted her head and peered down Pitney Road toward Marcus' house. She put her head down almost at once; the wind-driven snow hurt her eyes and face. She had seen very little, she thought—the house, still fifty yards off, and only barely visible through the snow. Another building, much larger, off to the right; a church perhaps:

And someone standing in the road in front of her only a few yards away.

She looked up slowly. "Tod?" she whispered, because her memory was reconstructing what she had just seen, filling in the blank spots out of the wind, and snow, and darkness, building her son up. "Oh, Tod," she wept. "Are you there, Tod?!" And then he was there, again. In the same spot. But his arms were hanging loose at his sides now, and his face was as blank and as white as the snow, and his mouth was hanging open wide, as if the muscles around it had been cut. Marian did not like what she was seeing.

"You're ob*scene!*" she screamed at it. "Give my son back to me. Oh, please, give him back to me . . ."

She fell to her knees. She held her hands out. She pleaded with the thing in front of her, "Who are you? Who *are* you?"

She got no response.

"You are my son, aren't you?" she said. "You *are* my son."

She felt pressure on her shoulder. "Marian?" she heard. "Stand up, Marian."

It was Terry. In an instant she stood, turned, and threw her arms around him. "Oh, my God, Terry. I'm sorry, I'm so sorry."

And from far to the left, barely audible beneath the noises of the storm, both of them heard, "Mommy! Help me, Mommy!" They looked in the direction of the voice. They listened. At last, they turned and started quickly back toward home.

35

Stephen Krull looked very confusedly at Sarah. "Sarah," he said, "the boy's gone."

Marcus pleaded, "Call him back!"

Sarah spread her arms wide. "We will," she told them, with great confidence. The group joined hands again, and bowed their heads. Sarah allowed a moment's silence, then lifted her head so her gaze fell on the second of three, large, broken stained glass windows in the east wall of the church. Snow was swirling in through the window. "Don't you see that we have beaten you, Mr. Death?!" She was smiling again, but her lips were trembling now, as if from the cold. "We are stronger than you, so much stronger than you . . ." She stopped. She could see that something large, and dark, and essentially formless had appeared in the window's lower left corner, as if, having pulled itself up the outside wall it was trying now to climb over the window ledge and then inside.

Her smile changed. It became a smile of awe, and of disbelief. "Mother?" she said. "Forgive me, mother, please forgive me."

It was the child that did it, Lucy, you know that, don't you?!

Yes, Jessica, I do, but my God—

Weyre Goodall sensed Sarah's sudden excitement. He lifted his head, looked at her.

"Mother?" he heard her say. "You do forgive me, don't you? It was only a little push, and I really did have to do it. But now..." Weyre followed her gaze to the window. He saw the snow swirling in, the pitch-blackness beyond. He looked back at Sarah. He thought she had never looked so very pleased.

"Now that I've called you back, Mother, it's all right, everything's all right."

My God, Jessica, she's only a child!

She's much, much more than that, Lucy. She'll bear watching. Mark my words. She'll bear watching!

"Sarah?" Weyre said. "What is it? What do you see?"

And Sarah answered, "She's alive. Mother is alive!"

Then, out of the corner of his eye, Weyre caught the suggestion of movement behind her, near the spot where the altar had once been. He strained to see. He saw very little.

Sarah screeched, "I have beaten you, Mr. Death!" and she threw her hands high into the air.

Andrew Liwush cocked his head quizzically to one side. He said to Lester Stanhope, who was standing near him, "Do you hear that, Lester?" Lester didn't answer. Andrew continued, half in anger and half in resignation, "He's trying to drive me crazy, I think he's trying to drive me crazy!" And he glanced quickly, expectantly around, until his gaze fell on the front doors of the church. He saw his brother-in-law there, chainsaw in hand, and whistling a scratchy, off-key version of "Melancholy Baby," blood clotted all over him like bits of old wallpaper.

"My friends!" Sarah called. But few still were listening to her. "She is alive. Mother is *alive!*" And although she hadn't run in decades, she ran now, and stopped below the window, and looked up, and reached—as if reaching for a life preserver—through the snow swirling into the church, toward the thing looking down at her from the bottom edge of the window.

"Red?" Weyre Goodall whispered to the thing he could see standing in the darkness. He saw a hand, an arm, a shoulder. And above it, almost directly above it, as if the shoulder itself were madly out of joint, he could see the suggestion of a skull, and eyes, and what remained of thin, pale lips. He heard, "It really is no fun alone, Weyre. Let's do it together. *Please*, let's do it together!"

Stephen Krull murmured, "We are all dying here!"

And Lily, who had been holding his hand very tightly, let go of it. He glanced at her. "Lily, I . . ." She pointed very stiffly, and tremblingly, at a spot just in front of him. He looked. He saw the thing she was seeing only for a moment, and unclearly, as if glimpsing someone else's dreams. He stepped back, away from it. "Jesus!" he breathed. He suddenly grew nauseous. And the thing in front of him vanished. He looked at Lily. She still was pointing at it. "Keep it away from me, Stephen, please keep it away from me!"

"Oh, Lily—"

The thing she was seeing was down on its haunches. Its arms were up, at its ears. It was hissing continuously at her, and every few seconds one of its feet moved forward, so it was waddling toward her very slowly.

"Lily," Stephen called, achingly aware of how really helpless he was, now. "Lily, there's nothing there." But she wasn't listening.

"Stephen?" he heard. He looked quickly to his left, his right. He couldn't pinpoint the source of the voice, and he didn't recognize it, at first.

"Stephen?" he heard again. "Stephen, there's a word for this."

Lily pushed at the air with her open hand. "Keep *away* from me, keep *away* from me!"

"There's a word for what's going on here, Stephen."

And then he recognized the voice; it was his brother. He smiled, slightly, gratefully, "Jim?" he said. "Where are you? I can't see you."

"You know what that word is, Stephen?—It's 'desperation.'"

Stephen heard a low, muffled thud nearby. He didn't bother to look. "'Desperation'?" he said. "What do you mean? Tell me what you mean, Jim."

Francis Eblecker's legs had buckled, and the air had rushed from his lungs, as if something had hit him hard, in the belly. Now he lay on his back, with his arms and legs outstretched, and the snow piling up around him.

Lily continued pushing at the air in front of her with her open hand. "Oh, please," she wept, "please, please go away from me!"

Judy Yount whimpered, "It didn't stay outside, John." But John wasn't listening. "It was supposed to stay outside." It was up on its rear legs, ten yards away, near the church's west wall. She imagined that it was sneering at her, and she imagined that there was a cold, brittle, and mocking laugh somewhere inside it waiting to come out.

Francis attempted a smile. He managed to roll his head to one side so his gaze was on the west wall. Irene Atwater Janus was in his field of view; he took no notice of her. He said, his voice a low, throaty gurgle, "Hey, Jesse, I like that. You play good."

Jesse paused and smiled back.

"'Desperation,' Stephen. Nobody *wants* to die!"

Irene Atwater Janus had opened many small wounds on her exposed arms, and around her calves and neck. None of the wounds was bleeding much—the cold air caused the blood to clot very quickly.

"John," Judy Yount said, "it really should have

stayed outside." John paid no attention to her.

"Stephen, listen to them," Jim said. Stephen listened. "It's like a zoo, isn't it, Stephen?" Stephen didn't answer.

"*Nobody* wants to die. But if you have to—"

Stephen put his fists hard to his ears.

"It's like a zoo, isn't it, Stephen?!"

"Please, stay away from me!" Lily whimpered. "Oh, stay away from me, please stay away from me—"

"Pay attention, Stephen. It's all right here in front of you."

"That's nice, Jesse," Francis said. "That's good. Play something else. Play *Rigoletto!*" But Jesse was changing. His skin was splitting open, and steam was escaping in various spots—around his nose, where the pores were largest, especially— and his hair was rapidly disintegrating, like tall grass wilting in the summer heat.

"You're being emptied, Stephen. All of you are being emptied, like bottles of milk. But there's more than milk in there, Stephen. Reach in. Grab hold. See what comes out. See what squirms around in your fist. Throw it down. Watch it rise up. *I'm* in there, Stephen!"

"Mother?" Sarah pleaded. "Come down. It's not safe. You'll fall. I don't want you to fall. I didn't *mean* it, Mother!"

"John, it wants to go back inside me . . ."

"I mean, Stephen, if you really *have* to die, like I had to, it's nice to think you'll still be able to get around."

"For Christ's sake, Winston, you're driving me up a damn wall!"

"Please go away, oh please go away . . ."

"Sure it hurts, Stephen. Sure it does. But that's life, my friend, that's life—"

"You'll fall, Mother, and you'll hurt yourself! I don't want you to fall. Oh, Mother, I'm so sorry. I'm so sorry—"

"And you sure as hell can't get around on broken bones, now, can you?!"

"My God, Red—that's obscene!"

"Nobody *wants* to die!"

"I'm cold, John. I've never been so cold. I don't think I'll ever be warm again."

"I don't know," Sarah murmured.

"See what they're trying to become, Stephen. *Zombies!* Goddamned, slack-mouthed, stick-in-the-mud zombies! It's a hell of a trade-off, isn't it? For life, I mean. But it really is too late. You know it. I know it. *They* know it!"

"Red, I can't, I don't want to, it's so stupid, it's so nasty—"

"Please stay away! Go back! Oh, please go back!"

"None of us ever will be warm again, Judy. Not ever again!"

"I'm cold, Mother. Come down here, hold me. Hold me tight. Forgive me, Mother. Please forgive me. I brought you back, didn't I?!"

"Freakin' goddamned *zombies*, Stephen! You wind them up and send them out into the world— Shit! *That's* not what Death is all about!"

"I don't know, I don't know!"

"*That's* what it's all about!"

"Play *Rigoletto*, Jesse. Jesse? Are you there, Jesse?"

"It's a goddamned embarrassment, Stephen, that's what it is!"

"Mother? Don't go away, Mother. Stay with me, hold me, make me warm, Mother. I brought you back, didn't I?!"

"Marjory?"

"Zombies, Stephen! They drool, and they suck, and they bite—"

"Winston, for Christ's sake—"

"Lord knows why, Stephen."

"Marge, I love you."

"John, I'll never be warm again."

"None of us will."

"No one *wants* to die, Stephen, but, hell, if you have to, I mean, if you really have to, it's nice to think you'll still be able to relax a little, watch the tube, enjoy a beer—"

"I'm so cold, I'm so cold!"

"But it's really just a pile of shit, right Stevey? Right? A big, pointed pile of shit ten stories high."

"Mother?"

"And don't blame *her*, don't blame *her!*"

"Stay with me, Mother. I need you!"

"All she did was give you answers. It's what you wanted, it's what all of you wanted!"

"Red? Where are you, Red? I'll do it with you now. I *want* to do it with you, now!"

"Right, or wrong, Stephen—no one much cared."

"Jesse?"

"It's gone back inside me, John."

"Like the commercial says, Stevey—'You asked for it, you got it—' "

"Come back, Jim."

"Goodbye, Stevey."

"I don't know, Mother, please, oh please—"

"Jesse?"

"Red?"

"Jim?"

"I don't know! I don't know! I don't know!"

Silence came into the church. And into the people inside it. Into each of them. One by one. It was the silence that comes before birth. And before death. It was the silence of transition. All movement stopped. A heartbeat came, and went.

Marcus screamed first.

And then Andrew.

And Harry.

And Lester, and Judy, and Irene, and Stephen, and Sarah—

And because one scream pushes on another and gets it going, like a string of dominoes—

Marjory hit the jeep's brake pedal very hard. The jeep slid a dozen yards on the snow-covered road and then came to a halt. Marjory rubbed a circle in the frost on the driver's window; she peered out, at the church, her mouth silently forming the name, "Harry," then the phrase, "Goodbye, Harry!" And she thought for a moment that she'd like to scream—for herself, for them all, for what they'd done. For what she was leaving behind. And what she was taking with her.

She saw that the storm was working itself up into a real frenzy. She put the jeep in gear. She drove out of Goode's Crossing forever.

It was a collective scream. A scream, first, of anguish, and of fear. And then a scream of knowledge. They had called Death. And Death had come. Into the village, into the houses, the streets, the sidewalks, the dust. And into them. Each of them. And so the scream continued, and as it continued, the tiny, dark eyes, in the small, oval gray faces darted this way and that—this was not what they had wanted at all, not at all. Not this . . . evaporation! This coming apart!

And so the scream continued. Because Life was tied to it.

Terry Hauser said, "Marian, I heard someone scream." He was in the kitchen, making coffee. Marian was at the table, distractedly fingering a salt shaker.

"I didn't hear anything," she said.

Terry leaned over and flicked the switch for the spotlamp on the back of the house. He parted the curtain on the window over the sink; he looked out. The storm abated for just a moment.

"Marian?" he said tentatively.

She didn't answer.

"Marian?" he said again, less tentatively.

"Yes?" she said.

"I see someone out there, Marian."

She put the salt shaker down. She shook her head sadly. "Terry, please—"

"Marian, someone's standing out there! Come here—" He stopped. He looked around at her, stunned. "My God!" He ran to the back door.

"Terry?" she said. She got up. She saw him throw the door open. When she got to the door he was halfway across the yard and all but invisible in the storm. "Terry," she called, "what is it?" She hugged herself for warmth, ran after him, stopped:

In the light from the spotlamp, she could see that he had his arms out. And she could hear that he was yelling something, but because his back was to her, and the wind was very strong, she couldn't understand him. "Terry?" she called.

She started running again.

She stopped, ten feet from him.

She saw him lean over the picket fence, saw him close his arms around someone, saw a pair of small, bare hands appear at his back. "Tod!" she heard. "Marian, oh my God, Marian!"

And she ran to him, trembling with happiness all the way.

As if it were something solid that had fallen from a great height, the scream stopped abruptly and sent pieces of itself skittering about in the church. The pieces were memories, and dreams, and guilt, and fears—all the stuff that Life is made of. Soon, they quieted. And, at last, the church was empty, except for places here and there where the darkness was particularly thick, and in motion— Life clinging tenaciously to itself.

In time it would stop.

36

Rick Armstrong, telephone lineman for the Greater Adirondack Communications Company, lying face down on Fox Street, outside what had once been Sarah Goode's home, could hear the chopper coming, though it was still a good distance away, and he knew that when it arrived he'd be carried off trussed to the skid, because no one wants to ride with a dead man. ("It's just like sleeping, Rick—just like going to sleep.").

He thought that it wasn't dying he resented so much as, simply, not living anymore. And that, he decided, was a pretty profound way to be thinking at that point in his life.

Around him, in the empty village, a tiny breeze came up and stirred the snow, and the dust. It quieted immediately, and the dust settled, the snow built itself up into the tiny drifts. Movement stopped.

"Just like a dreamless sleep," Rick said, though not loudly, or well.

At the Goode's Crossing First Presbyterian Church, there were a few footprints in the snow that had piled up toward the center, but most had been obliterated by the wind, and by time.

On Fox Street, Rick Armstrong sat bolt upright, surprising himself. "Jasper," he screeched, "I am sure going to haunt your ass!" Then he died.

And the chopper appeared blackly at the horizon.

There were shadows in the Goode's Crossing First Presbyterian Church, too. Shadows that rose very slightly, and fell, and quivered, and leaned at oblique angles. Shadows that were not shadows at all, but were places where the light refused to go.

At the playground, just beyond the southeastern edge of the village, a whisper rose up. It drifted from place to place; it halted, fell to the earth again, rose up. It was a particularly small and insubstantial thing, a memory, a good feeling, and it moved about under the skeleton of the swings, and in circles, slowly, on what remained of the tiny steel merry-go-round.

It disturbed nothing. It was not alive, or dead, and it could not laugh, or ask for love, or plead, "Remember me." That was for others to imagine.

At last, it fell to the earth again.

And it stopped.

Acknowledgments

Many thanks to Harriet McDougal, my editor at. Tor Books, who said some very kind things and got the ball rolling.

Thanks also to Stephen King, for his continued support. And to Bill Thompson.

And special thanks to Mike Cantalupo for a really great job of copyediting.